P9-ARW-494

RECEIVED

DEC 1 7 2013

By_____

HAYNER PUBLIC LIBRARY DISTRICT
ALTON. ILLINOIS

OVERDUES 10 PER DAY, MAXIMUM FINE
COST OF ITEM
ADDITIONAL $5.00 SERVICE CHARGE
APPLIED TO
LOST OR DAMAGED ITEMS

HAYNER PLD/DOWNTOWN

MARATHON

A LYNN BRYANT MYSTERY

MARATHON

GENIE DAVIS

FIVE STAR
A part of Gale, Cengage Learning

GALE
CENGAGE Learning®

Detroit • New York • San Francisco • New Haven, Conn • Waterville, Maine • London

GALE
CENGAGE Learning®

Copyright © 2013 by Genie Davis.
Five Star™ Publishing, a part of Gale, Cengage Learning.

ALL RIGHTS RESERVED.
This novel is a work of fiction. Names, characters, places and incidents are either the product of the author's imagination, or, if real, used fictitiously.

No part of this work covered by the copyright herein may be reproduced, transmitted, stored, or used in any form or by any means graphic, electronic, or mechanical, including but not limited to photocopying, recording, scanning, digitizing, taping, Web distribution, information networks, or information storage and retrieval systems, except as permitted under Section 107 or 108 of the 1976 United States Copyright Act, without the prior written permission of the publisher.

The publisher bears no responsibility for the quality of information provided through author or third-party Web sites and does not have any control over, nor assume any responsibility for, information contained in these sites. Providing these sites should not be construed as an endorsement or approval by the publisher of these organizations or of the positions they may take on various issues.

LIBRARY OF CONGRESS CATALOGING-IN-PUBLICATION DATA

Davis, Genie.
    Marathon : a Lynn Bryant mystery / Genie Davis. — First edition.
        pages cm
    ISBN 978-1-4328-2728-1 (hardcover) — ISBN 1-4328-2728-6 (hardcover)
    1. Women insurance investigators—Fiction. 2. Women mediums—Crimes against—Fiction. I. Title.
PS3604.A956965M37 2013
813'.6—dc23   2013021219

First Edition. First Printing: November 2013
Find us on Facebook– https://www.facebook.com/FiveStarCengage
Visit our website– http://www.gale.cengage.com/fivestar/
Contact Five Star™ Publishing at FiveStar@cengage.com

Printed in Mexico
1 2 3 4 5 6 7 17 16 15 14 13

3153620

MARATHON

Chapter One

The night had a lurid orange glow from the oil refineries down toward Texas City, and a fine mist of rain hung like a curtain across the sky. Although you couldn't see it from the parking garage roof, the Gulf of Mexico was out there somewhere, pale and luminous.

My hair hung wet in my eyes. I tried to shake it off my face, but I couldn't quite manage that, not and slam the owner of a late-model shiny black BMW against his car. The slamming had priority.

As soon as he hit the hood, the car alarm started blasting.

I thought he'd stay down, so I took a moment and swiped my arm across my face to clear the hair away. But he was gutsier than I figured; he drew himself up and swung a ragged left hook at my jaw. I sidestepped the blow, but the garage floor was slippery with oil and rain, and down I went.

I scrambled to my knees fast, but he jammed his foot on my chest, pushing me back. It surprised me to see he was wearing expensive loafers with little tassels. If I'd just stolen a cool million, I would've worn something like snakeskin boots.

I slipped my hand inside my leather jacket while he started ranting. "I asked you to go away! And now, now I'll have to . . . I'll just have to . . ." His voice trailed off with an unnamed threat. He sounded petulant, as if whatever he was planning to do, say throw me off the roof of the garage, was all my fault.

I pulled my snub-nosed thirty-eight out of my pocket. The

guy heard the resonating click as I cocked the weapon, and his jaw dropped.

"You're a woman," he said. "I didn't think you carried a gun."

"I can shoot it, too," I told him, keeping my voice light and reasonable. "Now get your foot off me."

He complied, but I kept the gun on him and scooted back on my behind, putting a little distance between us before I stood up again. "Spread eagle. Flat against the car."

He hesitated, just for a second, but it was long enough that I knew the fight wasn't out of him yet. So I fired, a nice clean shot right into the hood of his pretty car. The alarm sputtered out.

"That was giving me a headache," I said. "And so are you," I added.

Now he threw himself flat against the car. "I'll give you half the money," he whimpered. "Please . . ." I love it when men beg. I kept the gun on him and plucked my cell phone from my jeans. I dialed the cops, but the call didn't go through. I cursed under my breath.

"How'd you know I trashed my own warehouse? How'd you know . . . ?" he sounded like he was going to cry.

"Picked the wrong week to stop sleeping with your secretary."

After a minor earthquake in Simi Valley, California, William Devins, CEO of Software Systems Inc., put in a claim for nearly a million dollars with my client, his insurance company. Apparently, he stored his entire inventory in a warehouse on the West Coast located very near the epicenter, and had insured it for about twice what it was worth. And now, every last piece of software was ruined. According to my client, it looked like somebody had stomped on it. Apparently, somebody had, Devins and his then-girlfriend.

"I'll give you *all* the money," Devins pleaded. "Just . . . go away."

"I'm not the one going away, you are. About five years, would be my guess."

That part about the money was tempting, though. My PI work sure wouldn't buy me a car as nice as his. But I dialed the police again. This time the call went through.

Lieutenant Frank Wilson answered his private line on the first ring.

"Frank, it's Lynn. Yes, sure the signal's bad. I'm in the parking garage at Westheimer and Hillcroft, near the Galleria."

"You need a couple bucks, pay the attendant?"

I sighed. "I'm holding a guy who assaulted me."

Frank laughed. "Sure it wasn't you assaulting him?"

I laughed too. "Yeah, I'm sure. He's involved in a big-ticket insurance fraud. I think some of you downtown are gonna be interested."

"Okay. I'll send some guys."

I hung up, and stuffed the phone back in my pocket. My gun arm was getting stiff and tired holding the thirty-eight steady. I let my hand drop to my side, and curled and uncurled my fingers.

The rain was coming down harder now. It was early October, still Indian summer, really. Rain doesn't usually begin in Houston until close to Thanksgiving, but this was quite a storm. The rain stung my eyes, so I closed them against the downpour.

I didn't have to be looking at Devins to know he was trying to sneak away. His preppy shoes were making little slip-slaps on the wet cement.

"Always wondered if it was true," I said, eyes still closed.

He froze at the sound of my voice. "If what's true?" he asked, his voice shrill.

"If I'm good enough to hit a target with my eyes closed."

9

He was smack up against the car again and didn't move a muscle for the twenty minutes it took Frank's guys to show up.

And when they did, sirens blasting, brakes squealing, testosterone oozing from their pores, they weren't guys at all, they were two young women, Reynolds and Soba. The women were somewhere around twenty-three and cocky, still impressed with their uniforms and with the importance of doing everything by the book.

I knew how they felt because I felt that way about ten years ago, when I was twenty-three. By the time I left Houston PD, five years after that, I didn't feel nearly so young, and it took a lot more to impress me than a uniform or a book. It took even more to impress me now.

"You realize you made an illegal entry?" Soba asked, after taking my statement. "That theoretically at least, we could be taking you to the station along with Mr. Devins here?"

"Would you, please?" I asked. "I can follow you in my car and get us out of the rain."

Soba shook her head. "If you're coming downtown, we're taking you."

The four of us fit rather snugly in the patrol car. Fortunately it was a short ride to police headquarters, and when we arrived, I asked for Frank; Devins phoned his lawyer, who arrived before Frank.

Frank greeted me with a glare, heavy eyebrows drawn together like a knotted rope. "Devins' lawyer is considering pressing B&E charges against you!"

Frank is tall, with strong, muscular shoulders. He has a rugged jaw, and curly dark hair edging around the collar of his shirt. And big brown eyes. He's quite good looking when he isn't angry, but at work Frank is almost always mad about something, which makes it hard for anybody to get mad at *him*.

"I had keys," I said. "His secretary gave them to me."

"Uh-huh. Keys given to you by a disgruntled employee. I know it must've been a surprise, him attacking you when he finds you skulking around his office with proof of a million-dollar fraud." The sarcasm was dripping off his tongue. "What were you thinking?"

"I was thinking I'd be home by now, watching *Saturday Night Live*," I answered.

Frank was getting a little patronizing, a little patriarchal in tone. Just because he was my boss once, didn't mean he was my boss now.

"I'm only speaking out of concern for your best interests, Lynnie," his tone softened, the eyebrows parted. "I don't know what goes on in your head sometimes, I never did."

Frank was now getting a little familiar, a little sentimental in tone. Just because we were a couple once, didn't mean we were a couple now.

"Look, if you're gonna charge *me* with something . . ."

"Thing I really wish you hadn't done was shoot his car."

"Why? Is *it* gonna press charges?"

Frank and I eyed each other for a few minutes.

Finally I broke the tension, which was getting as heavy as the downpour hammering on his high-rise windows. "Am I free to go now?"

He nodded. "Sure. I'm gonna call it a night myself. Need a ride to your car?"

"That'd be nice of you."

"You hungry?" he asked.

I raised my eyebrows.

"We're friends, aren't we? Friends can get a little midnight snack."

My clothes were still damp and my mascara had run down my cheeks, but I was starving. So I hit the Ladies, washed my face, put the makeup back on, combed my hair, and smoothed out the wrinkles in my black tee shirt. The results weren't too bad.

I was blessed with a figure ladies' lingerie sales personnel describe as "statuesque," and gravity has not yet brought me down. I'm five foot ten, with broad shoulders and big feet, and I run every morning. I do free weights when I feel like it. I might not win a marathon, but I'm pretty sure I could finish one.

We headed for Hop Louie's place downtown. We always used to go there, and it hadn't changed much. It was still disreputably dark, lit up with pink neon, front door flanked by double gold dragons, menu the same since nineteen fifty-three. If you're a cop in Houston, or you were one once, you go there. The quantities are large, the prices reasonable, and you get forks instead of chopsticks.

"This is a good place for an assignation," I remarked.

"You should know," Frank said good-naturedly.

I shot him a look.

"I meant because of your work," he amended. "Along with the insurance cases, you've been doing a lot of domestic, I heard."

I was genuinely surprised he had a clue what I was working on. It was months since we last talked, and that was over a car repo I did, the car being stolen in the first place.

Frank ordered us the moo shu vegetables, the sweet and sour chicken, and a couple of the restaurant's signature chroma-key blue rum drinks, decked out with fruit and paper umbrellas.

We were dining with a crowd of louche, pale young hipster-artist types, an old woman feeding pieces of chicken to a small dog cradled in a green net shopping bag, and two transvestites.

Maybe it was the lack of competition that made Frank look good, or maybe it was the wicked umbrella drinks.

"I miss seeing you around," he said. "You used to stop by for lunch at least, every week or two."

"I've been on a diet."

"You're even prettier now than you were when I first met you," Frank flattered me. His eyes were getting something resembling a twinkle in them. It was a dangerous thing when he made his eyes twinkle like that. I looked away.

"No smarter though," I remarked. "Judging by the company I keep."

"Good, I like 'em to be a little stupid. That way I come off looking better."

After we had three or four little paper parasols each stacked up by our plates, we went back to his place, a worn monument to art deco near Reliant Stadium.

Sitting at Frank's kitchen table, we watched a rerun of an Astros' game on ESPN late night, and switched from the restaurant's rum to scotch; moving on to the bedroom we switched from being just friends to something more.

Looking into those liquid brown eyes of his was a lot more intoxicating than the alcohol. We were wrapped around each other, our hands and lips moving slow and sweet. I was floating high on his kisses; still, I made a perfunctory attempt to sober myself up.

"I don't know what I'm doing here," I said, but he was already lifting my tee shirt over my head.

"It's like riding a bike," he whispered, kissing my neck. "It'll come back to you."

He had my bra pushed down over my shoulders. He was nibbling all along my collar bone and between my breasts, his lips moving lower, and lower, and I was a complete and utter goner then.

When he went to sleep, I lay there in his bed awhile, watching shadows undulate across the ceiling. He was right; it had all come back to me. Including the reasons why I wasn't with him anymore. After a while I got up, made myself coffee, swallowed a couple of aspirin, and called a cab to take me to my car.

I rooted around in my purse for a pen and paper. I wanted to leave Frank a note, but what would be right? Thanks for being there? Thanks for dinner? Thanks for not arresting me? Thanks for the memories? In the end I just wrote "Thanks." Let him take it anyway he wanted.

I threw the pen back in my purse, right on top of two computer CDs of William Devins' accounting files, undeniable evidence of his scam.

On impulse, I plucked a plastic baggie from Frank's kitchen cabinet, stuck the disks inside, labeled the bag "Lynn's B&E," and tucked it behind Frank's backup bottle of scotch. In other words, if anything happened to me, which was maybe a little melodramatic with a case like this, but still, they'd be found, by a cop with a certain interest in the case.

The cab driver tapped his horn and I let myself out of Frank's apartment. By the time I stumbled up the stairs to my own apartment and climbed into bed, it was almost morning.

I was beat, but the caffeine and the alcohol were battling it out in my brain, and the caffeine was winning hands down. Besides, there were too many things I didn't want to end up dreaming about to even think about sleeping.

So I lay there in bed until it was officially Sunday morning, and the church bells at Our Lady of Guadalupe were ringing. I was hung over and pissed at myself. My eyes were tight and dry and my head was pounding; a hot shower and more coffee only helped so much.

It was nine a.m. when I jogged down the front stairs of my duplex. It needed paint and it had termites, and nobody would confuse its utilitarian design for architect Renzo Piano's work on The Menil Collection museum, but because of its proximity to a power plant and the jets of Houston Hobby, my rent is just about affordable.

The day was blue sky beautiful, and the planes were sailing silver through little wispy clouds. Downstairs I saw my neighbor Rita's door was open, and through the screen, New Age jazz blew out along with a heavenly whiff of banana pancakes. I stopped for just a second, taking a long, pleasurable inhale. She stuck her head out the door and caught me.

Like me, Rita is in her early thirties. Our similarities end there. Small boned and curly haired, she's employed as a baby nurse, bringing joy into the world instead of tending to its miseries. Rita was young when she married food truck driver Paul Benson, and was pregnant with their now-fourteen-year-old daughter, Amber. They have better credit than I do, and a Himalayan cat they adopted as a stray.

. I knew all of it except the part about the cat before Rita told me, but I didn't let on. It's conditioned behavior, doing a background check on everybody around me.

"I thought I heard you. Come in and have breakfast," she said.

"I'm not that hungry," I lied. The pancakes smelled delicious, but I wasn't sure I wanted to go in. Rita wasn't just my neighbor, she was my best friend, and I would surely end up confessing that I'd gone home with Frank, for God's sake, a habit I thought I'd outgrown. I wasn't sure I wanted to confess just yet.

Rita was eying me suspiciously. I never pass on her banana pancakes. "You don't look good," she said.

"Little too much to drink last night, that's all." I tried to manage a smile.

"You saw Frank, huh?"

So much for saving my confession. "Yeah. We had ourselves the usual train wreck." I wanted commitment, the kind of relationship that was going somewhere, not constantly derailing.

And I knew full and well I couldn't have that with Frank. Didn't I?

She shook her head at me. "Have you always considered yourself a glass half-empty sort of person?"

"It depends what's in the glass," I said. "Last night it was altogether empty. And I mixed rum punch and scotch. I should have one of those 'Just Say No' bumper stickers pasted on my forehead."

"Or possibly on another part of your anatomy," she winked. "I don't imagine Frank was real interested in your forehead."

I laughed, but laughing made me wince. And thinking too much about Frank made the laughter turn perilously close to tears. I told myself that's what happens when you miss a night's sleep.

"Give me a rain check on breakfast, okay? I've got paperwork," I said.

I walked as fast as I could over to my office, which is only a mile and a more gentrified neighborhood away. Up at Fernando's, boys on bikes were waiting at the counter for smoothies, and a pretty Mexican girl was necking with her boyfriend. A toddler sucked on a piece of red licorice at one of the outdoor tables while his mother slathered on the sunscreen. I waved at the kid and the kid waved back. It was hard to stay miserable on a gorgeous day when little kids waved at you.

I stood there for a minute and squinted up at the shining sky awhile. Then I closed my eyes, just letting the sunshine sink in. A hundred spots of silver and gold, hot and bright, danced against the surface of my lids, like someone had thrown me a bucket full of precious coins and they were within my reach. It was just an illusion, of course, rather like love.

CHAPTER TWO

My office perches over what was once a battered movie theater and is now a battered movie theater polished up and divided into eclectic office space and specialty retail shops selling handmade chili-pepper-shaped soap, Tex-Mex cuisine, and punk couture.

It's a one-hundred-and-fifty-foot workplace room with peach-painted walls and the upscale address my apartment lacks, which makes up for its minuscule size and the fact that it's almost impossible to find a parking space.

I opened the window and the hall door for a little fresh air, and had just turned on my Mac to type my report for Fidelity Insurance, when the phone rang.

"Bryant Investigations," I answered. My heart hammered. Who else would call on a Sunday morning except Frank?

"This is Joe Carver with Fidelity Nationwide. Is Lynn there?"

I stifled a sigh. "Hey there, Joe. I'm writing up the Devins' case now."

"That's what I'm calling about. Look, Lynn, the thing is, we're trying to duck the publicity here."

"I understand. Keep it quiet. Ignore phone calls from major news sources."

"A little more than that. We're working on damage control."

"What kind of damage?"

"Well, you see, we can't have our contractors going against the letter of the law. That visit you made to Devins' office . . .

17

you shouldn't have done that."

My hangover headache came out of semi-remission and raced across my forehead. "I know, things got a little out of hand. I can drop the assault charges, it was no big deal."

"It's not the charges. You threatened his life."

"He threatened mine."

Carver cleared his throat. "The thing is, Lynn, I mean, we'll pay you on this one, but, uh, we need to disassociate ourselves from your agency for a while."

"Disassociate."

"The other case files I gave you, well . . . we're going to want them back."

I drew in my breath sharply. I'd had a slow summer; I was counting on those cases. There went the rent, both apartment and office.

"I just saved you a million dollars," I choked.

He gave a short laugh. "It might cost us a lot more than that in canceled policies if it gets out that individuals in our employ brutalized our clients."

I hung up the phone. Carver didn't call back.

I could just hear Frank saying I-told-you-so, but in reality, Frank wasn't saying anything at all right now, was he?

And if he walked in the door right that minute, I wouldn't give him a chance to mouth off at me, anyway. I'd keep his lips busy in a completely different way, before he could even explain why it had taken him so long to show up. Not that I wanted him to show up in the first place. I slumped over my desk and put my hands over my face. My temples throbbed away.

And that was when Karen Shaw gave a tentative knock on my door and walked in, wearing a hot pink halter top and silver pants.

I sat up straight and started shuffling papers, trying to look as if I was actively engaged in some business pursuit other than sulking.

She was simmering with a seductive sexuality, but her face was a little worn. She was somewhere between forty-five and forty-eight, tall, with a great body in those tight clothes, and long, thick blonde hair. Her eyes were a killer blue and her mouth was a sweet rosebud. But she was mid-forties all the same.

"Talent agency's down the hall," I told her, "but I think they're closed today."

Karen smiled, like I just paid her the best compliment in the world. "I'm looking for Lynn Bryant," she said.

"My mistake then. You found her. How can I . . . ?"

"I'm Karen Shaw, and I need your help," and then she started to cry.

"Have a seat." I'd just lost my biggest account; I couldn't afford to turn business away.

I handed her a Kleenex from a box on my desk, and she dropped down into a chair.

"Usually I'm not in on Sundays," I began, but she cut me off with a wave of her hand.

"I knew you'd be here," she said. "I found your name in the phone book and you just felt right."

My hair prickled along the back of my neck. Great, a lunatic. A hangover, a one-night stand with Frank, getting fired by a flunky at Fidelity Nationwide, and a lunatic.

"Well that's nice, but my point is that I can't spend a long time today, I've got a lunch date." I kept my voice breezy, and my smile upbeat. "Why don't we schedule an appointment for another time?"

I flipped the pages in my empty Day-Timer. I found that with most crazies, you rescheduled them, they never showed up. Whatever insane impulse sent them to your doorstep in the first place had long since been replaced with another impulse by the time they were supposed to see you again.

"I know what you're thinking, but I'm not crazy," she said, looking up. A last tear dripped down her cheek. "Although I might be soon, if I don't get some help. I saw a woman get murdered last night."

"Then you should be talking to the police, not me," I said. "I can call someone for you right now." I reached for the phone. It was an excuse, anyway, to call Frank and act like nothing at all had happened between us.

She locked her gaze to mine. She looked desperate but not crazy.

"I can't go to the police. They'll never listen. I can pay you," she said, and she pulled a fat wad of greenbacks out of her purse, and laid them, an offering, on my desk.

The phone buzzed its dial tone in my hand.

"Just let me tell you what happened," she pleaded.

I let my hand slip the phone back in its cradle, and I nodded almost imperceptibly. I supposed it wouldn't hurt to listen.

If it was all hundreds, like the bills on top, there was probably two grand there. It wasn't as good as I would've gotten from Fidelity on the files they now wanted back, but it was good enough. Besides, it was a long time since I'd done anything resembling a homicide investigation. I used to be good at them.

"We were standing on my porch, Johnny and I," Karen said, her voice husky from crying. "We were . . . kissing. Well, more than kissing. He was touching me all over and—I begged him not to stop."

I felt myself color, but she went on like she was reciting her grocery list.

"I so didn't want him to let go of me, even for a second. We were out there a long time, I guess, and the rain started coming down harder and harder." She stopped there, as if looking for confirmation that, see, she wasn't crazy, it really was raining last night.

"I know," I said, "I was out in it too."

"So we . . . decided we better go inside. I took my keys out but I . . . I dropped them. They fell in the bushes. We'd had kinda a lot to drink." She looked hopeful I'd understand. "But that doesn't change what I saw."

"Go on," I said. Who the hell was I to judge, me, the consumer of umbrella drinks and Frank's J&B.

"I leaned down over the bushes. It was hard to see in the rain. Johnny asked if he could get them for me, but I said I had them, and I did have . . . have something. But it wasn't the keys. It was a hand. A woman's hand. It was all white and swollen, but the fingers were still twitching. And then I heard this scream.

" 'Don't kill me,' she said."

"Jesus! And you haven't called the cops?" I was reaching for the phone again, but Karen put her own hand on mine and stopped me.

"I screamed, I couldn't help myself. Johnny knelt down beside me. He asked me what was going on, because all he saw were the keys in my hand. The woman—she'd disappeared."

I made a choked sound. "Look, Ms. Shaw, I really don't think that I can help."

"But I've been seeing her for a few days now. And I saw her off and on all last night. Somebody beat her to death. With a belt, decorated with those silver things . . . conchos, I think you call them. Kicked her too, there were boots kicking her, work boots, metal-toed. There could've been a knife, as well, I'm not sure."

"Perhaps a therapist."

She sighed, impatient. "I don't need a therapist. I have plenty of insight into the human condition, including my own. I'm a psychic. I get paid for investigating people just the same as you do, except that what I investigate is on the inside, and what you see is on the outside. I know very well that when I see this woman's death it isn't really happening, not in the present, not in the here and now. But I think it either has happened or will happen. I'm not sure which. And the fact that I'm seeing these awful images tells me that there's something I'm supposed to do for the poor woman. At least I have to try."

She shoved the money across my desk. "I want you to come out to my house, see if you can find anything. Any evidence. Anything," she hesitated and then she spat the word out like it was something dirty, *"real."*

She was probably a lunatic, but you never knew. Sometimes the police brought in psychics the way they brought in bloodhounds, when they didn't have anything else to go on, and they were hoping somehow they could sniff out a clue.

The bloodhounds often worked, the psychics usually didn't pan out. Still, I already saw one thing real, her money.

I picked it up. "My rate's fifty an hour. I take three hundred as a retainer to start."

"That's twenty-two hundred dollars there in your hand," she said. "Keep it all. I know you'll earn it."

"I'm not sure this case is going to warrant that kind of outlay." Whether she was crazy or not, I wasn't going to cheat her.

"Take it. You need it," she said. "I insist."

I chewed my lip. How the hell would she know I needed it? Well, she said she was a psychic, right?

"I'll write you a receipt," I said. "I can't promise anything, but I'll be glad to . . . to take a look around."

She smiled an absolutely radiant smile that lit her up and made her look years younger. I found myself smiling back.

"I knew you'd help me." She touched my arm. "I don't need

a receipt. I trust you."

"If I can't find anything, I'll give it back," I promised, "less my retainer, of course."

"When can you come over?" she asked, giving me her address.

I looked at my watch, almost eleven a.m. "I have some work to finish here," I said, "I'll be over in a few hours." I wanted to spend a little time finding out who Ms. Shaw was, before I just showed up at her door.

She nodded, relieved. "I'll see you later then," she agreed, shaking my hand. Her handshake was firm and generous.

"By the way, you shouldn't be so angry at him," she told me. "I believe he really does care."

I felt the little hairs prickle on the back of my neck again, but I didn't say anything and she didn't say anything more either.

CHAPTER THREE

I watched from my window while Karen Shaw climbed into the backseat of a taxi idling outside.

Then I popped a couple more aspirin, dry, and sat down at the computer for a while.

Karen's residence and place of business was in Channelview, off one of the canal streets. She'd lived there a long time, apparently buying the house back when such houses were still pretty cheap, a refuge for hippies and freaks, and then later, gangbangers, and later still, artists.

Before she moved to Houston, Karen lived in a small West Texas town near Big Bend National Park called Marathon. I looked it up, and saw Marathon was not too far from Fort Stockton, south of Santiago Peak and about an hour and a half off U.S. Route 10. In the town's online yellow pages there were no Shaws presently listed.

Karen didn't own a car and had no DMV record, at least not in the last five years. My computer wouldn't take me back any farther.

She was listed in several database registries that promoted psychics, spiritualists, and metaphysical healers, but unlike most of them, she had no advertisements running, no web page of her own. But her name turned up in many a chat-room archive, long, flowery messages praising her insight and wisdom, claims that Karen was instrumental in saving marriages, finding lost sisters, connecting with soul mates; and that she herself was a profound and old soul. Other than that, there was nothing.

Then I logged into a website of classified police files, using a security code I'm not officially allowed to use anymore.

There I discovered that Karen Shaw had been arrested, once, over ten years earlier, for operating a fortune-telling business on the street without a license. She also filed a report about two years ago, regarding a fatal automobile accident she said she'd witnessed. It was at a bad intersection up near Lake Livingston, and Ms. Shaw was described as "incoherent at the scene." The accident report was continued on another web page, but that page wouldn't load on my browser.

I exited the high-tech highway, locked up the office, deposited Karen's money at the corner ready-teller, and realized I'd left my car back at my place. By the time I slunk back to pick it up, Frank still hadn't called, and I was beat.

I topped off the gas tank of my serviceable Corolla sedan. Like my usual attire, my car is blend-into-the-background black. I headed for the Loop northbound to Channelview and Karen's place.

I merged smoothly into traffic that just about immediately reached the apotheosis of speed. For the next forty-five minutes, it never again moved faster than that initial record-breaking twenty miles per hour.

Although I'd promised Karen I'd see her in a few hours, over five had passed when I crawled off the freeway and took the turn down Rose Avenue to Karen's place on Seaver. Everything felt damp in this neighborhood, with the channel so close. Dragonflies and moths skittered around. There was a faint smell, too, something like a goldfish bowl that needed cleaning.

Karen's house was a little blue stucco tract home with ragged-looking shrubs planted along the sidewalk. Nobody had done what you'd call gardening in a long time, but the house was freshly painted. There was a narrow open porch on the front, which must've been where she and her boyfriend were fooling around. A big overgrown hunk of night jasmine ran the length of the porch.

I poked around in the bushes before I knocked on her door, but I found nothing.

No one answered the door when I knocked. The shades in what must've been the living room were drawn, and a neon sign suspended in the front window that read "Psychic Readings" was turned off.

I walked around to the back of the house. There was a sun room, glassed in, with a separate entrance. I knocked on that door, too; again, no answer. For a moment I thought she'd given up on me, but as I turned away, the door swung open.

I leaned inside. "Ms. Shaw? Karen?" I heard somebody stirring around, and I walked in.

The sun room was clearly where she gave her readings.

A candle, tarot cards, and a crystal ball were laid out neatly on a velvet-colored table, a folding chair on either side. There was a small crucifix on the wall directly behind the table, and a bundle of herbs. I sniffed them; they smelled like sage and lavender, and I could've stood there a long time inhaling the fragrance. It reminded me of something, some early childhood thing, a little sachet my mother kept in my underwear drawer.

There were shelves crammed with books, crystals, candles. It was a small room but neat. When I lifted a crystal in my hand it caught the sunlight through the windows behind me and sent a rainbow of light bouncing off the walls. Not a speck of dust on it.

I heard a faint moan. I set the crystal down, took my gun out of my purse, and headed for the sound.

It was coming from the other side of a swinging door, which led into the kitchen. Unlike the sun room, the kitchen was a mess. There were the remains of what must've been a spaghetti dinner shoved to one end of the table, more dishes stacked in the sink, empty wine bottles, glasses, dirty pots on the stove.

Wrapped in a short silk robe with a Chinese dragon on the back, Karen was slumped in a kitchen chair, face-down on the part of the table that wasn't covered with dirty dishes. Her hand was clutching a seriously depleted bottle of bourbon.

I told myself I'd never drink anything stronger than Coca-Cola ever again.

Karen moaned once more. I put my gun back in my bag, and shook her shoulder. She lifted her head, groggy. Puffy-eyed, she looked her age now.

Still, she managed a crooked smile. "I had a feelin' I'd see you again today."

"We had an appointment," I said. "Sorry to be so late."

"Jesus," she pushed the bottle away from her, and pulled her robe tighter. "I kind of forgot." She was smoothing her hair, making an attempt at least to sober up.

"You shouldn't leave your back door unlocked like that. Anybody could walk right in."

She shrugged. "What's outside can't be as bad as what's in here." She tapped her head.

"Rough afternoon?" I asked, but before she shaped an answer, the front door slammed and then the swinging door burst open. I had my gun drawn by the time the guy took a full step into the kitchen.

"What the fuck?" he said, surprised.

"Please," Karen murmured. "Put the gun away. This is my friend, Johnny Ross. Johnny, this is the private detective I told you I was going to see, Lynn Bryant."

"Good to meet you," he said and extended his hand.

He didn't look that thrilled, actually. He was in his late twenties, which put him four years younger than me, and a good seventeen years younger than Karen. Tall and slender, he had light brown hair, wavy and down to his shoulders, high cheekbones, and nice green eyes. There was something edgy about those eyes though, like there was something he had to look out for, but he just wasn't sure what it was. It was possible being with Karen did that to a guy.

He was wearing tight-fitting Levi's with a rip in both knees and a white tee shirt. His body was muscular without being pumped. He wasn't the type of guy who went down to the police academy gym and bench-pressed two-twenty like Frank, but he was no stranger to physical labor, either.

Both his jeans and tee shirt were splattered with paint, paint rimmed his fingernails, there was even a streak of paint in his hair. My guess on his profession was house painter, which would explain the fresh coat of blue on Karen's front porch.

Now that he was sure I wasn't going to shoot him, he flopped down in the chair next to Karen and picked up the bourbon.

"Are we out of milk?" he asked.

Karen sighed.

He touched her shoulder, tender. "You were up all night. I thought you were gonna try to get some rest."

"I couldn't close my eyes . . . I kept seeing . . . you know." Karen shook her head, which made her cringe. "After I went to see Ms. Bryant I, well, I tried to make it stop." She looked at us, chagrined. "Passed out on the kitchen table for a few hours, I guess."

Johnny looked from me to her, from her to me. "I'm not sure what good this is going to do, having an investigator nosing around."

I wasn't sure what good it would do either. "If you'd like me to leave, come back tomorrow," I began, but Karen interrupted.

"I'll take a cold shower. I'll be okay."

She rose, a little unsteady, and put her arms around Johnny's shoulders. He lifted his hands up and stroked hers. They both seemed to need each other so much, to care so much, that it hurt to look at.

Karen broke away first. She gave him a quick kiss on the cheek, and hurried through the swinging door. Almost immediately, a shower started running in the back of the house.

I turned to Johnny, who was studying me with the scrutiny of a bug he thought he might dissect. He was trying to figure me out, or more likely trying to figure out what I was doing with Karen. Since I wasn't quite sure myself, I turned the tables on him.

"You were with her, last night, when she saw . . . the body?"

He started stacking the dishes at the table.

"Yeah, I was with her." He eyed me, speculatively. "Whatever she's seeing, it's been going on for over a week, and scaring the living shit out of her."

"I know she's scared."

He carried the dishes to the sink. "So she's scared and you come along, taking her money, thinking she's a fool?" he asked.

"She came to me, and I'm not that kind of a person."

He shrugged, like he might believe me, but it didn't matter. He started collecting the pots and pans.

"Has she ever done this before?" I asked.

"What do you mean?"

"Called in an investigator, to look into something."

"No," he said, and he seemed pissed off. "And it's a bad idea now."

"Why do you think so?"

"Because you can't understand."

"And you do?"

He carried the pots and pans to the sink and added them to the stack there.

"You honestly believe you can find what she's seeing?"

"I don't know. I already looked around. There's nothing in

29

the bushes."

"Oh, you looked in the bushes, good plan. You're wasting your time."

I heard the shower shut off again.

"I've wasted it before," I said.

As soon as Johnny did the dishes, he left her house, in one hell of a hurry it seemed to me. Meanwhile, I poked around the crawl space beneath the house, and explored the back yard, parting the shrubs and bushes. It was postage-stamp small and bore the traces of a long ago garden lost in the weeds.

Then I looked in her garbage can and her recycle bin. I wandered through her neighbors' yards. I parted their shrubbery too, to the furor of a dog inside one of the houses.

The only thing I found was a loose board on her front porch steps. "You should get this fixed," I told her.

"There's a lot I should fix," Karen admitted, as she mainlined coffee. "Did you come up with anything at all?"

I shook my head. "No bones, blood stains, or murder weapons around here."

Karen shrugged, as if she'd expected as much.

"I'll do door-to-door next, ask your neighbors if they saw—"

She interrupted me, vehement. "No. Don't involve them. No one saw it but me."

Now it was my turn to shrug.

"Why me, though?" Karen asked. "Why are the visions coming to me?" She seemed to be asking herself more than me.

I raised my hands and lowered them again. I didn't believe in visions in the first place, but if *I* was going to have one, I hoped it would show me the winning lottery numbers rather than someone being beaten to death with a belt.

I also believed that you saw what you wanted to see in life. That was true whether you were my landlord ignoring termite holes, or me, imagining myself receiving citations for my dogged investigative work.

I tried to think of a nice way to tell Karen that perhaps she just wanted to see some woman being beaten to death with a belt, although why she would want to see that, I couldn't say.

"It started after I saw the two girls . . ." she said.

"You're seeing girls, too?"

She laughed, lightly. "I mean really saw them, in the flesh. They came in for a reading a few days ago, a birthday present for one of them, but it was the other one, the one who gave me the money, that I started to read by mistake. I thought her mother was trying to contact her in some way. She said she hadn't seen her in a number of years. But the birthday girl wanted to leave and . . . I didn't even finish the reading. It upset me, to be unable to finish. The next day I had the first vision."

"The girl might be a place to start. Who was she?"

Karen shook her head. "I don't know. I'd never seen either of them before, usually people call for an appointment, but they were a walk-in."

"Did you get a name?"

Karen sighed. "No. They never said their names. They paid in cash."

"Can you describe them?"

"They were both seventeen. The one having the birthday had blue streaks in her hair. The other one was pretty, and had dark hair. They didn't come in a car."

"Anything unusual about them, clothing, jewelry?"

"Just jeans. Tee shirts. That blue hair."

"That's not much to go on, and you don't know if they're connected to this woman you're seeing in the first place."

"You're right, of course."

"If they walked, they must be local, live nearby . . . ?"

"The pretty one said they came on the bus."

So I went through the motions. I walked to the bus stops closest to Karen's, and took down the route numbers going in both directions.

While the sun set a livid red, I whipped out my cell, sat down on a bus stop bench, and called the RTD. Eventually, despite it being Sunday evening, I found someone in dispatch who agreed to get me the names of drivers working those routes on the date Karen said she'd seen the girls. I left my cell and office numbers, and promised to call back myself tomorrow, and that was that.

I walked back to Karen's. I told her what I'd done, and she seemed satisfied, as well as more or less sober. I saw her eying the bottle of bourbon though, now tucked away on the kitchen counter.

I headed for the door. It was full dark now, and I was hungry. Besides aspirin and coffee, I hadn't had anything to eat all day, and I'd spent enough time on what was probably a fool's errand.

"What are you going to do now?" she asked me, licking her lips.

I practiced my patience. "Well, since you don't want me to question the neighbors, I'll check back with the RTD tomorrow, see if I can turn up any leads on those two girls. If I can find them, I'll question them. I'll also check the files in the county morgue. Look into any unsolved crimes in your immediate neighborhood." It sounded pretty lame and it was. "I don't know what else I *can* do," I admitted.

I gave her my card. "Call me if anything else happens. I'll let you know if I come up with something. And if not . . . I'll only charge you for my time today, and we'll hope everything just . . . goes away."

I was ready to bolt, and bolt fast.

Then she smiled at me, that big, radiant, incredibly persuasive smile. And all of a sudden, I didn't want to get away from her so fast. Her smile was like a blessing or something; it felt ridiculously good that she was bestowing it on me. I almost thought she was going to pat me on the head and go "there, there, you did your best," and everything would be all right in my world again.

No wonder a man over fifteen years younger wanted her.

"If you're done for now, will you come have dinner with me?" she asked, still smiling.

And so I found myself walking along the street with her. Things were mostly quiet, even around the bars; but the few layabouts hanging around on the corners all had their eye on Karen. It was a warm night and she had changed into an orange sundress with big blue flowers that fit tight across her hips and breasts. With her makeup on, and her hair in a French braid, her afternoon debauch wasn't so noticeable. A couple of guys whistled, and she laughed, seeming to enjoy the attention.

Karen leaned close to me, confidential. "I'm glad I came to you," she said. "It makes me feel like I'm doing something, anyway. I know I'm meant to do something about this. And I was meant to find you to help me. Do you ever feel that way, that something is absolutely meant to be?"

I could still smell the bourbon on her breath, beneath the coffee and what must've been breath mints. "Sure," I said, "but usually I'm wrong."

"You're being flip. That's not true." Her eyes met mine, and held my gaze. "Although you don't trust your heart enough."

"There's not a lot of things I trust."

"Name one thing you do."

"Instinct."

"Not bad," she said. "What else?"

I patted my purse. "And my Smith and Wesson."

She laughed. "Stick with instinct, you'll be fine."

She guided me to a coffee shop at the end of the street, its neon lights just springing on.

"They have the best grilled cheese in town," she told me.

I'd just been thinking about how much I wanted a grilled cheese sandwich. Pickles, cole slaw, maybe a chocolate shake.

"Great milkshakes too," she said.

I was a little unnerved.

Karen opened the door to the coffee shop and a bell rang. A waitress in roller skates rolled over right away and led us to a table with a view of the parking lot out back. She dropped menus in front of us.

"Anything you want's on the house, Karen. You were right, my boyfriend came back."

Karen smiled, and picked up the menu. Her hands were shaking. The waitress gave her an understanding nod. "I'll get you some coffee."

She swept away before I had a chance to order that grilled cheese. There was a little tray of oyster crackers and Tabasco and jam on the table. I opened a package of the crackers and ate them.

Karen looked at me, her eyes sympathetic. I thought she was feeling sorry for me because I was eating the crackers, which were pretty stale.

"You shouldn't try and hide it," she said.

"Hide what?" I crunched.

"How pretty you are. In that baggy tee shirt. And this man that you care about . . ."

"Whoa," I said, "I don't think we ever said anything about an exchange of services."

"You don't want to hear right now?"

"I absolutely, totally, completely, positively *never* want to hear."

"He loves you," she said, gently. Then, before I could get too riled up, she amended, "But I'd have to do a spread with the cards to really see what's going on. I'd like to give you a reading."

I crumpled up the cracker wrapper. "No thanks," I said.

"You don't believe in all this, do you?"

"No."

"Yet you're here."

"I believe you believe in it. But honestly I don't think that's what's going on. I'm thinking you could be seeing a repressed memory . . . something you saw when you were . . . half asleep or . . . something."

"Or near to passing out?"

I nodded.

"I suppose it doesn't matter where you think this is coming from," she spoke slowly and carefully, measuring her words. "It just matters that I'm not alone on this. I feel it very strongly, that I shouldn't be alone."

"What about Johnny?"

"He wants me to step back. Stop trying to see more, do the opposite, really, and close my eyes to it."

"Maybe he's right."

"He's afraid for me, I think. I'm scared, too. But to live a life worth living you can't turn away from things that frighten you."

"Sometimes that's the wisest choice."

She inclined her head as if to say I might be right. "I don't consider myself wise. I have a gift. When you're given something this precious you . . . you . . . can't abandon it."

Her eyes welled up with tears, but she swiped them away.

"When I was young, I didn't know what I had. I didn't understand it, and I didn't want it. There were other things I wanted, but I couldn't have them. This is what I got instead. I've done good with it. I want you to know that. I've done a lot of good."

I crumbled one of the crackers in my fingers. "You have many customers?"

"Clients," she corrected me. "I could give readings twenty-four hours a day if I was up to it." She dropped the menu on the table. "I'm not up to it right now."

"Have you had this type of experience before—seeing something that wasn't there?"

"A few times. But rarely with this intensity."

She put her hand over her eyes for a moment.

"You're not seeing things right now, are you?"

She shook her head, no.

"Did it ever occur to you," I tried not to insult her straight off, "did it ever cross your mind that you're seeing these . . . visions . . . when you've had too much to drink?"

Karen laughed. Apparently I'd said something really funny. "I only drink to make it stop."

She looked at me, and I guess I didn't seem like I completely believed her.

"That's what happened this afternoon. Johnny left me alone, and I could hear that woman screaming, begging, and I just have to stop the voices sometimes. I hear them everywhere, whether I want to or not."

Oh God, I thought. I'd taken the money of a complete lunatic, and now I was about to eat dinner with her. I just hoped she wasn't contagious, like she had the flu.

"I thought you would understand. We both try to help people, don't we? This woman that I'm seeing, she needs our help. I just hope when we can give it to her, it's not too late." She managed a smile, added, "Maybe it never is."

"Even if you are . . . plugged into something . . . I need a name, a place, a date, something to go on."

"So do I," she said. "I had hopes that *you'd* give me that."

I cleared my throat. "Here's the thing. It may be impossible to figure out who this woman even is. I think your friend Johnny's probably right. About stepping back and all. Really, my best advice to you is to let time take its course and probably these visions will just . . . move on. I can't find something if it isn't—real."

We were both silent for a moment, and then suddenly Karen was crying, inconsolably.

"Look," I said, "I don't mean to upset you."

But clearly I had. She was sobbing now. She stood up so abruptly her chair tipped over. "Maybe Johnny *was* right. Maybe nobody can help me."

The waitress shot me a look of pure hatred as Karen stormed out in tears. I left a couple of dollars on the table for the coffee, and reluctantly I followed Karen, but at a distance. Man, I was starving.

I honestly expected her to head straight to a liquor store, or any bar that was open, but she walked past two of each on her way around the corner to St. Anne's Catholic Church.

I slipped in the back and watched her for a good fifteen minutes, her head bowed, her lips moving in silent prayer.

When she left, she looked better, calmer. She wasn't crying anymore. She walked fast out of the church, and went straight to a florist's. It was a cavernous store, busy even on a Sunday night. Karen bypassed the cheap roses wrapped in cellophane and the potted orchids and slipped into the back room.

I lurked behind a display of cactus as Karen set a little basket filled with sage branches and dried lavender on the counter and pulled out her wallet.

"It's working?" the old man behind the register asked, flashing a toothy grin. "It's protecting your spirit?"

Karen nodded, but I thought she was lying.

She walked back toward her place, but changed her mind and doubled back on the street before hers. Then, at last, she stopped at a liquor store. She bought two bottles of bourbon, and a bottle of Chilean chardonnay.

I bought a sack of barbecue-flavored potato chips, which were better than nothing. I got a little buzz off the MSG, which helped me handle the drive home.

Back at my place, Rita's door was still open, and Amber was sitting at her electronic keyboard, picking out the notes to something that sounded like *Pomp and Circumstance.*

Amber waved. I waved back. I saw Rita in the kitchen, cutting up lemons. Probably going to make lemonade. The idea was appealing, but my headache was back full-tilt, and my knees felt stiff; I was that tired.

Inside my place it was quiet, except for the faint, muffled sound of the keyboard downstairs. I leaned against the door and left the lights off. The only illumination was moonlight filtering in through my drawn blinds, striping the butter soft, beige leather sofa I'd bought at a police auction, the flat-screen TV I rarely watched, and the watercolor desertscape I bought at a crafts fair, when I was hired to make sure the artist wasn't cheating on his wife.

I headed for the kitchen. I was still hungry; the chips I'd consumed just hadn't done the trick. But the idea of cooking, even scrambling an egg, seemed daunting.

Maybe I really wasn't that hungry after all.

I decided on a hot bath, leaving the lights off so I wouldn't have to see how bad I looked in the mirror. I took off all my clothes and climbed in the tub, by then half-wishing I'd knocked on Rita's door. A lemonade would be nice, and I wouldn't have to make that myself.

When the water started to cool, I stepped out of the tub and finally turned on the lights. I picked my clothes up off the floor and threw them in the hamper, which was full. Laundry.

Another chore I wasn't up to taking on.

I pulled on a pair of sweatpants and a tee shirt. I decided it was bed time, even if it wasn't quite ten o'clock. But then somebody rang my doorbell. I figured it was Rita, and maybe I would take that lemonade, but I threw open the door and there was Frank. Great, here I was wearing sweats, with my hair still wet from my bath, and no makeup on.

My face fell, I guess, because he took a step back. "You were expecting someone else," he said, kind of stiff.

I laughed. "Not in the way you're thinking." I opened the door wider, and he stepped inside.

"To what do I owe the pleasure?" I asked. I combed my fingers through my hair. My heart was hammering and I knew I was blushing, just a little.

He looked so damn good in a dress shirt and tie. There was just something about Frank's tough-guy persona all dressed up; it was like the wrapping paper on a birthday present you just knew you were going to want even more when you could take it all off and see what was inside.

"Not pleasure, exactly," he said.

"You were just in the neighborhood?" My heart rate slowed.

He shook his head. "I need you to drop those assault charges against William Devins."

Honestly, it had never seemed worth the effort to pursue them, anyway. I just wanted to keep Devins from running away before Fidelity Nationwide could get to him, and I could get my bonus. Yeah, I sure did get a great bonus. I got fired.

Now I was glowering at Frank, just thinking about it.

"It's a bad idea," he said. "A no-win for you."

I knew that; how dim did he think I was? After all I was the ex-cop with a gun; Devins was the whiny guy in fancy shoes. Who'd believe he had me pinned down on the garage floor? Who *wanted* anyone to believe it?

Still, it wasn't a good idea to let Frank know you agreed with him, ever. He'd just continue to press the advantage until he came to something you couldn't agree to, or at least regretted having agreed to, in the morning.

"Why?" I said to him. "Why is it a no-win?"

Frank dropped down on my sofa and put his feet up on my coffee table like it was old times and he was thinking, still, about moving in.

"Devins' secretary has recanted her statement to you, says you pressured her to make such accusations, and then stole her keys. Devins' lawyer is this hardball little guy named Kincaid, and he claims Fidelity Nationwide has backed way off, the VP of Claims is saying that he in no way sanctioned your, and I quote, 'extreme investigation.' We can't do anything with this case."

He had that paternal tone in his voice again. I didn't like it much.

"I talked to Fidelity this morning," I said. "You don't have to tell me what's going on."

"Look, I'm not trying to piss you off here. The point is, Kincaid says if you don't drop your charges, he's filing against *you*. Not *considering* doing it, he'll *do* it. I'm just keeping you in the loop."

From anybody else, I would've appreciated it. What I wanted from Frank was something entirely different than legal advice. And clearly, he had no intention of providing it.

I sat down on the edge of the coffee table and shoved Frank's feet off. "Just waxed it," I lied.

The eyebrows went together like someone had tied them and he spat out, "I don't know what I'm doing here."

"It'll come back to you," I said meanly.

He didn't look as hot as he probably thought he did in that Pierre Cardin knockoff silk tie.

Frank got up and went for the door. "You know, I almost believed last night might mean something."

It meant a lot more than I cared to tell him about, not when the only reason he'd come over to my place was to tell me how to run my business. "Old times," I said. "It meant for old time's sake."

He looked me over, up and down, very cooly, just once. "You never did want *me*, did you, Lynnie? Just the information I fed you between the sheets."

He stomped down the stairs. So that's what he thought about me. Okay, I'd live with that. I'd rather he thought I had no feelings than that I had far too many.

I closed the door behind him carefully, and listened to his footsteps fade away.

It was true that once, when I was still police, I was investigating a shooting connected to the nephew of a certain local-area, well-regarded-downtown, Chief of Police. So I was told to back off.

But I didn't back off. Frank said I was like a dog with a bone; I wouldn't give it up until I'd chewed it through. I strongly believed, and still do, that you don't see that something stinks and let it lie there stinking.

Frank had given me some information that I used to press my advantage in the case. Thus armed, office politics be damned, I brought the kid in, and the prosecutor nailed a conviction. Everyone started treating me differently after that. So I resigned, with a smile on my face.

Did I ever look back? Sure. And mostly what I saw was Frank telling me not to take things so personally; there was only so much you could do, and nothing more.

I supposed not taking things personally included ignoring the fact that right around that time, he started keeping his office door locked in the middle of the day, so I couldn't just walk in on him, or him and whoever he was with; and the way the new file clerk brushed her hand across his shoulder, and the way he smiled when she smiled, too.

CHAPTER FOUR

I didn't sleep well, but at least I slept, and late. I hadn't set the alarm, and it was already after ten when I took a quick shower and pulled open my top dresser drawer. Empty of all black tee shirts. My entire working wardrobe was in my hamper. I pulled on yesterday's jeans and found a serviceable pale-blue cotton sweater. It felt like I was wearing a neon sign; it was that much more colorful than my usual attire.

I had too much to do to hit the laundromat first thing, but I threw my clothes in a plastic bag, hauled it to my car, and tossed it in the trunk. I'd get to it eventually.

First, I'd go see Devins' lawyer before I just caved in and dropped those assault charges. I was not going to go away quietly with my tail tucked between my legs. I might tuck in my tail, but I was going to bark a little first.

En route, I called the RTD again and this time, I was able to get the names of the drivers on Karen's bus line the day the two girls visited her. I left messages for all the drivers, describing the girls I was looking for, explaining they were potential witnesses in a homicide case.

Then I called Karen. I wanted to tell her that unless I got something off the bus drivers, I'd be sending her a check, less my three-hundred-dollar retainer, no hourly charges. I decided there was absolutely no point in holding out hope to the hopeless just because I was broke.

There was no answer. Maybe she didn't have an answering

machine. Maybe she just intuited who called.

It was raining when I reached River Oaks, and the offices of William Devins' lawyer, John Kincaid.

He shared a suite near the country club with a bunch of other lawyers, but you were supposed to think the swell address and the receptionist and the thick carpet were all his, not just a cramped reception cubicle and windowless office as small as mine.

He did have a secretary, a skinny white-blonde secretary who wore glossy lipstick and no bra, and had French-tipped fingernails so long I wondered how she could type with them.

She knocked on Kincaid's door, announcing my name. The door was directly behind her desk, so all she had to do was swivel her chair, not actually stand up.

Kincaid flung the door open. He was quite short, and had his hair slicked back, and his suit was a cheap knockoff. I wondered why Devins couldn't do any better for a lawyer. Of course, he might not want to. A better lawyer than Kincaid might ask a higher caliber of questions. Perhaps Devins didn't want to be bothered answering them.

He ushered me into his private chamber, lined with tennis trophies and towering stacks of file folders.

"I guess you know I'm the one that filed the assault charges against your client," I told Kincaid.

"I know your name," Kincaid settled on the edge of his cluttered desk, and swung his legs back and forth like a kid. "What are you doing here?"

I hadn't quite decided until that moment.

"I want it in writing," I told him. "And notarized. That you will not come after me anyway, if I withdraw my charges."

"Why would I bother?" he sneered.

"Because you're not just intimidating *me*. You're attempting to intimidate a Fortune five hundred insurance company. So that your client gets to keep the million bucks he stole and you get to keep whatever portion of that million dollars he's paying you."

He sighed impatiently. "Fidelity Nationwide has made it extremely clear that they will not second-guess our claim in this matter."

"Ah, but if they should, say, dawdle a bit with their payment, and if Devins forgets to go play nice with his girlfriend again, or this time his wife turns on him, well, then you have the option of trotting me out again, and complaining about my behavior."

"A very slim possibility." His legs stopped swinging, and he smiled an unctuous smile. "But hypothetically, supposing such a scenario occurred, in what way would it benefit me to have a document drawn up exonerating you?"

"I have the files," I said.

His smile dropped off his face like someone had slapped it.

"You have the what files?"

"Your client cleaned off his hard drive, but he kept encrypted accounting files in his floor safe. His secretary told me. I knew she would say I coerced her confession as soon as you, or somebody, informed her she was an accessory to insurance fraud. I didn't go to Devins' office on a Saturday night to say pretty please, will you confess, too? I was after something more substantial. Proof no one could take back."

Kincaid blanched. His mouth twitched like it was trying to find his smile again but he had to settle for a scowl.

"You seriously expect me to believe that?"

I smiled. "No. But why don't you call Mr. Devins and ask him if the numbers that access his safe correspond to the letters in 'Smell It.' I don't even like to think what that means."

Kincaid apparently decided to believe me all of a sudden.

"I'll have the paperwork you requested drawn right up. And you can . . . we can . . . arrange an exchange of the files for your paperwork."

"I want the statement from Mr. Devins first. And I want another statement made by Mr. Devins, or from your offices directly, and I want it issued to Fidelity Nationwide and the attention of Mr. Joe Carver."

Kincaid's mouth dropped. "What kind of statement?"

"I'll give it to you word for word," I suggested.

Kincaid reached for a legal pad, and scribbled what I told him.

" 'Dear Mr. Carver, this is to inform you that not only does my client, Mr. William Devins, have absolutely no complaint, nor does he intend to file any complaint in regard to Ms. Lynn A. Bryant of Bryant Investigations, but that to the contrary, he has nothing but praise for her diligent efforts.' That's it. Keep it simple. You can use your own proper legalese of course."

"Just what do you think you're going to accomplish by having me write something like that?" Kincaid's voice was tight.

"I just want it on record."

I marched to the door, which was admittedly a rather short march. Then I added, "By the way, if you think the files are at my home or in my office, think again. I'll be back this afternoon around four. Make sure the documents are drawn up and delivered by then."

Kincaid gave a short nod and made a sound like invisible hands were strangling him.

Heartened by the thought, I decided to give Karen Shaw's case another go.

I swung downtown and made a stop at the county morgue, spending a few unfruitful hours looking for anything that looked remotely interesting in death certificates culled from Karen's neighborhood, but came up empty. The sheer number of people who'd died in uninteresting ways, not to mention the stale air and inadequate fluorescent lights, were depressing.

Outside, it was seriously raining. I tried calling Karen again, but there was still no answer.

I thought I might as well drive over, see her in person. But driving down Wayside, the driver's side wiper blade stopped working. The wiper made a terrible, fingernails on the blackboard sound for about thirty seconds and then it just smeared the windshield, so that everything was a blur of raindrops, kinda pretty like a Monet landscape, except that you didn't usually have to drive through a Monet.

I pulled into the first gas station I came to, bought a package of wiper blades from the mini-mart, and installed them myself, huddling under the canopy between the gas pumps.

A skinny red-haired guy in a black Explorer honked at me, trying to get at the pump.

His power window slid down. "You shouldn't be doing that here."

"Go around to the pumps on the other side or wait a minute. I'm working as fast as I can."

He chose to wait, engine running, exhaust spewing my way. His impatience was rewarded; I was finished fast.

I got back in the car, started the engine, shifted to reverse, and bam! My head slammed against the windshield. Mr. Impatient had backed his SUV into my car, which, having been in reverse itself, and my foot off the brake, crunched back into a beige Altima behind me.

My head hurt. I climbed out of the car gingerly, as if the act of exiting the vehicle could cause further injury. My hood was majorly crumpled and so was the trunk. I doubted the damn car was even drivable. The red-headed guy jumped out of his own car, yelling, as if it was my fault, and the Altima driver was exiting the mini-mart, running toward her car, screaming.

On top of everything else, now I was going to have to deal with another insurance company.

A patrol car eventually arrived and the other drivers stopped screaming and yelling. The officer drew a diagram of the accident, very slowly, and very carefully, ignoring all of us. Occasionally the officer looked up, and I smiled wearily, trying to bond with him and at the same time send the message that if he'd just hurry it up and I could get my car towed to the repair shop, pick up a rental, and go on with my life, it would be much appreciated.

Just as he finished his meticulously drawn diagram, a call came in over his radio. The dispatcher read his unit number in with a list of others. "One Adam Twelve . . . Possible one-eighty-seven . . . thirteen forty-four Seaver, Channelview . . ."

A one-eighty-seven was a homicide and the address was Karen Shaw's.

I showed the cop my PI license, and explained that the address I'd just heard come over his radio was that of a client of mine, and I really needed to be on the scene.

As I expected, my car didn't run, and he was generous enough to give me a ride over.

At Karen's, there was a row of official vehicles lining the curb: an ambulance, two squad cars, plus the one I arrived in. There was also a dirty grey Ford, which would've been the plainclothes detectives' car.

One of the two plainclothes guys was bald and wearing a striped tie. He was talking to one of the paramedics. The other one had an early Beatles haircut and was wearing a raincoat with the collar turned up. He was listening while Johnny spoke, the two of them huddled under an umbrella. He was the guy in charge, Detective Hale.

Johnny's shirt and jeans were soaked through, apparently he'd been out in the downpour without benefit of that umbrella for some time.

I thanked the officer who'd given me a ride, and flashed my license at the uniforms, who were busy drawing a line of police tape across the porch. I flashed it again as I stepped up next to Johnny.

Johnny was pale and agitated, and he kept wiping at his nose and his eyes. I heard part of what he was saying.

"I was working at Lowe's market, on Sheldon, trying to finish up the exterior trim before the rain really started coming down . . . and I just got this feeling . . . I don't know. I had to see her. Left the ladder up and everything. Jumped in my van but . . . I couldn't get the engine to turn over. So I walked. And then I ran . . ."

"How long did it take you?" the detective asked.

"I dunno. About fifteen, twenty minutes."

I felt something bad twisting around in my stomach. I interrupted. "Where's Karen?"

Johnny spun toward me, and at first he didn't even seem to know who I was. He blinked several times; he seemed to be clearing not just the rain from his eyes but the blur in his mind as well.

"She's gone. She's . . ." his voice trailed off. He just stood there with a stunned, sick look on his face.

I knew exactly what he meant, but I had a hard time getting my mind around it. I heard a buzzing in my head. It struck me that the woman Karen saw being murdered in the rain was herself. She wasn't having a vision exactly; she was having a premonition.

I'd heard it from people many times: "I just knew he was bad" or "I had a feeling, that night, that someone was there." I had never heard anyone say "I saw my own death," but then after they were dead they wouldn't be telling me.

"Any idea who hurt her?" I was talking to Detective Hale now, who shook his head.

"It appears the lady hurt herself," he said.

Johnny started to cry, big racking sobs that shook his entire body. "No," he said. "No."

I stood there getting soaked right along with him, and put my arms around him and held him a long time, until he stopped.

Because I was there on the scene so fast, the cops had to grill me too, how long I'd known the deceased, how it was I'd been privy to the police radio dispatch, all that. Eventually they finished with me, and moved on with taking prints and taping things off, just in case Johnny was right the way he'd called it in, and Karen wasn't her own victim.

This was what I knew so far. Karen died from deep, jagged gashes cut on her wrists with a pocket knife. She'd also died pretty drunk. There was no blood-alcohol reading yet, but the coroner was a tough, no-nonsense old guy, and he knew his stuff.

I thought about her lying passed out, face-down on the kitchen table. I thought about her saying how she'd go crazy if nobody helped her, and how I hadn't helped her.

I felt guilty somehow, like I'd let her down. I felt like I'd let myself down, too. Maybe it was that suicides always made the survivors feel guilty. But maybe I just plain didn't believe it *was* a suicide. Not with all of her talk about her gift, and helping people. It just didn't fit that she'd throw that away, not deliberately. I could see it if she'd mixed pills with booze, anything to stop the screaming sound she was hearing; I could see it being an accident, her lying there dead. But intentional . . . no.

Johnny kept saying, over and over, "She couldn't have done it. She wouldn't do it. She didn't do it!"

He kept insisting the knife found next to her body wasn't hers. It was pretty, a silver pocket knife with rose quartz and turquoise chips in the handle.

Johnny claimed the only knives he'd ever seen in her house were the ones in the kitchen drawers.

I'd asked Detective Hale why he was so sure it was a suicide. He rolled his eyes, but I persisted.

"Look at how deep those cuts are on her wrists. Someone put a lot of force into making them."

"Yeah, so?"

"The woman seemed pretty fragile even when she was sober, and she was apparently far from sober when she died. It'd be hard for her to make cuts that deep."

"Not if she was determined to make 'em."

"They look like they were made from above, don't they? She would've had to stretch out one wrist, and lean across the table to cut herself like that. Then she'd have to do the same thing with the other wrist, while she was bleeding."

"Okay, that's what she did then," Hale said.

"She wouldn't have had the strength to do that," I pointed out. "Superficial cuts, die of blood loss over time, okay, I'd believe that. But cuts that major, wounds that fresh? There's two empty bottles of whiskey here. If she was as drunk as I'm guessing she was today, as drunk as the coroner is estimating, she wasn't even conscious at the time of her death. Meaning she wasn't capable of blinking, much less slashing her wrists."

I'd only known her, what, a little over twenty-four hours? Only spent about six of those hours in her company, but man, I agreed with Johnny. I so didn't buy the suicide scene. Of course it was possible I was a lunatic myself. Or maybe I just missed working homicide.

Finally, the coroner took the body away. Johnny went shuffling off down the street, dazed, with his hands stuck deep in his pockets. And then it was just me, standing on Karen's porch, drying my face and hair with a towel the coroner gave me, watching the water drip off the eaves, and waiting for the last of the official-looking vehicles to drive away.

Detective Hale shoved his card in my damp hand. "Call me tomorrow, I'll give you what we have," he promised.

I thanked him.

"You need a ride some place?"

"I'm waiting for my lift now," I lied.

I looked at my watch, feigning impatience. "Traffic must be bad."

As he drove away, I shoved his card in my purse, pulled out the neat skull key ring that held my collection of lock picks, and went to work on opening Karen's front door.

What I'd always liked best about police work, what I'd always been most impressed by, wasn't the badge or the uniform or the book; it was that little motto, "to protect and serve." Mostly now I served divorce papers.

Karen Shaw needed me to protect and serve her, and I hadn't done either very well.

I thought about her going to the church, the florists, and yeah, the liquor store, too. In her own way she was trying to protect herself. She might've been better off buying pepper spray, or a gun, and taking target practice. I could've told her that. I could've at least tried to take her seriously.

I thought about her amazing smile, and how she wanted to give me a reading, and I refused it. That was stupid, it might've given me more insight into her, into her case, if not more insight into me.

What struck me, now that she was dead, was that I did see it as a case, not just some crazy person picking me out of a phone book to unload on. Now I wasn't so sure that the protection she wanted was just from the demons in her own head.

But now it was too late, and even though I'd taken her money and not earned it, there was nobody to help anymore. It was time to walk away from this mess.

But hey, nobody really walks in Houston. Everybody drives. And my car was out of commission anyway. I could spare a little time to look into the circumstances of her death.

I twisted my pick a little bit deeper in the lock, and Karen's front door clicked open. I slipped inside, closed the door carefully behind me, and walked down the hall in the dim, rainy light.

I walked through the kitchen, pushing past the swinging door. It squeaked, something to do with the dampness.

In Karen's reading room, the curtains were all open and the windows were rain-splotched and ugly and dark. I turned on the light. It was dim, but it caught a crystal ball lying on the floor like it had been thrown there.

I moved around the room. Hanging above the door frame was the fresh bundle of herbs I'd seen Karen buy. A small sprig of the sage and lavender broke off as I walked under it and dropped at my feet. I picked it up and tucked it in my bag.

I sat down at her velvet-covered table. There was candle wax dripped over the sides of a little dish, the candle completely melted down. The wax was cold and hard.

There was one empty bourbon bottle on the table. The glass it had been poured into lay shattered in a million shiny bits on the floor. One of the larger pieces of glass was blood-stained, and there were little pools of blood soaked into the indoor/outdoor carpeting. Another bourbon bottle, also empty, had rolled against the table.

I thought about the murder Karen kept seeing in her head.

What if the dying woman she'd described wasn't a premonition of her own death, but the *reason* she was dead? The woman she saw had been beaten and kicked to death with a belt studded with silver conchos, and heavy work boots. A western look, similar to the style of the knife found next to Karen's body.

I'd theorized to Karen that she was seeing something she'd forgotten she'd seen, possibly something she'd witnessed drunk one night. What if that was true? What if someone knew she knew about this other woman's death, someone clever enough to set up this suicide scene and kill her to make sure no one ever figured out the truth?

I picked at the candle wax on the velvet cloth. There was something missing from the table.

"The cards," I said out loud. "Where are her cards?"

I stood up and started looking at the shelves, thinking she'd put them away there. My eyes scanned the herbs and powders and crystals and all those books; there were runes and the I Ching and a pair of dice even, but no tarot cards.

In the far corner, tucked between the bookshelves and the wall, there was a pale-blue Old Navy backpack with a Powder Puff girls figure dangling from its zipper, a peeling sticker of a marijuana leaf, and the inked-on notation "Go Cougars."

The Cougars are the University of Houston's football team, doing very well this season. I'd been to a couple of games; Rita's daughter, Amber, wanted to go to school there. The backpack sure didn't look like something Karen would carry around.

I was about to pick it up and look inside, when I heard a scratching noise, followed by a heavy thunk. The thunk came from the kitchen; I wasn't sure about the scratching. I dropped the backpack and pulled out my gun.

I walked back into the kitchen, holding the door between the two rooms carefully so it wouldn't squeak behind me.

The window over the sink was open. A gust of wind made the curtains billow, rattled dishes neatly stacked in the drainer, and sent raindrops flying in. It had also blown a potted plant over on its side. I straightened it, and saw a piece of paper tucked under it, a receipt from a liquor store.

I heard the scratching sound again, coming from the direction of the front porch. It was somebody trying to break in, somebody who wasn't as good at it as I was.

I stuffed the receipt in my purse and slipped out of the kitchen. Inching my way down the hall, I saw a figure through the front window. It was crouched on the porch, fumbling with the lock I'd so recently had at myself.

Something that looked like a putty knife was pried in at the door jamb. There was more scratching around and then the door popped open.

The grey light from outside made the man just a dark silhouette as he stepped through the doorway. He dropped the putty knife on the hall table. His hand grazed the wall, feeling for the light switch.

The lights snapped on and Johnny froze, seeing me standing there with my gun trained on him.

"What are you doing here?" I asked him.

A look of almost unreasonable longing crossed his face. He didn't even seem like he noticed the gun.

"I thought if I put my face on her pillow I might still . . . catch the scent of her."

I lowered my gun and looked away, embarrassed. "How come you don't have a key?"

"She never gave me one."

"How'd you get in before?" I asked. Surprise made me look at him again.

"The front door was already open. Which was unusual."

"Front, huh, not the back?"

"Not the back."

I dropped my gun in my purse.

"Back door was open yesterday, when I found her in the kitchen."

"She does that sometimes, leaves the back door unlocked."

"Not very safe, is it?"

He was calm now; his eyes were remote, dark, troubled.

"Not a lot of things are."

"That's an argument for going sky diving, not for leaving your back door unlocked in Channelview."

"I don't think I want to play this game right now. Yeah, I shoulda bought her a couple of deadbolts and told her to use 'em. I fucked up. I fucked up a lot, okay?"

"All right," I said, "everybody does, huh?"

Then like he was honing in on the big way I'd screwed up, he said, "What are *you* doing here, anyway? Your client's dead."

"Karen Shaw paid me twenty-two hundred dollars to investigate the murder of a woman whose body wasn't really there. Well, now there's a body and I still have her money."

We walked into the kitchen together. He took a glass from a cabinet, filled it with tap water, and drank.

"How long were you together?" I asked him.

"Little over three years," he said.

We were both still thinking of the key he didn't have.

"She liked her privacy," he allowed. "And it was all or nothing with us. We were either together every hour or we . . . we stayed away sometimes."

I nodded. I supposed you could make a case for Frank and me being together off and on for ten years now, which was pitiful really; you'd think one of us would've moved on, gotten married, discovered we were gay, something. A lot of times we stayed away, too.

"I thought I was good for her," Johnny said, his voice barely audible, so that I had to lean close to hear.

"I'm sure you were," I said, wondering if he was or he wasn't all the same.

"Oh yeah, I was good for her all right. Look what she did."

His voice was so full of self-loathing it hurt to hear it.

I said it before I was even sure I meant it. "No. You had it right with the cops. She didn't slash her own wrists. Someone just made it look that way."

Johnny didn't move, didn't even blink. "I thought nobody believed me."

"There was no sign of a struggle. But then she was almost certainly passed out cold. How much of a struggle would there be?"

Finally, Johnny blinked. "But who? Who would've done something like . . . ?"

"Perfect strangers don't stage suicides. It was someone she knew, someone she let in."

Anguish dripped off of him like the rain on his jacket. "She wasn't giving a reading when she was that messed up . . ."

"I didn't mean for a reading."

He looked at me now, and his eyes widened. He smacked his hand down on the counter. "If she was lonely, she would've called me," he said.

I left him standing there in the kitchen, and walked through the rest of the house. Without the police around checking everything out, I was free to pull open drawers and look in the cupboards, but there wasn't much to see.

I started in the bathroom. It was tiny, clean, white-tiled. Aspirin, Band-Aids, cold pills in the medicine cabinet. A hamper spilling sheets and towels. Both the sheets and towels looked muddy, but there didn't appear to be any blood on them. My guess was she changed them after the night in the rain with Johnny.

There was a small, orderly living room, Mexican blankets on the walls, a Victorian-style maroon velvet settee, bookshelves here too, but of a less metaphysical nature than those in her reading room. Here was Crane, Louis L'Amour, the Kama Sutra.

Which took me into her bedroom. The bed was neatly made. The bed didn't look slept in, the pillowcases were pristine. Maybe the sheets had been changed as recently as that morning. I wished I could get the cops back in to run an analysis on any trace fibers or hairs on the contents of the hamper.

Her dresser featured a painter's hat that must've been Johnny's, and half a bottle of rye. It was bourbon in the reading room, bourbon that I'd seen her buy at the liquor store. Maybe she wasn't particular about her booze, or maybe this bottle belonged to somebody else. Had the cops dusted this one for prints?

Along with the liquor and the hat, there were tubes of lipstick, tweezers, eye shadow, foundation, a hair brush, and a Bible on the dresser.

The top drawer held lacy undergarments, a cross, a diamond tennis bracelet that I bet Johnny hadn't given her, a couple of removable tattoos in the shape of hibiscus flowers.

She had a couple of sweaters in the next drawer down, and in the bottom drawer there were tax returns, some letters, and what appeared to be the deed to her house.

I leafed through the paperwork. She made somewhere around fifteen thousand a year, at least that was what she'd declared to the IRS. Not much, but the house was paid for. In fact, she'd paid for it in cash; there was a receipt on the date of the sale. That was sort of interesting, but since it was almost thirty years ago that the house was purchased, I didn't think it had any bearing on her death. She would've been real young when she bought the house though, which was more interesting.

The letters were all thank-you notes for something wonderful Karen had done or discovered in people's lives. They were kind of the opposite of mail I sometimes got, from people who claimed I'd ruined their marriages or business deals.

There was nothing resembling a will, and I supposed before

the state took hold of the property, I should do a search for any living relatives. It was always possible that one of them was her killer, and that the motive for Karen's death was as simple as claiming this paid-for house.

Her closet was crowded, filled with dresses and shirts, vivid with florals and heavy on the spandex. In the middle of the closet, the clothes were pushed back and there was a prominent empty hanger. I wondered if that was where she kept her robe, the one she'd died wearing.

I walked out of the room and up the hall. Johnny was still standing in the kitchen by the sink.

"Where did she keep her robe?"

He looked at me, blank for a minute. "Hook in the bathroom," he said. "But she was . . . wearing it."

Although I doubted anyone murdered Karen for a dress or a slinky shirt, the empty hanger seemed significant. If not the robe, what had hung there?

Johnny drifted back to Karen's bedroom, and I let him go. I figured he deserved the privacy he was after.

I walked out onto the front porch again.

There was Johnny's truck, parked crooked at the curb. He'd managed to get the engine to turn over after all.

The wind came up and blew a big shower of rain right into my face. I ducked my head down and at the same time my foot caught on that loose board I'd found the day before, now slippery with the rain, and I went slamming down three steps and flat out on to the sidewalk like I had a rug snatched out from under me.

I flailed my way up, feeling dizzy. The side of my head throbbed; I must've grazed it on the railing when I fell.

Karen's plastic trash can was next to the stairs. I grabbed onto it, steadying myself.

I leaned too hard, and it wasn't on even ground. The can

pushed off under my weight and down I went again.

It was like slipping on the same banana peel twice, and in this case there actually were banana peels flying all over the lawn.

In fact, the contents of an entire bag of garbage were flying around: liquor bottles, old soda cans, crumpled tissues, candy bar wrappers, a broken hair clip, a pizza box, old newspapers, and a slinky red dress balled up like a rag, and torn along one seam. There was something else the police should run some tests on.

I picked it up, to get it out of the rain, and right next to it, I saw a newspaper folded neatly around something small and square. I peeled the wrapping away. Inside there was a small box. And when I lifted the lid, inside, there were Karen's tarot cards.

The cards and the dress. It was funny that she would throw them away. I set both objects on the porch, and then, this time, moving very carefully down the steps, I tottered through the mess of trash and collected my belongings. Detective Hale's business card lay sodden on the grass. My gun and my hair brush and my cell phone were under the bushes. The same bushes where Karen saw the disembodied hand.

I dropped down on my knees, and grabbed everything, and stuffed it all back in my bag. I half expected to grab a hand myself.

I must've stood up too fast, because the earth was whirling around again, green and wet and muddy, and for the third time in five minutes I was lying flat on my ass.

I was only vaguely aware of Johnny coming out and clattering down the steps and picking me up, of his voice, concerned, muttering ". . . get you to a doctor."

Then I passed out.

CHAPTER FIVE

"Astros six, Angels three . . ." The baseball game was on television, the volume turned low. Johnny was hunched on the edge of what seemed to be a lawn chair, watching the game in the rear corner of a big, bare loft space. Next to him, there was a wobbly looking table and a couple of kitchen chairs, a hot plate, and a dorm-type fridge.

Across a vast stretch of wooden flooring splattered with paint, there was an easel. Canvases lined the wall: seascapes, city skylines, but mostly portraits, most of them of Karen. They were quite good, I was surprised by how good they were, but then I'd been figuring Johnny for a house painter.

I was lying on a swaybacked sofa somewhere in the middle of the room. I lifted myself up on one elbow, still looking at the paintings.

"Those are beautiful."

Johnny tore his eyes away from the game. "I never thought I was any good. I was just painting houses when I met Karen."

Okay, so I wasn't that far off.

He smiled to himself, remembering something. "She told me I had a gift."

I had to admit it. "She was right."

"She was a great believer in gifts," he said.

I sat up all the way and moved my fingers around my head, gingerly. There were two sore spots, one larger than the other, both on the left side of my head. I only remembered hitting it

61

once when I fell.

It took a little effort to get up, but I managed, and staggered over to Johnny's paintings. I picked up one of the portraits of Karen. Yeah, he really was good.

A wave of dizziness hit me and I put the painting down fast, and leaned against the wall.

Johnny came right to me. I snapped at him. "I'm fine."

"Take it easy. You took quite a fall," he said.

"I took a coupla falls."

"You were out cold. I wanted to take you to the hospital."

"Why'd you bring me to your place, then?"

"You asked me to take you home," Johnny said.

"I probably meant my home."

"You probably did, but I had no idea where that was. Your business card only has a phone number. I couldn't find your driver's license."

I had a vague recollection of handing it and my insurance card to the officer at the scene of the gas station collision. I didn't recall taking it back before we tore off to Karen's house.

Johnny had my elbow and he was leading me over to the sofa again. I saw my pale-blue sweater was all muddy and grass-stained. And I realized that my laundry was still in the trunk of my car. And my car had been towed long ago to the repair shop I'd requested, Three Crowns Auto Body off Sam Houston Parkway.

"Damn it," I said.

"You want to go to the hospital now?" he asked me, misunderstanding.

"Haven't paid my medical this month. I'm sure I'm fine."

"You're not seeing double or anything are you?"

"Why, don't you have a twin?"

On the television, a soft roar went up, cheers from an appreciative crowd. Johnny studied me, concerned.

"I was joking," I said, and I slumped back down on the sofa.

I waited until another wave of dizziness passed before I spoke again. "I found Karen's tarot cards in the trash. Any idea how they got there?"

Johnny shook his head, puzzled. "No. She always kept them with her."

"Unlikely, then, that she'd throw them out?"

"Completely unlikely."

Our eyes locked and we just sat there.

"What about the dress? Red dress, pretty? That was in the trash, too."

He nodded. "I saw it when I picked you up."

"Was she in the habit of throwing out her clothes?"

This time he smiled. "Yeah, sometimes. She'd get this idea that a dress was bad luck or something. Had negative karma."

I frowned.

"I know you think that's stupid, but how many times have you worn something and something bad happened, and you decided you'd never wear it again?"

I looked down at my sweater. It was in that category. I shrugged.

"She wore that dress the last night she . . . the last time I saw her. We had an argument. I can see why she'd get rid of the dress. I can see why."

After a long time, he added, "God, I wanted her different."

I jumped on him. "Stop drinking so much? Stop sleeping around?"

His eyes burned like I'd slapped him and it stung. "I wanted her to stop hurting so fucking much."

"Tell me what Karen was seeing."

"She already told you."

"I want *you* to tell me." I leaned back on the sofa.

"She saw a woman being beaten with a belt and kicked to

death. The woman was lying some place muddy in the rain, and there was a knife lying there too. Sometimes Karen only saw a hand, or a foot, or the shoes doing the kicking. That's all she told me before she lost it."

"Lost what?"

"The vision. She'd stopped seeing the woman. That's what she told me anyway, when she met me last night."

"Where'd she meet you?"

"The Empire Lounge. It's walking distance from her place. She'd already been drinking . . . quite a bit."

"More than usual?"

"She didn't drink all the time." He sounded defensive. "But yeah, more than usual."

"And?"

"And she was real upset, I said we had an argument." He rubbed his hand across his face. "More than just an argument. She was furious. I was pretty angry myself. She stormed out on me. It was the last time I saw her until—until it was too late."

I prodded him as gently as possible. "What was it that had her so worked up?"

"She'd given a reading Sunday night after you left, and it didn't work out right."

"Do you know who it was she read?"

He shook his head.

"Okay, so why didn't the reading go well?"

"She said she couldn't focus. That she hadn't just lost that one vision, she'd lost her gift. Lost it forever. I didn't believe her. But I wished I could. If only she had . . ." he stopped himself, passed his hand across his mouth like what he really wished was that he could take back the words he'd said.

"You thought it would be for the best?"

"Yeah. That's just about exactly what I told her."

"Why do you feel so bad about saying it?"

"She said without her gift, her life was over. And damned if she wasn't right."

Johnny drove me home around ten. The rain had stopped again and big puddles of moonlight were splattered all over the ground.

Rita watched me from her doorway, her arms folded across her chest. "You could've called me," she fumed.

"Called you?"

"I was worried!"

"About?"

"You!"

She sounded so mad I didn't know where to go with it.

"I'm fine," I said. "I had a lousy day, but I'm fine."

"Frank came by," she blurted. "He told us you'd been in an accident. He told us your car was totaled!"

Boy, word got around. It must've been Detective Hale who told Frank. I felt momentarily gratified that Frank cared enough to stop by. But then he hadn't cared enough to be sitting out on my front step waiting to make sure I was okay, put his arms around me, and tell me he was glad I was all right, now was he?

"My car wasn't exactly totaled. But I can't drive it."

I realized that one of the two bumps on my head must've come from the accident at the gas station.

"Then a patrolman came by and left this," she fished my license out of her pocket. "It was in an envelope, but I wanted to see what it was."

"I left it in his car. This has been a really long, sad, confusing day."

She nodded, still not entirely placated. "Look at you," she said, taking in my dirty sweater, the grass I was even now picking out of my hair. Her eyes widened in disbelief. "You're wearing blue."

"Must be bad luck," I said, thinking of Karen. I slumped against the railing, and launched into an encapsulated version of my day: car accident, client dead, police investigation, tripping on a loose board, ending up at Johnny's place.

"You think this guy, this artist, the one who gave you a ride home, who now knows where you live. You think he might have killed that poor woman?"

"No. He's devastated. I think he loved her more than anything in the world."

"People who are in love don't always act rationally," Rita said.

I got her point and took it. "So what else did Frank say?"

She laughed. "That a lawyer named John Kincaid was turning purple."

"Oh boy. I forgot all about him."

"And that he was gonna put out an APB on you if you didn't call in."

"Kincaid is?" Maybe it was the couple of blows to the head, but I was confused.

"No, you moron." She socked me on my grass-stained arm. "Frank. He was even more worried about you than I was. He was on duty or he would've stayed around longer."

I called Frank, but I got voice mail at the office, subject out of service area on the cell phone, and the answering machine at home.

Yeah, he was worried all right. He was probably with a date by now, and just wanted to make sure I wasn't going to barge in on him at an inopportune moment.

I left a message at the home number. "Frank, it's Lynn, I'm fine. Car's not, but I am. I'm investigating a suicide that looks more like a murder. Karen Shaw, Channelview. I'm guessing you already know that though, from the detective in charge.

Anyway, I'm going to sleep. I'll get back to Kincaid tomorrow. You, too."

I hung up, feeling vaguely annoyed. It was so like Frank not to be there. He got me to call him, then he wasn't around to answer the phone.

It wasn't that much different from the times he'd gotten me to say, yeah, I'm crazy about you, too; and then he'd disappear, queasy on the whole subject of commitment. He was too busy to talk about it, banging away on one case after another, or one file clerk after another, more than likely.

I was going to leave a message at Kincaid's office, but I kinda liked the idea of that lawyer all purple-colored.

I put an ice pack on my head and I called Frank two more times, and hung up when I got the machine.

Rita took me to the car rental office on her way to work in the morning. With my laundry as yet undone, I was wearing a sleeveless yellow turtleneck and a tight, white denim skirt, scrounged from the back of my closet. Sneakers looked ridiculous with that outfit, so I was wearing my flip-flops. I still felt ridiculous.

I slithered out of Rita's van and into the car rental place, where I discovered that my insurance policy did not pay in advance for rentals. They would reimburse me. Well that would be absolutely swell if my credit cards weren't maxed out. While it was possible to pay for the rental with a check, thanks to the late Karen Shaw, I couldn't guarantee the rental without a credit card, and that credit card had to have some credit available on it. Or they wouldn't let me rent a car.

Rita gave me a fallback position. If I dropped her at Texas Medical, she'd let me borrow her Dodge van. I promised to take very good care of it. I also promised I'd pick her up at five.

First stop, Three Crowns. They still hadn't finished evaluating the damage to my Corolla. I tossed my PI license around, and name-dropped the names of various police, and generally led them to believe not having my car ready was messing with official law-enforcement-type business. The manager agreed to get his estimate faxed over to my insurance company by noon, and start on the work immediately after.

"I just need to grab something out of my trunk," I said. The manager waved me toward one of the service bays.

I was less than thrilled to see that my car was up on a lift. It was a real treat to shimmy onto the hood of another wrecked car just to reach my trunk, wearing that tight skirt.

But eventually I did, and I retrieved my damn laundry, hoisted the sack over my shoulder like Santa, and threw it in the back of Rita's van.

"Whatcha got in there? Couple dead guys?" the mechanic joked. He'd been hanging around through the whole thing, drinking a Dr Pepper and never offering to help.

"Room for one more," I smiled sweetly.

Next stop, Kincaid's office. Unfortunately, I had to forgo the sight of him apoplectic with rage.

"He's in court," the secretary said, flashing her talons at me.

She handed me an envelope that contained the documents I'd requested, and even a FedEx slip indicating that the letter praising me to Fidelity Nationwide had in fact been sent.

"Where's your half of the bargain?" she asked me, her eyes narrowed.

"Coming up," I said. "Coming up. When's your boss due back?"

"Not 'til five," she said.

"I'll be here before five with the CDs," I promised.

"That's what you promised him yesterday," she reminded me.

Now I was torn between two scenarios for the rest of my day.

Option one, go downtown while there was no traffic to fight, withdraw the charges against Devins, thank Frank for his concern, lift my evidence off Frank's kitchen counter, and swing by Kincaid's again on my way to Channelview to canvas Karen's neighbors.

Option two, go directly to Channelview, guaranteeing myself a hellish afternoon in rush-hour traffic in a van with no iPod jack, and grill Karen's neighbors, which I was itching to do, first thing.

Option two it was, hands down. Besides having the benefit of exercising my investigative muscles, it kept me from having to deal with Frank right away. Dealing with Frank too early in the morning sometimes made me lose my focus.

I drove over to Karen's house and parked. The place looked forlorn, with the remnants of police tape trailing off the porch and the shades drawn. I crossed her tangled lawn to the house on the right, the side closest to Karen's reading room. An elderly man was sitting in a glider on his front porch, working a crossword puzzle.

I introduced myself, and handed him my card. He didn't bother to look at it, just tucked it in his shirt pocket.

"My name's Ryan, Sean Ryan," he said. He set the crossword aside and shook my hand. He was wearing a plaid short-sleeved shirt, and was somewhere between seventy and eighty.

I asked him if he'd seen anything out of the ordinary recently involving Karen Shaw.

"You mean, out of the ordinary for most people, or for her?"

"For her," I smiled.

He pointed toward a tangle of rose bushes on his front lawn.

"See those roses? My wife planted 'em, just before I lost her. One day last week I was out trimming 'em, and I started feeling sorry for myself. Karen came out of her house, stood right next to me, just like I called her. I asked her if she needed something."

69

He paused, put his hand over his chest. "I swear, she spoke to me in my own wife's voice, told me she loved me." He choked up and made no effort to hide it.

She hadn't used Frank's voice, thank God, but she did tell me Frank loved me, too. Possibly it was the sort of thing she went around saying all the time.

"By out of the ordinary, I meant did you witness any arguments, shouting, anything like that? Especially in the last week or two."

"Couple nights before she died, I guess. That'd be the night before you came here the first time."

So he'd seen me, digging around. That was good, even when he wasn't out on his glider, he was watching.

"Her and that painter fella, they were drunk, out there on the lawn. They were having themselves a time. She sure was a fine-looking woman . . ."

"Yes, well," I wanted to deflect this line of thinking as quickly as possible.

"I didn't watch or nothin'. But he had her right down there on the grass and . . ." he caught a look at my face and he stopped himself. "Closed the blinds. But then I heard her scream. Looked out my window again, but they were already in the house, I guess."

I assumed it was what was going on in her head that made her scream, not something that Johnny did. But I made a note of it.

Mr. Ryan offered me some iced tea, and chatted about his late wife a little longer. "I'm hoping Karen's with her now. Talking about what an old goat I am, and looking down to make sure I keep up the roses."

I shook hands with him again, and promised I'd let him know if I found out anything more about Karen.

"Woman like that, so much life to her, you know. She had a

problem, she needed something, all she woulda had to do was ask me. Sad, what happened . . . sad."

I agreed with him, thanked him, and headed across the street.

The house directly across from Karen's was empty, a "For Rent" sign in the window. At the house next to that, a young guy was squatting in his driveway, draining the oil from his Harley.

He had a buzz cut and slightly crossed eyes, and he was wearing a tee shirt that read "I ain't no (Hell's) Angel."

"Hey doll," he said, "whatcha got for me?"

"Actually it's what you may have for me," I said, which took his attention away from the motorcycle, fast.

He stood up and wiped his hands on a rag. "What're you talking about?" he asked.

"I'm a private investigator looking into the death of your neighbor across the street. Karen Shaw." I handed him my card.

"Go ahead, look. Who's stopping you?"

"I was wondering if there's anything you can tell me about her, or anything you saw that was unusual in the last couple of weeks."

"Well, she had some kinda fight the other day with a guy out on the front lawn. The guy kept grabbing at her. Dress was hanging half off her and her feet were all muddy; man, she was a sight. Thought she might do me a favor and fall right outta the dress. But no luck there."

I inclined my head, just slightly. "This was two nights ago, right?"

He shook his head. ". . . no, early in the morning. Yesterday, same day she bought it."

"You sure about that? The time of day and all?"

He raised his eyebrows. "Yeah, I'm sure. Just got off work, work night shift, messenger over at the airport. Five-thirty-two a.m. on my digital," he said, slapping at the Timex on his wrist.

"Young man, light hair?"

He shrugged. "Guy had his back turned the whole time. Too far away to see his hair color that time of morning. Sun's not all the way up yet."

"Long hair? Short?"

"I don't remember." He shook his head. "I was watching her, you know."

"That's okay, you're doing great," I said encouragingly, but he stopped talking and ran his eyes over me, taking in the tight white skirt. "You want a beer? I got some right inside."

"I've got to keep working," I said. "But thanks anyway. Now you said this guy was grabbing at Ms. Shaw. Did she seem afraid of him, was she trying to get away from him?"

"If she was, all she woulda had to do was call out."

He reminded me of old Mr. Ryan all of a sudden, willing to help Karen out of a jam if she'd only just said something.

"She was cool. Kinda crazy but cool. I keep a baseball bat in the garage. I coulda shown that guy the road, real fast."

"So she wasn't in trouble . . . ?"

"I dunno. Not that she told me about. The guy kissed her, and they went inside again. I fed my cat, stripped down, took a shower, and went to bed."

"Would you have heard, at that point, if she cried out, anything like that?"

"Don't think I woulda, tell you the truth. I had my head-phones on. I'm trying to teach myself Spanish. There's a girl at work, see."

"Ah," I said. "No habla English."

"I guess." He scratched his chin, puzzled.

Clearly the tapes weren't working too well.

I moved on, walking a small circle around Karen's place. There was a cute young couple with a baby who hadn't seen or heard a thing and didn't even know Karen's name; a young woman who was home sick with a cold, who'd been out of town for two weeks.

I hit pay dirt with the neighbor directly behind Karen's house.

The small ranch style home was identical to hers, but decorated with an absurd collection of lawn gnomes standing around in little groups as if they were ready to start singing Christmas carols or plot a government takeover.

The woman who answered the door was about my age, with a pointy nose and chin. She bore some resemblance to the gnomes, except that her expression was less cheerful.

"What do you want?" she said, coldly.

I explained and half expected her to slam her door in my face. Instead she stepped outside next to me, tugging along a full-sized dirty white poodle intent on wrapping its leash around her legs. This would've been the dog I heard barking when I was looking under everybody's bushes two days back.

"Sally Adowski," she said, without offering her hand. "It's time for Sally Boo's walk, but you can come along. She's named after her Mama," the Sally with the last name informed me about the Sally who bore the sobriquet "Boo."

Sally willingly picked up where the biker left off. "Yes, of course I heard something. I'm a writer. I'm home all the time. There was crashing and banging inside the house, sun wasn't quite up yet. And later in the morning, she had one guy in the house with her, and another pounding on the door."

"This is yesterday. The same day she . . . ?"

"Left this mortal coil? Uh-huh. I already said so didn't I? Twice you asked me that."

"Can you describe . . . ?"

"I heard it, I didn't see it. Bad enough she woke me up so early, and then just when I was trying to take a nap . . . Sally here was barking and barking . . . I gave up and took her for a walk. Went around the block like we're doing. Saw there was a delivery van in her driveway."

She sniffed her disapproval. "Red's Liquor store."

I remembered the receipt I'd picked up in Karen's kitchen and put in my purse.

I retreated to Rita's van, and rooted around in my purse until I found the receipt. I was surprised to see the address. Red's wasn't the place around the corner. It was over near the airport.

The receipt was for a delivery order, called in the morning of the day Karen died. She'd bought two bottles of overpriced bourbon. There was Karen's signature on the bottom, and that of the delivery guy, someone named "Creed." I decided to go check the place out.

Trying to avoid the Loop traffic, I sailed down Navigation Boulevard until I hit a red light right in front of the Empire Lounge, where Johnny said he and Karen had spent their last evening together.

I swung over to the curb. Might as well check out the Empire before I went to Red's.

The bar was a solid yellow stucco box, with a greasy little sign on the door that told me nobody under twenty-one was allowed, and that the hours were eight a.m. to two a.m.

As I stepped inside, a wave of juke box R&B washed over me along with the smell of beer and sweat. It was dark inside, which was a good thing, because it hid the look on the faces of all the daytime regulars hunched over their beer and shots.

The place had Christmas lights hanging from the ceiling and a stage with a drum set on it. I sat down at the narrow bar and ordered a beer from the bartender, who was a plump guy in his thirties already losing his hair. He had a sleek moustache though, and a cool Hawaiian-type shirt with a martini-glass pattern. I asked him a little about the place.

"Is it always this quiet?"

"This time of day."

"You have a band, nights?"

"Five nights. Tonight it's the Deadbeats."

Should fit right in with the crowd, I thought.

"You work days, only?"

"You a cop?"

"Private," I said.

"I usually work nights," he told me, as if this would exonerate him from any blame in anything.

"Were you here on the night before last?"

He sighed, crossed his arms over his chest. He looked bored and resentful.

"Who you after? Some guy skipped out on his bail? Guy stepped out on his wife? Guy messed up on his alimony?"

"Not after any guy. I'm just after information." I took a hit of the beer, trying to look friendly. "I'm looking into the death of one of your regulars, Karen Shaw."

There was a new look on the bartender's face now, that could almost be taken for gratitude. He reached across the bar and shook my hand.

"It should be looked into. She didn't off herself. Be bad karma. She was into karma. She told me about my past lives. That's why I'm here, working off past lives."

"Me, too," I said, glancing around the bar, "evidently."

"What you need to know?"

He opened a beer for himself, took a long pull. He set a bowl of peanuts out on the counter between us. I munched a few.

"I understand she was in here two nights ago, with her boyfriend, Johnny."

"Yeah, they were in." He shook his head. "Man, she looked hot. Had on this red dress, fit her just so, you know. Lotta makeup, hair curled, looked absolutely fuckin' gorgeous. Johnny couldn't take his eyes off her, and I swear to God neither could any other guy in the place."

"Yeah, she had that quality."

"But close up, she looked real upset."

"How could you tell?"

"Her eyes, man. Just this look in her eyes. I asked her if she was okay, and she said she was great, but I didn't believe her. Something real sad about her the other night."

"So anything happen?"

"Yeah, yeah. Things do seem to happen, did seem to happen, around Karen. Johnny got in a fair number of fights in this very room around the holidays, defending her honor so to speak. Lotta broken glass." He smiled at the memory.

I took another swallow of my beer. "So two nights ago, was there a fight?"

"Not that kind." His smile faded. "She was dancing to the music, band was doing a cover of the Red Hot Chili Peppers. She kept slipping right up against Johnny, touching his hips, sexy. But it was like her heart wasn't in it, she was trying too hard.

"Johnny told her she should just sit down. He was right about where you're sitting, sketching her. Looked like a nice picture, but she grabbed the pencil out of his hand, said real loud, 'C'mon. Let's celebrate!' "

He set his beer down on the bar with a solid thunk. "I'd already given her a refill two or three times, and she'd had a few before she came in. But she wanted another, so I poured it. Before she could even lift the glass, Johnny kinda grabbed her wrist. He said 'Tell me what we're celebrating.' I could tell he was worried about her."

"And did she tell him?"

"Yeah. She started going on about how they're celebrating 'cause there's no more voices in her head. No more seeing things. Johnny wanted to know what she meant. And that was when she started crying. I remember it perfectly. She said, 'I'm just like everybody else now.' "

"Ah," I said.

"So Johnny tore off the sketch, gave it to her. He told her she'd never be like everybody else, and I had to agree with him there. I threw in my own two cents, said 'Yeah, Karen you're special.' She laughed and pressed that picture up against her, but then she started really crying. She said her gift was gone . . . you know what she was talking about, right?"

"The psychic stuff."

"Yeah. She said it was like somebody turned out a light on her, and every place was dark. I felt real sorry for her. I handed her a napkin to wipe her eyes, but Johnny waved me away. He figured it was none of my business, I guess."

One of the old guys at the end of the bar rapped his glass three times. "I get another before I die?"

The bartender shrugged, rueful, like see what I have to put up with, and walked on down to the old man.

"Hear anything more?" I asked the bartender, when he returned.

"I wasn't trying to eavesdrop, you know. The band took a break, and I cared about Karen, so naturally I was paying more attention to what was going on with her than, say, what was going on with him." He pointed his thumb back down the bar toward the old man.

"I understand," I said. "And what you heard could really help me find out what happened to her. So anything at all . . ." I let my voice trail off, and waited for him to go on.

He chewed a few peanuts thoughtfully, and then he did. "Well, Johnny told Karen not to worry, and she said she couldn't help it, she kept thinking about that poor girl. 'She was just in high school. I couldn't help her, and now I'll never help anybody,' she said."

"What girl?"

"I dunno, sounded to me like some girl came to see her for a tar-oh reading and Karen couldn't, you know, perform."

I flashed on what Karen told me about the two seventeen-year-old girls who came to see her right before she started having her visions, and the unfinished reading that upset her.

And then I thought about the blue backpack sitting in the corner of Karen's reading room. I never looked inside. What if it belonged to one of the girls, and it could lead me right to her?

The bartender went on. "Anyway, Johnny was just trying to calm Karen down, you know, saying maybe it was all for the best, that kinda talk. But then she got really angry. I thought she was gonna slap him. She asked him how he could say something like that if he loved her. Maybe he didn't really love her. At that point anybody would've heard her, she was screaming at him, anybody would've heard. At first he just kind of sat there and took it. She was shaking Johnny's shoulder, and pulling on him. 'When did you stop loving me? Answer me.' Stuff like that. And finally Johnny spoke up. 'Why should I?' he said. 'You have all the answers. And you're always right, aren't you, Karen?' At that point he was really pissed, too, you know."

It seemed strange that Karen would doubt Johnny loved her. I didn't for a second; it was written all over him, a full-body tattoo. She probably just doubted everything right then, without those voices in her head that she relied on to guide her.

Why *had* she lost them all of a sudden? Had the whole psychic-to-the-universe trip just gotten to be too much for her, with those scenes of a woman's ugly murder popping up around her?

The bartender cleared his throat.

"They say anything else?" I asked.

"No. She stood there awhile, and he just sat there, and neither one of them looked at me, or at each other, and they didn't say another word, either of 'em. And then she left. Johnny started to follow her. He pulled money out of his pocket to pay the tab. Then I guess he changed his mind. He left the money lying on the bar, sat back down, and started drawing again. I poured him another before he left. Must've been a full hour later."

The sunlight made me frown as I stepped out of the bar. I climbed in Rita's van and just sat for a minute, staring at Amber's soccer ball and cleats, lying on the floor by the passenger seat. I looked at them long and hard, as if they were a great work of art, and I was studying them for some secret truth about human nature.

I was thinking about Johnny, how he'd cried in my arms because Karen was dead. Karen was wrong about him not loving her, I knew that. Still, it didn't mean she hadn't pissed him off so much that he killed her.

My heart said Johnny wasn't that kind of guy, but my head said he still needed an alibi. He told the police detectives he'd been painting Lowe's market. I'd go there second, after I swung by Karen's house again. Red's Liquor had moved down my list a little further.

Karen's neighbors were gonna think I was moving in, but I had to take a look at that backpack.

Mr. Ryan had vacated his glider, but I went around the side and picked that lock instead of the front, where nobody could see me.

Inside, I saw Johnny had swept up the broken glass, and left an enormous bouquet of daisies in a vase on the spot where she died. I knew it was Johnny, because he'd also left a picture he drew of her propped up next to the vase. I felt my eyes welling up. But he still needed an alibi.

The backpack was in the corner next to the bookshelf, just where I'd dropped it. I picked it up and opened it. Definitely not something that belonged to Johnny or Karen. It contained a pink hair brush marked "Lovely Girls," a notebook filled with algebra problems, a small stuffed dog that had seen better days, seven pencils, most of them with the erasers chewed off, one pen, a roach clip, a quarter and two dimes. No I.D.

I cruised through Karen's house one more time. Nothing new, but the bottle of rye on the dresser still bothered me. I looked at the dress and the tarot cards Karen had thrown out, now lying on the floor by the front door. Johnny must've brought them in off the porch after I fell. The dress was torn jaggedly in several places and mud-stained. My guess was that the fight with the mystery guy in the front yard the morning she died caused the damage.

Taking the backpack, I locked up and headed for Lowe's market. While I drove, I called back all the RTD bus drivers I'd left messages for regarding the blue-haired girl and the dark-haired girl seen on the Channelview route a week earlier. I left my numbers again.

Next, I called Detective Hale, the guy in charge of Karen's case. I suggested he look at the sheets in the hamper, the rye bottle in the bedroom, and the torn dress. I didn't think mentioning the teenage girls would get me anywhere but laughed at. I also didn't mention breaking into Karen's house to find these items, and Det. Hale didn't ask.

He was already getting sniffy. "Give it a rest, why don't you. Only reason we paid as much attention to the scene as we did was the woman's boyfriend going on about how she couldn't have killed herself. Better to be thorough with somebody that insistent. But we've been thorough enough now. Only prints on the knife were hers."

I tried to be persuasive. "If you catch some killer out there stalking single women, think what a good guy you'll be, man of the hour, huh? As opposed to just passing this one off as a suicide and waiting for the killer to strike again."

He snorted and repeated a version of what I'd told Johnny. "If it was a homicide, and I'm not even saying I consider that a real possibility, it wasn't some stranger wandering around looking for a victim. Not with the scene we found."

I couldn't really argue with that, since I believed the same thing. So I asked him just one last question. "You get a blood-alcohol level on Karen Shaw yet?"

"Yeah," he said. "She was pretty loaded, point twenty-seven."

"A woman with that reading probably couldn't pick up a knife," I noted, "much less use one, you think?"

There was a shuffling of papers and slamming of file drawers.

"Evidence shows she did," he said.

"You have a time of death?"

"Not long before her boyfriend showed up at the scene. Around two o'clock in the afternoon."

"Huh," I said. "About that time she shoulda been practically comatose. Check out the sheets and the dress and the bottle of rye, please?"

He didn't say yes or no, he just hung up.

I parked in front of Lowe's market. The neighborhood was a blend of rent-controlled, older, motel-like apartments, and snazzy, gated condos. A glass-windowed high-rise abutted a garage that promised free smog checks if your vehicle didn't pass the emissions test. About half the business signs on the block were in Spanish. Euphemistically speaking, it was called a "mixed use" neighborhood.

Lowe's was a small corner store that had not been owned by anybody remotely named Lowe for a long time. It was a half bodega, half used-clothing store. However, the exterior trim did look pretty fresh.

Inside, a woman with her thin black hair stretched into rollers was watching Telemundo on a little, black and white camping TV. I identified myself, and asked if she was working the previous day. She gave an almost imperceptible nod.

"Did you have a man named Johnny Ross painting around here yesterday?"

Her eyes moved sideways, just slightly. "Uh-huh."

"Do you know what time he left?"

She rolled her eyes. "He left before he was done with the job. He do the front, not the back. Says he's gonna come back today after he finishes another job. Sloppy."

"Would you know what time it was when he left?"

"Sure I know. *Pedro el Escamoso* was just coming on. Three o'clock. Ross left his van, his ladder, everything. We had canvases up, protect the paint from the rain, all that trouble, and the job not done. When he came back, it was almost dinner time, and he wouldn't talk to me."

"He had a personal emergency," I said.

"Oh, right, I'm supposed to be sorry. Nobody else has no emergencies."

"One more thing. Did he leave any other time during the day that you're aware of, take a lunch break, or anything?"

"His van was parked out front all day. My best space. If I woulda known he'd take so long on a little touch-up job, I would've told him to move it."

"But how about Johnny himself, he was out front all day, too?"

She drummed her fingers on the counter. "I follow him, you think, know when he takes a pee?"

"A long break. More than say twenty minutes. Surely you'd notice that."

"You think I have nothing to do but watch the lazy-ass painter go about his business?"

I leaned across the counter, for emphasis. "That you *saw*, did he leave the premises anytime other than around three in the afternoon?"

"That I saw, no!" She turned back to the television again and locked her eyes on it. "Best of my knowledge, he was up on his ladder dripping paint on my customers all day long."

More or less, Johnny Ross had himself an alibi.

On my way down to Red's Liquor, I snagged the cell phone again and called Frank. I got his answering machine and I was just as glad this time. I tried to keep things light and breezy.

"I'll be by pretty soon, I need to get something from you and then I'll put the whole thing with Devins and his lawyer to bed, okay?" As soon as I said the word *bed* I regretted it, but his voice mail cut me off and didn't give me the option to re-record the message.

Red's was a big place, across the street from a major-chain grocery and drug store. It was close enough to Hobby that the planes coming in and taking off made the van windows vibrate.

I had to park on the street, not in the lot, because there was a familiar white truck blocking the entrance, and a long-haired guy up on a ladder painting the words "Twenty-four hours/ Open Day or Night." I was pretty sure the guy was Johnny.

Maybe Karen had ordered from the store because Johnny had brought her attention to the existence of a place that delivered' round the clock. Or maybe Karen told Johnny that the place needed a new sign painted.

While I was thinking these possibilities over, a young guy in a baseball cap and a tee shirt, both imprinted with Red's logo, went storming out of the side entrance to the store. He had greasy hair and a mean look on his face, halfway between a sneer and a pout. He could've been the poster boy for the expression "he looks like trouble."

He stalked into the parking lot, and marched right up to Johnny's ladder and shook it.

"What's your problem?" Johnny called down.

"You blocked my truck, dude. I got deliveries."

Johnny started down the ladder. I slipped low in my seat, so he wouldn't see me watching.

The delivery boy was staring up at the sign Johnny painted with a strange look on his face, the sneer twitching into something close to amazement. "That's kinda fancy," he said.

Johnny looked up at what he'd painted. I turned the side-view mirror this way and that until I got a good view of it, too.

To the left of Red's logo, there was a fully realized, full-color mural of a woman holding a wine glass. The woman's face was clearly Karen's.

"The right word's *ironic,*" Johnny said to the boy.

"I don't get it."

"That's okay, neither do I."

Johnny pushed past the kid, heading for his truck.

The delivery kid was rattling on. "The woman looks like somebody . . . I know—that slut down in Channelview."

I knew Johnny was gonna hit him way before the kid did, and the kid took it hard, slamming back against the building.

Johnny pinned him there.

"Don't you call her that. How do you know her?" Johnny was shouting so loud I could've been parked halfway down the block and heard his end of the conversation.

I thought about getting out of the van and putting a stop to it, but I wanted to hear how the kid knew Karen, too, and preferably without parting with another twenty. Plus I didn't like the look on the kid's face.

"Made a delivery. That's all." His voice was lower than Johnny's, so I had to strain to hear him.

"All the way to Channelview?"

"Yeah. You're painting the sign! We deliver twenty-four hours. Anyplace in greater Houston, for a price." He gave Johnny an ugly leer on the word *price* and Johnny raised his fist.

I was gonna have to stop this. I had the van door open but before I could jump out, Johnny took a step back, and just stood there staring at the guy, his fists clenched.

The kid was backpedaling fast, doing a good imitation of somebody who was sorry. "Didn't mean anything, I swear. Just the way she was dressed. Have a big mouth, that's all."

I didn't buy it, even from a distance, but apparently Johnny did. He moved over to his ladder, and lowered it. He looked up at the mural he'd painted, and his face took on a dreamy quality; he seemed almost happy.

The kid scurried around the van, hightailing it back to the store. He kept one eye on Johnny while he ran. He reminded me of a rat; his eyes were beady, and he had little whiskers on his chin.

When he got to the door, he called back, loud enough for Johnny to hear him over the traffic noise and the sound of the ladder coming down.

"You're Johnny, aren't you? She called me Johnny, while I was kissin' her . . ."

Johnny wheeled, his face dark with fury. The guy ducked inside the store, and I saw him flip the paper "Open" sign to "Closed."

I stayed slumped down in the seat. I watched Johnny slam the ladder in his truck and climb in the front, still glowering.

He revved the motor a couple of times, and raced from the lot with his tires squealing.

I sat tight, waiting for the kid to walk out of the store again, so I could take my own shot at questioning him.

Johnny was barreling up the street; he couldn't seem to get away from there fast enough. And then he made a U-turn. A real radical one, bouncing the rear wheels of his truck over part of a traffic island.

My mouth dropped as the truck sailed right past me, jumped

the sidewalk, and smashed straight through Red's front window. An alarm blasted.

Pieces of the window and the bottles on display sprayed out all over the sidewalk. Liquor and little splinters of multicolored glass splashed back to where I was parked, and scattered on the hood of Rita's van.

Across the street, people rushed from the drug store and gawked.

I was out of the van as soon as the debris stopped flying, in plenty of time to see Johnny jump out of his truck, scramble through the broken window, and grab the delivery boy inside the store. He slammed the kid down right in the middle of all that spilled booze and broken glass.

"Did you hurt her? Did you hurt her?" Johnny roared.

"No, I didn't hurt her. She wanted it. She wanted . . ."

I was picking my way through the rubble pretty quick, but I wasn't fast enough to keep Johnny from decking the kid so hard his head snapped back.

Another guy was peering over the checkout counter, his eyes wild as he took me in. I hoped he didn't have a gun back there, and if he did, that he wouldn't start shooting.

"Everybody cool it," I said. I grabbed Johnny's arm, hard, and twisted it behind his back, like I was gonna cuff him.

"He's gonna kill me!" the delivery kid shrieked.

He still looked like a rat, but now he looked like a rat who was caught in a trap and talked like a little girl.

Johnny fought against me. He was strong for a thin guy, and he was giving it his all. I hoped I wasn't gonna have to knock him out.

His face was cut from broken glass, and he was breathing hard. I gripped his arm tighter. Tight enough that it hurt, and he stopped pulling quite so hard.

"What the hell are you doing?" I asked.

"Trying to kill him," he said, through clenched teeth.

The kid cowered and sniveled and tried to widen those beady little eyes at me. He clearly thought I was his guardian angel.

"Are you a cop? I didn't hurt that freakin' psychic. Swear."

"What did you say?" I scowled at him and he didn't look quite so confident that I was there to save his ass.

"Ask her if you don't believe me! She wanted it. She wanted . . ."

"I can't ask her. She's dead," I said.

I looked at the kid, hard. I wasn't sure if he was surprised or not. His eyes twitched but that was about it.

"Don't hit him again," I warned Johnny, and I let go of his arm.

The kid covered his battered face with his hands, but Johnny didn't go near him.

"If it'd bring her back, I wouldn't stop," he told me.

I believed him.

There were police sirens wailing, real close. Johnny leaned against the counter, just waiting for them. I saw he had dark circles under his eyes, and his whole face looked older, exhausted. I doubted very much that he'd slept last night.

I pulled the delivery receipt out of my pocket and squinted at the name on the bottom. "Hey," I said to the kid, "are you Creed?"

He nodded. I waved the receipt in his face.

"This what you delivered to the woman on Seaver?"

He squinted at it and managed another affirmative shake of his head.

"What time was that?"

"Ten a.m. or so."

I waited. He waited too, panting.

Finally he gave up. "She was nuts. She put a knife to my throat, cut me . . ."

A knife. The hairs rose up on the back of my neck, much as they had when Karen Shaw was alive and telling me she just "knew" I'd be in my office.

An ominous look shadowed Johnny's face. He straightened. "Or you put a knife to her throat. But she still didn't want you, did she?"

I moved between them. It wasn't because I thought if Johnny smashed Creed, the universe would fall out of whack or anything, it was because I really didn't think Johnny would do that well in prison. Sure, he could fight, but he was way too sensitive.

"What kind of knife?" I asked.

Frightened, the kid tried to answer us both at once. "It wasn't my knife . . . it was small, had jewels on it. She took it from her pocket. And I . . . all I did was kiss her. Then I got out of there . . ."

Johnny shook his head. His eyes looked bleak and dark, like he'd been through a nuclear winter. "He's rotten," Johnny muttered. "You can smell it on him."

Creed fell silent and tried to make himself smaller than the speck of bacteria he was.

The police sirens throbbed right outside now. Seeing the blown window, they came in with their weapons drawn, and I pushed Johnny back, and down, so they'd know he was already submitting.

"I'll post your bail," I told him. "It's time to cooperate."

CHAPTER SIX

By the time the police finished their investigation, it was almost four. It seemed to me that when I used to run a crime scene, I ran it faster, but maybe that's just pride talking, or at the time I hadn't been in a hurry to return a borrowed van to my best friend. Rita needed it to pick up Amber and take her to an AYSO game.

The arresting officer told me Johnny wouldn't be processed for a couple of hours, so I zipped past the airport and drove south.

I called Kincaid's secretary, who didn't like it much when I said I wouldn't make it in until tomorrow.

I left a similar message for Frank. Where the hell was he, and why didn't he have his calls forwarded to wherever he was? Weren't the police supposed to be accessible, in case anybody needed them, to, say, save their lives, or something?

I called the body shop, too. They'd rushed it, and the car would be ready tomorrow, but not until noon.

It was ten after five when I pulled up in front of the employee entrance at Texas Medical, and Rita was waiting. "I'm gonna have to pick Amber up from the library first thing to make her soccer game. No time to drop you off. You're late."

"Only fifteen minutes."

I gave her the quick rundown of my day, and asked if I could borrow the van again after soccer was over.

"To bail the guy out," I explained.

She waggled her eyebrows at me, but she didn't say no.

We pulled up in front of the library and Amber bounded over to the van like a long-legged colt. She slid the door open and climbed in the back.

"You're getting awfully personally involved here, aren't you?" Rita said to me.

"With the guy who's stopped by two nights in a row? Her old friend Frank?" Amber asked, eager.

"Hello to you too, Amber. No, not with my old friend Frank. With helping a man who was involved with a client of mine that passed away yesterday. And your mother's wrong," I added.

Amber plucked at the backpack I'd lifted from Karen's. "What're you doing with Hayley Corelli's backpack?"

"Hayley Corelli?" I repeated stupidly. "That's her backpack?"

"Yeah. Where'd you get it?"

"It was left at my client's . . . Amber, who's this Hayley, and how do you know that's hers?"

"She sits in front of me in algebra. I saw the thing every day all last semester. Anyway, last week, she said she lost her backpack and that was where her math homework was. Nobody believed her. But I guess maybe it was true."

"What does she look like?"

"I don't know. Nothing special. Taller than me. Kind of a stoner. Oh. She had her hair dyed blue."

"I have to find her," I told Amber, as Rita wedged the van into a space in front of the soccer field that I wouldn't have even begun to attempt in a vehicle that size.

"I could give her the backpack." Amber grabbed her ball and cleats from beneath my feet.

"I need to talk to her. You don't know her phone number or where she lives do you, honey?"

Amber shook her head. "She's not like my friend or something."

"Thank God," Rita threw in.

"I'll have to go to the police with this," I mused. "School won't give a PI the address of a minor, but if I can convince the cops . . ."

Amber grabbed her own backpack from the rear of the van and tossed it in my lap. Hers must've weighed about seventy pounds.

"Just look her up in the student directory. It's in there, somewhere."

I was on a lucky streak. Hayley Corelli lived close enough to the soccer field that I could walk over. The house was in a snazzy new subdivision with a faux-adobe look. The planters were landscaped and there was a windsock with a Saguaro on it floating from the edge of the roof.

Even luckier, Hayley herself answered the door. She was indeed a year or two older than Amber, and she wasn't pretty, but she had a certain wild energy flashing out of her that was appealing. The blue hair had to go, though. I introduced myself, told her I'd found her backpack and asked if her parents were at home.

"Nah," she said. "Working. They work late."

I asked her if I could talk to her for a few minutes; she agreed, and I stumbled inside, narrowly avoiding a basket of laundry, which reminded me that my own laundry bag was now in the back of Rita's van. I sidestepped a skateboard and a cardboard box and a stack of *House & Garden* magazines. By the look of the living room, with pizza boxes, clothes strewn around, and newspapers spilling off the coffee table, the subscription was wasted.

"They work a lot," she said.

"You could pick up a little," I suggested.

She snickered.

I handed her the backpack, and showed her my license, assured her she wasn't in any trouble, but that I was investigating an incident that happened in Channelview. She seemed suitably bored.

"So what you were doing at the house where I found your backpack."

"The psychic's?"

"Uh-huh."

She put her hands on her hips and swiveled ever so slightly. "Well, it sure wasn't my idea to go there. It was Addy's."

"And Addy is?"

"Adrianne. My friend from Marathon." She yawned. "She came to visit for a week. Gone now."

My pulse accelerated at the mention of Karen's hometown. I tried not to look too interested. "Marathon, huh. And your friend knew Ms. Shaw, is that it?"

"Addy read about her on some online chat room, somebody said the psychic was good. More like a good psycho, you know?"

I smiled. "Why don't you tell me."

"It's not that interesting."

"I'd really like to know. And I did come all the way over here."

Hayley shrugged. "Sure, why not. We went to see her for my birthday. That's what Addy came down for, to help me celebrate. We were really good friends when we were little kids. Anyway, they have year-round school up there and this was one of her breaks. She was supposedly gonna go to class with me here, but we ditched, hung out at the mall, and it wasn't as much fun as I thought it'd be. Addy's just . . . lame. I thought it was 'cause her dad was so strict and all, but it's her, too." She shook her head, dismissive. "Still, I thought it was an okay idea of hers, get my fortune read for my birthday, so we took a bus, went all the way out to the psychic's house."

I nodded encouragingly. Hayley yawned.

"Addy forked over twenty-five bucks for the reading. So, some psychic, right, she thought it was *Addy* come for the reading, said 'Sit across from me.' "

"Did you correct her?"

"Sure. Said Addy was just there to watch, it was my birthday present. And I sat down, and the psychic sat down, and Addy stood there and shuffled her feet. She has that habit."

"Uh-huh."

"And I thought it was the shuffling or something, the woman kept looking up at her. So I told her to sit down and she did, and the fortune-telling freak started to finally pay attention to me. Asked me palm or tarot, and I said palm, and she started running her hands across my hand and it felt real weird, and she wasn't saying anything. Addy got bored and flipped through these tarot cards lying on the table.

"And that woman, she dropped my hand, and lifted a card off the deck. I said 'hey,' tried to get her attention back, but she wasn't listening. She got all twitchy. She looked at the card, put it back, and grabbed, and I mean really grabbed, Addy's hands.

"Addy started apologizing. Said she didn't mean to touch anything. Still this bitch wouldn't let go of Addy. She was shuddering and shit. It was like she wasn't seeing Addy at all, but some messed-up thing in her own head, you know? Addy was tryin' to pull away and the candle went out and I just got up and said 'screw this,' you know."

"So what happened?"

"So the woman looked up like she didn't even know she was in the same frickin' room as us, and finally she dropped Addy's hands. And Addy just kinda sat there, like she was stunned, you know. So I grabbed her, pulled her out of the damn chair, and I told her, 'let's get the hell out of here.' We were halfway to the door when the freak called out 'I think it's your mother, trying to reach you.' "

Hayley snorted, derisive, "What a joke, huh? But Addy got all freaky, and asked 'What about my mama? I haven't seen her in three years.'

"I'd had enough, you know? I told Addy, 'forget it, let's just get our money back.' So the woman took Addy's money out of her pocket and threw it down on the table, and started staring into her frickin' crystal ball. She was speaking in this high squeaky voice like she was Addy's mom or something, saying how she only wanted to protect her kid."

"Protect her from what, did she say?"

"Nah. It was all just a trick to get more money, you ask me. But I wasn't biting. I took the dough, and Addy's arm, and I'm telling you I was practically dragging her out of that place. No surprise now that I forgot my stupid backpack, huh?"

"Perfectly understandable," I said.

"Then I had to work on calming Addy down. She was so upset she actually called her daddy, even though she swore she couldn't wait to get away from him. Called him all teary and I don't know what went on, but he said he'd come down and get her if she wanted.

"I was like fine, whatever, but finally she said no. Wasn't 'til the next morning I realized I'd lost my backpack. I figured I left it either at that house or on the bus, and I sure wasn't gonna go back to freakazoid's."

"Does your friend always get so upset about her mother?"

"Yeah, Addy has a thing. I mean her mother disappeared on her when she was like fourteen. She's nine months older than me, even though she acts like such a big baby. She's a senior now."

"Her mother disappeared?"

"Ran off with some guy or something. That's what my parents say, anyway."

Hayley looked at her watch. "You need to go. Parents'll be home soon. You see psycho psychic, tell her I said 'fuck off.' "

"She's dead," I said, and waited for a reaction.

Hayley's eyes got big. "No way. Totally?"

"Uh-huh. Totally dead. That's how it usually goes."

"She have like a seizure or something?"

"No. Nothing like that."

"Huh."

"Think you could give me Adrianne's address? Phone number, something? It's no big deal, but I'd like to talk to her too," I said.

Hayley shrugged. "I guess."

I pulled a steno pad out of my bag and she wrote down Adrianne's full name, address, and phone number. "It's long distance," she pointed out.

"I got that, yeah."

"But you might catch her here in town," she said. "I don't think her bus leaves for another hour yet. I just didn't feel like going downtown with her, you know. Like I said. She was kinda lame."

I ran back to my place.

What if Adrianne's mother was the one with the lead role in Karen's visions? And what if there was a reason Adrianne went to see Karen that had nothing whatsoever to do with her friend's birthday?

If the girl thought Karen knew something about her mother's disappearance, it added a great deal of credence to my theory that someone with the motive to kill Karen knew something too.

I wanted to catch the girl at the bus station and get the story.

Out of breath, I knocked on Rita's door.

"I'm in a big rush," I said. "Gotta question somebody before she leaves town. Then get Johnny out of jail."

"Very alliterative," she said, dangling the keys to the van.

I snatched them and started jogging down the sidewalk.

She followed me. "Please don't have sex in it or anything, okay?"

"Yeah, right, with who?"

"With Frank. You might run into him."

"I might run *over* him but never mind, not in your van."

"And no sex with this mopey artist guy either."

I unlocked the van and slid behind the wheel. "He's madly and deeply in love with my dead client. I'm not attracted to him. I feel sorry for him."

"No pity sex in my van."

"Yes, mother," I said.

Driving downtown the sky was beautiful, pink chunks of cloud floating like cotton candy over high-rise office buildings of blue and emerald glass. Downtown Houston reminded me of Oz floating along the freeway.

Traffic was heavy and I made it to the bus station with only about ten minutes before Adrianne's bus was supposed to leave. I double-parked Rita's van with the flashers on, and hoped I wouldn't get a ticket.

I went up to the ticket window, and asked where I could find the bus that was leaving in ten minutes for the town of Marathon.

The slender ebony-skinned woman behind the window twirled her hoop earrings. "No such bus," she said.

"Big Bend area. Leaves very soon . . ."

"Big Bend? You gotta give me a town, honey. A town that actually a bus goes to."

I gave up and went out to the bays where the buses were lined up and waiting for departure. Dallas nope. San Antonio nope. San Francisco nope.

And then, in the next to the last bay, there was one marked Fort Stockton/West Texas. Okay, that would do.

The bus was just boarding now, and there was a little scene going on between an overweight woman carrying a baby and the driver, who was demanding that he be shown a ticket.

Behind them, there was a young girl in a jeans skirt and jacket and a Youth Lagoon tee shirt. She was very pretty. Pale, almost translucent skin, full mouth, sweet, heart-shaped face.

There was something embroidered in rhinestones on the back of her jacket, "Arianne." The "D" had fallen off, but no fooling me; it was the kid I was after.

I pushed through the crowd waiting to board.

"Adrianne?" I called.

She looked at me, and she got this expression on her face, like she was afraid of me, afraid of something. Whatever it was that scared her, it scared her enough that she jumped out of the line for the bus and took off running through the station.

I followed her, but she was fast, unexpectedly fast. "Stop," I shouted, elbowing my way through the crowd. "I won't hurt you! Your friend Hayley told me where I could find you! Just wanna ask you some questions."

Instead of stopping, or even slowing down the least little bit, she gave something equivalent to a high jump, launched herself over a bench, and kicked it into supersonic.

I pumped it up to stay with her. "Damn it. Stop running!" I dodged a guy with a shopping cart full of cans and bottles, but I guess he must've dropped some of his booty along the way.

I heard the crunch before I felt it, but I'd stepped on something that went right through the heel of my flip-flop. Broken glass. I thought of the broken shot glass at Karen's. The broken glass in the liquor store. What was it with this case and broken glass?

It looked like there was part of a beer bottle sticking out of my right heel.

I lurched forward, but just a few steps. It hurt too much. "I'm a private investigator." I shouted after Adrianne. "Stop . . ."

The kid, of course, kept right on going.

I dropped down on a bench, and tugged the piece of glass out of my foot. My foot bled copiously.

I limped as fast as I could, back toward the bus platform, still thinking I could grab Adrianne. The blood dripping off my foot made everybody get out of my way, but the bus was already pulling out, and the bus driver didn't stop when I slammed my fist against the door.

I saw Adrianne in the back of the bus, her head down like if she didn't see me, I wasn't there.

I limped outside to Rita's van. There was, of course, a ticket under the windshield wiper. I snatched it up and resisted the urge to crumple it. My lucky streak was over.

I stopped at a drug store and coated my heel in Neosporin and gauze, and then I went to bail Johnny out from Central Booking.

As soon as I posted bail, a dapper-looking man in a well-cut blazer appeared, a pleasant smile etched on his model-handsome face. He introduced himself to me as Hallie Johnson, the delivery boy's lawyer. I'd never met him before, but I knew the name.

"My client said you'd promised to bail out his assailant. So I've been waiting for you, Ms. Bryant." He said it like I should be flattered.

He made a cheap retainer like Kincaid look like dog food.

The thought of Kincaid made me grimace. I still hadn't brought him his disks. The charges against William Devins were still on record.

The lawyer saw my wince and mistook it as directed at him. "I assure you, there's nothing painful about what I'm going to ask you." He led me to a secluded corner and spoke with hushed intensity.

It turned out that Creed wasn't just any delivery boy. He was the son of Red's Liquor's owner, Wesley Redham.

"Mr. Redham is a major, and I do mean very major, contributor to a certain city councilman. And neither of them, in this election year, needs the hassle of charges being filed against Mr. Redham's son."

"No one ever needs a hassle like that," I agreed.

"I really don't believe that young Creed would attempt an assault in the first place."

"You don't?"

"He's not the type of person to—"

"To attempt an assault and not succeed?"

Hallie sighed. He flashed a sympathetic dimple at me. "Look. We want this whole mess to go away."

My foot throbbed, and I was tired. No matter what mess went away, Karen would still be dead. "Meaning?"

"Well, as you already know, Mr. Redham delivered an order to Ms. Shaw around ten o'clock yesterday morning. The bill totaled fifty-four dollars, and she didn't have enough money on hand to pay for it."

He paused, wetting his lips and trying to read my expression.

"Go on," I prompted him.

"She was scantily dressed. A little robe, not much under it, and I gather Mr. Redham suggested that the transaction did not have to be taken care of entirely in cash."

"Ah," I said.

"Ms. Shaw apparently acquiesced at first, and allowed Mr. Redham to kiss her. But she called him by another man's name. The name of the man who caused two hundred and ninety six thousand dollars' worth of damage to Mr. Redham's store this afternoon, in fact."

I huffed, impatient. "I'd almost buy the ninety-six thousand, but I don't see the two hundred playing. Inventory, some shelves, a window. No structural damage. I looked around."

Hallie Johnson nodded, respectful. "We would double-check the amount of course, before any civil suit were to be filed. But my point is that none has to be."

"Uh-huh. So Ms. Shaw called your client by the name Johnny and he backed off?"

He straightened his tie.

"Well, not exactly. He told her something along the lines that she could call him 'anything she fucking wanted,' quote unquote, and things proceeded from there. A few moments later, she changed her mind, pushed him away, and attempted to stab him. He was the true victim."

"Oh, I get it. Attempted rape, self-defense, true victim."

"It was a consensual liaison that didn't progress nearly as far as you're assuming."

"Because of course you're taking Mr. Redham's word."

"I have no reason to doubt it. Ms. Shaw is deceased. He didn't have to say anything at all."

I shrugged. That was true.

"In any case, she pulled a knife on Mr. Redham and held it against his throat. He still bears a small scar from the incident. He was literally in fear for his life. Fortunately, someone came to Ms. Shaw's door and knocked repeatedly. He cried out for help."

"Oh, okay. So there could be a witness that might have seen Mr. Redham attack Ms. Shaw?"

"No one came to his aid, Ms. Bryant," he said quickly. "Whoever was knocking stopped, and left. No one saw anything that went on inside Ms. Shaw's home. But it may have been the presence of someone knocking on the door that caused Ms. Shaw to release Mr. Redham with only a superficial neck wound. She reportedly told him that he was free to go, that she wasn't going to kill him. Naturally, he ran."

"Naturally."

"At any rate, we won't be pressing a case, criminal or civil, against Johnny Ross. We'll write it off as an unfortunate accident. But he cannot turn around and accuse my client of attacking his deceased girlfriend. For which he frankly has no proof whatsoever. And he cannot harass my client in any way, not through physical intimidation or the threat of legal action."

"None of this is up to me."

It was Hallie's turn to grimace.

"My client saw, firsthand, that you have a relationship with Mr. Ross. That you have influence over him."

"I may not have *that* much influence," I said.

"Oh, I bet you do." Hallie flashed his dimples again, and smoothed his sleek blonde hair.

"What if I find out that your client murdered Ms. Shaw?"

Hallie brushed the lapels of his lovely suit and eyed my tight white denim. "The boy did no such thing. He was back at the liquor store, quite shaken up, I might add, several hours before the police estimate her time of death."

Not that Creed couldn't have faked an alibi in his own father's store. But while I could see the kid pawing at Karen, I couldn't see him hanging around, waiting until she was dead drunk and then staging a suicide. He wouldn't have the brains or the patience.

"Are we in accord then?" Hallie asked.

"I wouldn't go that far, but there's no point that I can see in bringing Mr. Redham into this case."

That was all he needed to hear. He smiled, shook my hand,

and stood. He was halfway across the lobby, and I doubt that he heard me when I added "at this time," under my breath.

CHAPTER SEVEN

Johnny stepped out into the night, looking bewildered and bone weary. He was strapping his watch back on and staring at it, like he was surprised it still worked. "Felt like I was in there forever."

I didn't tell him how much longer it would've felt if the charges stood and he got convicted.

"Thank you," he said. "For getting the charges dropped."

"It wasn't really me. Creed's lawyer wanted to make sure we don't spread the word about his client attempting to assault Karen. I don't think he had anything to do with Karen's death, so we cut a deal. But all bets'll be off if you go after that kid again, okay?"

Johnny rubbed his hand across his face. "I wouldn't . . ."

"You were thinking about it. I heard you protected Karen with your fists. Why should it be any different now?"

"I got in a couple of bar fights, that's all. I shoulda known better than to hang out with her in some of those places."

"Yeah, you should've, because she obviously didn't. Bet there was a real wholesome crowd of regulars at the Empire."

Johnny looked at me, chagrined. "She went where she felt people needed her."

"And the drinks were cheap."

"Sometimes I couldn't stop her, Lynn. And sometimes I guess I didn't try."

He crossed the street to a bus stop and stood there, looking up the road. The only thing moving was a paper bag, blowing around the corner. Outside Men's Central Jail, this part of downtown Houston at night wasn't a real hotbed of activity. If Johnny waited around long enough, he'd probably run into an addict or two, but public transportation didn't travel this route past rush hour.

I toyed with the idea of leaving him there to figure it out on his own while I dropped in on Frank.

But Johnny looked pretty forlorn, slumped at that bus stop.

I felt bad for him, and he made me realize how forlorn I probably looked myself with my foot all bandaged up, and how little I wanted Frank to feel as sorry for me as I was feeling for Johnny.

"Come on," I said. "I'm in the garage."

I was hungry and I figured jailhouse food probably wasn't very satisfying, so I swung off the I-45 at Clearwood and pulled into the loading zone in front of Taquerias Arandas.

"Stay in the van. I already got one ticket tonight. If the cops come by—"

"I might run," he told me.

"How about you just drive the van around the block instead."

He nodded.

"I'll get us a couple bean and cheese burritos. Want yours wet or dry?"

"Doesn't matter."

I got them wet, added onions, and grabbed some sodas.

When I slid back in the van, I opened up the windows so Rita wouldn't smell the onions. I had a feeling that eating raw onions in her van would be almost as bad as having sex in it.

Johnny scarfed down the burrito before I'd even pulled away from the curb. He gulped his soda. Then, fortified, he started asking questions. "Hey, Lynn. What were you doing at the liquor store, anyway?"

"Investigating. Found a delivery receipt in Karen's kitchen. Thought it was worth following up."

"I wonder why she called Red's. She always went to the same place, around the corner from her house."

"You mention Red's to her? The free delivery thing?"

Johnny shook his head. "I got the job to paint the sign weeks ago. But I never said a word about it. She thought it was a waste, me painting signs. But there's the rent, you know. Sometimes you just have to take any kinda work to get by."

"Yeah, believe me, I know," I said.

He gave me the ghost of a smile. "I can't believe she's gone. I keep thinking somehow I've got it wrong, and she's at home now, she's calling me." The smile disappeared.

"I found the girl she gave a reading to."

"The girl?"

"The client Karen saw right before she started having her visions. The one she brought up to you at the bar Monday night." I was hoping for a reaction but there was none.

"And? Did the girl say anything?"

"I haven't had a chance to speak to her yet. But I'm thinking she might have some personal connection to Karen."

"What do you mean?"

"She lives over in Marathon."

Johnny looked at me, waiting for more.

"That's where Karen was from."

"Oh. Near the mountains, she told me. Never said where exactly."

We were both silent and I was almost at his place, a loft in what was once a pottery factory not that far from Karen's house.

"Well, here you are. Stay out of trouble, okay?"

Johnny looked down at his hands. He hit his open palm with his fist. "I hated the look on that kid's face this afternoon."

"I don't think Creed did it," I said, gently.

"I don't know what to think," Johnny said.

"I don't think you killed her, either."

"Jesus," he stared at me now, surprised.

"You had to realize I was looking at you."

"I guess I don't realize much of anything right now," he opened the van door, but he didn't get out. "Are you keeping on with this?"

" 'Til I feel like she got her money's worth, anyway."

"I have a little saved, when that runs out."

"You need a new truck."

"I need to know, Lynn. Anything you find out. Even if it turns out she did what the cops think she did."

"I talked to some of her neighbors," I told him.

"Did they see anything?"

"They saw you and Karen in the front yard together. The night it rained. Why'd she scream?"

"She saw something. Something she didn't want to talk about at first."

"The woman's hand?"

"Yeah, that's right."

"What time was it? Around dawn?"

Johnny shook his head. "Around two, I guess. I don't remember the exact time."

"But you'd remember if it was light out?"

"Of course I'd remember if it was light out . . ."

"One of the neighbors swears he saw her outside right at daybreak. What about the next night? Did you see her after she left the bar? Stop by early in the morning, the day she—"

Johnny cut me off. "I didn't see her until it was too late," he said flatly.

Either Johnny was lying, or there was another guy fighting with Karen in the wee hours of Monday morning. A guy who tore her dress. A guy who could've killed her. The thing was, it could've been any guy.

Johnny cleared his throat and got out of the van. "The funeral's tomorrow. Nine a.m. Tranquility Garden, in Bayview."

I wasn't sure why, but I promised I'd come.

It was still dark when the alarm went off. I was even less sure now why I'd promised to attend the funeral.

I turned on my cell before I turned on the lights. There was a message from the detective working Karen's case. They'd pulled the bedding, dress, and the bottle of rye and were working on prints, fibers, etc., as I'd asked. The case did not at this point warrant any expensive DNA testing, but should I come up with any additional evidence that Ms. Shaw was not a victim of suicide, I should call him. Detective Hale sounded resigned, but civil.

There was another message from Frank, telling me he wished I'd call again, he'd take the phone into the gym with him, the handball court, even the shower. He was working on a big smuggling case, but he would have all his calls forwarded. He'd sent three text messages saying approximately the same thing. I was surprised he hadn't written on my Facebook wall, too.

There was also a voice message from one of the RTD bus drivers, confirming what I now already knew, that there were indeed two girls, one with blue hair, one with dark hair, who rode his route both to and from the Channelview stop. He remembered them because the girl without the blue hair was crying.

I left a thank you message for Detective Hale, and a message telling the bus driver I'd be in touch if I needed anything more. I texted Frank a smiley face and told him I'd call him later.

Next, I called Adrianne's number up in Marathon. I let it ring over and over. I called the operator, checked the number, and asked the operator to dial it, too. No answer. You'd think, seven a.m. on a ranch, someone would be up and around to answer the phone.

I drank coffee, peeled an orange, and got myself ready for Karen's funeral.

Although I still didn't have a clean tee shirt or jeans, I did have a decent black cocktail dress. I'd last worn it to the police charity auction a year ago, as Frank's last-minute date. He'd called me the night before the auction.

"I couldn't quite get up the nerve to call, 'til now," he'd said.

It was noisy in the background and I knew he wasn't at the office. I asked where he was.

"Had to have a couple beers, get my courage up," he told me.

"Right. Your real date blew you off this afternoon. Or . . . wait . . . just ten minutes ago."

"It's not true, Lynn. I thought you might wanna see some old friends, get your name around. Good for business, huh, never know?"

I went straight to the mall and I found the perfect black dress; it would break Frank's heart to see me in it and know he couldn't have me.

Of course, as it turned out, I doubt his heart broke, and he had me anyway.

There'd been no occasion to wear the dress since, but it was just about right for Karen Shaw's funeral. I added a faux-pearl necklace, pulled my hair off my neck in a clip, slathered more antiseptic on my heel, rebandaged it tightly, and crammed my feet into a painful pair of black pumps.

Because of the shoes, and the dress, and the fact that Rita had already gone to work, I splurged and took a cab to Three Crowns Auto Body.

The mechanic gave me a low whistle when he saw me all dressed up. "Wish I was going wherever you're going," he said, and winked.

"I'm attending a funeral," I replied.

His face fell and he disappeared beneath the chassis of a Plymouth.

It took me longer to get my car out of the service bay than it took to get Johnny out of jail, but then I didn't have any smooth-talking lawyers handling the paperwork.

It was good to have my car back looking polished and new. I pushed the speed limit to make up for lost time and drove out to Tranquility Garden.

There was a mixture of fog and smog in Bayview that put an unpleasant steaminess over everything. But the grey sky and the clammy promise of drizzle felt right for a funeral.

There were ten different funerals scheduled for nine-thirty a.m., but I had no trouble at all finding Karen's. It was the one with the three-hundred-some people of all ages, races, shapes, and sizes, none of them except me wearing black.

The waitress from the diner down the street from Karen's was there, already in uniform. I saw people in business suits, saris, muumuus, moth-eaten Chanel, leather mini-skirts, leather chaps, and lots of tattoos.

None of them were wearing a tee shirt that said "I killed her."

Johnny arrived in a taxi and stood apart from just about everybody else, wearing what was probably his best, least paint-covered pair of jeans, a clean dark-blue tee shirt, and a dark-blue suit jacket that didn't fit him very well. He looked gaunt, and though he hadn't shaved, he'd cut his hair to just above the collar line.

It struck me that he must've hacked it off as some form of mourning, but at the same time he looked better. With the long hair off his face, you could see what nice cheekbones he had.

A limo pulled up and a very pretty Vietnamese woman in a

neat beige pantsuit stepped out, followed by a Caucasian man, with a Bible in his hand.

The man marched to the casket and bowed his head. He read from Ecclesiastes, and paused, and some people called out "Amen."

With perfect timing, and perhaps they'd rehearsed it, the beautiful Vietnamese woman started singing a cappella in her own language, something that sounded like a dirge.

It was all very different from the last funeral I'd attended, my mother's, years back. We'd just moved to Houston, my father having exchanged his Army career for an advisory position in aerospace, and before we'd even settled into our new home, my mother was diagnosed with the cancer that consumed her. And before she'd made any friends to mourn her, we were burying her silently, alone.

Ten years to the day she died, I had to place my father in an assisted living center, the politically correct way to identify the nursing home in which he now resides.

I visit him every week, and once in awhile there's a glimmer of recognition in his eyes when I say "I love you." Somehow it's easier to say it now, when I know I'll get no response, than it was all those years after my mother died, when I kept hoping he'd say it back.

"I'm not a demonstrative person," he'd say.

Unlike my father, everyone at Karen's funeral was being very demonstrative indeed. All around me people were weeping, moaning, and calling out Karen's name.

The song ended and the woman who was singing proclaimed "I would not have had any of my children without Karen to guide their spirits into this world. She herself was a song."

There was a chorus of tearful agreement, and the waitress from the coffee shop threw me a glance so sharp I almost felt the sting. "She was an incredible person, worthy of the greatest respect," she said loudly.

Everyone seemed to have a story to tell, about how Karen had helped them, guided them, or made them better people. They told their stories, and then slowly everybody left, until it was just me and Johnny. And we had nothing to say.

Finally Johnny spoke. "You heard. She helped every damn person here today. But in the end, any way you look at it, she couldn't help herself. And I couldn't help her, either."

"Maybe we can help her a little now," I said.

"You're the one," Johnny smiled at me, sadly. "Not me. You're the one that can still do for her."

I offered him a ride, but he said he was going to stick around awhile.

I watched him sit down cross-legged on the grass near her grave. Then I kicked off the too-tight black pumps and climbed in my car. My injured heel throbbed and I felt silly and overdressed in the little black number.

I got lost driving out of the cemetery and ended up making a circle past Karen's grave again. Johnny was still there and there was a sparrow pecking at the grass in front of Johnny. He held out his hand to it, but it flew away.

I made it out of Tranquility Garden and back on the highway on the second try, and going for the gold, I tried calling Adrianne again from my cell. There was still no answer.

I rolled down the windows, popped the sunroof open, and let the wind blast at me.

Maybe it was the whole funeral scene, and life being too short to hang around waiting, or maybe it was what Johnny said, that I was the one that could still do something for Karen. For whichever reason, I decided I might as well just drive all the way across the damn state over to Marathon and corner the girl.

Was I gonna solve this case or not?

★ ★ ★ ★ ★

I went home, took off the dress and heels, and switched to shorts, my flip-flops, and a tank top that read "Cabo San Lucas" and sported a giant marlin on the front. I didn't have a lot of clothing choices left, and there wasn't much to pack, either.

I drove over to Texas Med and went up to the sixth floor, maternity, and had Rita paged. She was annoyed before I even opened my mouth.

"No, you can't borrow the van again! It smells like onions! You used up all the gas. I was late this morning and—"

"I got my car back. I just need to get my laundry out of the van."

She marched me to her locker, impatient. "I have three women all dilated to nine centimeters."

"I wouldn't have bothered you now except I've gotta hit the road."

She took in my attire. "You're going to Cabo?"

"No. Little town out near Big Bend."

"Why?"

"Because of the murder case I'm working on."

"The psychic with the soulful boyfriend? You bringing him along?"

"You sure do ask a lot of questions. No, I'm not bringing him along. What do you think I am, a grave robber or something?"

"You don't have to sputter. That would be *cradle* robber, because he's younger than you, and a rebound if he was interested in you, and fun, if you were interested in him. You never know until you actually spend some time with a guy who isn't Frank."

"You're insane. You're morbid. You want me to get into a relationship with a guy whose lover, my client, just died in a horribly gruesome way."

"I didn't say you had to have a relationship with him. Maybe just a fling. It might do you both some good."

"He's not the 'fling' type. And neither am I. Don't you have babies to birth?"

She tossed me her keys. "Just leave 'em at the desk, okay?"

I transferred my laundry from Rita's van to my trunk again. There had to be laundromats somewhere in West Texas.

My plan was to drive out, talk to the girl face to face, see if she knew anything, nose around town a little, see if there was anything I didn't already know about Karen that would prove useful, turn around, and come back home again. It would be . . . hah! . . . a marathon driving trip, but I could pull it off. And I had this feeling in my gut that the trip would yield the information I needed to find Karen's murderer.

But first there was Frank to visit, the charges against William Devins to rescind, CDs to retrieve, and lawyer Kincaid to be mollified.

I zipped onto the Loop. For once it was clear sailing, and I was across the street from Frank's office and parked in the police garage in under twenty minutes.

Officer Reynolds was inside Frank's office, dropping a file on his desk. She looked me up and down.

"Vacation?" she asked.

"Sort of," I nodded. "Frank around?"

"Around in a meeting. Be back in an hour or so."

I sighed. I didn't want to sit around for an hour, but then I didn't want to barge in on some meeting dressed the way I was dressed, either.

"Don't suppose you'd get him for me?"

"Don't suppose."

Still, she got the paperwork I needed at least, I dropped the charges, and I left a note on Frank's desk. "Sorry I missed you. I left something at your apartment the other night that I need back. Call my cell and I'll explain."

Kincaid was just gonna have to wait for the damn CDs.

I was backing my car out of its parking space when I felt something thump against the side. I stopped, afraid I'd hit something, and there was Frank himself, out of breath, like he'd just run a mile.

He didn't smile of course, just moved up next to my front window, wringing his hands together like he would've rathered they were around my neck.

"Can't you ever stay in one place long enough for me to talk to you? I had to run down here to catch up with you," he shouted. His shouts echoed off the parking garage walls and bounced back. I turned off the engine, and drummed my fingers on the steering wheel.

"This has got to be a record," he said, finally catching his breath.

"Record for what?"

He leaned in my window. "For getting involved in two major messes at once. William Devins and the Shaw case."

"Karen Shaw was my client. And I just withdrew the charges against Devins. I made a deal with his lawyer. All I have to do now is give him the computer files I stole."

"You stole files? And you admitted it?"

"They were the basis of my deal cutting."

"That's evidence of breaking and entering!"

"That's documenting Devins' crime."

"B&E!"

We could go on like this all afternoon. "By the way, Frank, I need to swing by your place to—"

He cut me off with a thump of his fist against my roof.

"Hey, I just got the car out of the body shop. Unless you wanna front the deductible this time, no more dents, okay?"

He jammed his hands in his jacket pocket. "I'm glad you're

all right," he said. "I was worried about you. No whiplash from that accident, anything like that?"

I shook my head. "See? Just fine. Now about swinging by your—"

Again he cut me off. "You coulda lost your license over this insurance shit," he said.

"Yeah, yeah. I lost the account over it, bad enough."

He took one of his hands out of his pocket again and wiped his face with it. "God, you get me hot and bothered," he said.

"Used to like that about me," I managed a smile.

He smiled too. "I might as well say it. I miss you, Lynnie. I miss you a lot."

That surprised me, and so did him leaning down into my window, and kissing me. But what was even more surprising, I was kissing him back.

We took a breather and he opened my car door and unlatched my seat belt, and we went back to kissing again, and then he was bending over me, his head bumping the ceiling of my suddenly way-too-small car, my back pressed up against the emergency brake.

He moved the driver's seat into the "recline" position. I was unbuttoning his shirt, and he was working down the band of my running shorts. We were going at it like a couple of high school kids high on hormones, when his elbow hit my horn and we both jumped apart like it was a gunshot or something.

"Maybe we oughta move this into the backseat," he suggested.

I tugged at my shorts. "Right here?"

His fingers traced the marlin on my shirt. "C'mon. You telling me we've never done it in the police garage before?"

I sat up, or sat up as much as I could with Frank still half on top of me. "No, you must be thinking of some other girl."

He laughed, but I wasn't particularly amused. I gave him a

little shove and he bonked his head on the ceiling again. He slid out of the car, and tried to pull me with him, but I shook my head.

"We'll go in my office and lock the door."

He might've still had a chance if he hadn't suggested that particular spot for an assignation. All those afternoons when his door was locked, and I wasn't with him. Now I *knew* he was thinking of another girl.

"I gotta go."

"We're not that far from my place," he said, sounding desperate now, "or hell, I'll spring for a room at the St. Regis."

"Like I said, you're thinking of someone else."

He sighed. "You really do make me nuts," he said, standing there, breathing hard, with his shirt unbuttoned. "But I realized the other night . . ." his voice trailed off. He turned those big brown eyes on me.

It was a practiced technique of his. I'd seen it when he questioned perps; I'd seen it in the boardroom, and the bedroom.

Somebody else had to finish his sentence for him, or let him off the hook. I didn't do either one this time.

"What did you realize?" I asked.

"You must've felt it too."

"Felt what?"

"Come on, Lynn. Don't make me—"

"Actually get it together to say how you really feel?"

"Exasperated!"

"Okay, finally we're in agreement."

He exhaled sharply. "Lynn, look, the point is, I care, I really do, and I don't want anything bad to happen to you."

"I'm touched."

"Just because you lost one account doesn't mean you can't find some other steady work."

"Thanks for the pep talk."

"What I'm saying is that you don't need to take every case that comes your way. No matter how strange and ugly."

"Karen Shaw's murder?"

"It's a suicide."

"I don't think it is," I said.

"Why? You have any evidence to the contrary?" He started buttoning up his shirt.

"I'm getting there."

"Is it real, actual evidence, or are you just reading people's minds, like the victim?"

"If I am, I don't like what I'm reading in yours."

"The guys working this case are absolutely positive she offed herself, Lynn."

"They're wrong. She was too loaded, for one thing. I just don't believe she did it, and neither does her boyfriend."

"They're closing the books on Karen Shaw. You've been making it way too hard on Hale. You keep pestering him to run more prints, analyze what you found in the woman's garbage. I told him to go ahead, but he asked me how long this is supposed to go on. How long does he have to keep looking for something that isn't there? What was I supposed to tell him?"

"To do his job?"

Frank took a step back, knotting his tie. "People still associate you with me, Lynn."

Now I was seething. I turned the key in the ignition again and gunned the engine. "Oh, that's the thing, huh. I do something you think is stupid and it makes *you* look bad."

"I didn't mean it that way. I'm trying to look out for you."

"Who asked you to do that?" I backed up fast this time, almost taking off his foot and part of a squad car. It was good to see him jump.

"Lynn, come on."

I ignored him and burned rubber out of the garage, and the place was history, and so was Frank, just like he should've been for years.

And then Houston was history too, a blur of traffic and buildings behind me. I was halfway to San Antonio before I remembered William Devins' stinking CDs.

CHAPTER EIGHT

"Good news," I called Kincaid's secretary when I stopped for gas. "Lynn Bryant, here. All the paperwork is taken care of downtown and your client is off the hook on the assault charges."

"Wow, that only took two days longer than it should've taken. CDs?"

"Coming soon. But not today. I'm on my way to Marathon right now."

"I'm on my way to a nervous breakdown. Take a long-distance run some other time and get in here with those files."

"I'm working on another case, honey. Marathon is a little town in the western half of this great state of Texas. Day after tomorrow, I'll be back in Houston, grab those disks in my hot little hand, and—"

She actually hung up on me. I would've called her back, but I lost my cell signal as I passed the Colorado River; the hours slipped by and I never got it back.

It was an oddly liberating feeling. Nobody could reach me, and I didn't even have to try to reach them. I could stay entirely focused on Karen Shaw, on proving she was murdered, and proving I was right in the bargain. Screw Frank, Kincaid, Detective Hale, everybody.

It got full dark before I knew night was coming, with the sun setting in the west ahead of me but behind the mountains. Outside of the big cities the plains spread eerie in the moonlight, a vast wash of brown field, white salt deposits, and occasional small towns, splotches of life on a mummified land.

Occasionally I saw pieces of somebody's bountiful past strewn along the highway like debris tossed out a car window. Roadside motel courts crumbled and abandoned. An old barn, desiccated by time and heat. A beautiful farmhouse with a wraparound porch and boarded-up windows. Crossing the Stockton plateau, what had to be Mt. Santiago appeared to the south, edged with stars, its jagged peaks resembling the spires of a cathedral.

It was past midnight when I made it to Marathon, and maybe it was the long drive, or the fight with Frank, or how early I'd set my alarm clock that morning, but I knew it was far too late to head south thirty-three miles on a two-lane road toward Big Bend, and find the ten miles of road that led to the ranch where Google said Adrianne Cannon lived with her father.

I idled at the town's one stoplight. Despite its diminutive size, Marathon boasts a small historical museum, a large and pretty park, an old railroad depot, and a sheriff's station and jail. Also gracing the shoulders of Highway 385, which serves as the town's Main Street, is a big, attractive-looking bar with a gold-plated wooden Indian guarding the door, a couple of junk-slash-antique stores not nearly as impressive as the railroad depot, a cute little café with gingham curtains, and an old-fashioned two-story yellow-brick hotel.

According to an iron plaque hanging over the front door, the Gage Hotel was built in nineteen twenty-eight. According to the clerk who answered the night buzzer, there were thirty-six rooms, the least expensive with shared bath, of which twelve were available. My room was small, with a handmade quilt spread over a brass bed. There was no phone or television, but there was wine and sponge cake set out in the lobby every evening. There was a well-regarded restaurant, but it was, of course, closed.

The lobby boasted a massive stone fireplace with a cow skull painted powder blue hanging over it. There was a circle of comfortable arm chairs surrounding a coffee table with wine and cake still sitting out, and a stack of Zane Grey Western novels on it. I downed two small glasses of zinfandel and ate three large slices of cake for dinner, and went straight to bed.

Morning. No need to set an alarm. I woke when the first train thundered into the depot. Six a.m. two days in a row.

I took a fast shower and washed out my underwear in the sink, and dried it with a hair dryer. I put on the one clean piece of clothing I'd packed, a diminutive sundress. I thought it might be feminine and non-threatening enough to endear me to Adrianne's reportedly conservative father, and who knew, even to the girl herself.

I was still limping, but the gash on my heel looked like it was coming together okay.

I grabbed a cup of coffee and some tasty biscuits from the café down the street, and headed for the Cannon ranch. I caught a glimpse of a small lake as the bumpy two-lane road narrowed quickly, going through a series of switchbacks until it twisted between a massive outcropping of black rock. I was glad I hadn't made this passage at night. Rusty highway signs warned of rockslides and flooding. Bony cactuses stretched out their long arms like supplicants.

I was gripping the steering wheel tightly when the roughly paved road disappeared entirely into washboard dirt and gravel.

Little rocks spumed up, pinging against the underbelly and doors of my newly sleek car. I had that body work done at the wrong time.

The dust rose in great clouds, making everything out of my windshield wiper's reach a thick grey. Even with the wipers going, it was hard to tell where the road ended and the edge of a cliff descending hundreds and hundreds of feet began. I managed to creep up to fifteen miles an hour, and that felt like speeding.

At last the road descended again, and then a narrower road led off to the left. Over it, a curved wooden sign had horseshoes bolted to it, and the words "Cannon Ranch" spelled out with big rusty nailheads. The sign reminded me of Adrianne's rhinestone jacket.

I turned and went the last ten teeth-rattling but mercifully flat miles until I reached a large unpainted frame house, with a big barn and a horse pen behind it. There was an enormous vegetable garden in front, with a canvas hooked up over it to keep the full hit of the sun away.

When I parked in front of the ranch house and opened my car door, the thrust of the heat hit me like someone had punched me in the jaw. The temperature must've risen by twenty degrees since I'd left Marathon.

A lizard darted in front of my feet as I crossed the yard to the house. Like everything else around, it was brown and dusty.

The house had an ample porch with an old milking bench on it, and a faded welcome mat. A leather braid hung on the door dripping with silver bells. I shook the braid, but nobody answered.

I knocked and knocked again, and there was Adrianne, still pretty and pale, in baggy overall shorts and a tee shirt printed with "County High Track Team." I would've bet top dollar she was the star.

When she saw me, she tried to slam the door shut again, but I pushed against it, and got my foot wedged inside. She was strong as well as fast, and we were pretty much even with the pushing and shoving.

"You better knock it off now," I said. "I just want to talk to you."

But she wasn't listening. She was staring down at the porch.

Without thinking, I'd used the foot with the gash on it as a wedge, and it had started bleeding again. There was a big puddle of blood oozing out of my sandal.

"Shit," I muttered. It hurt, too.

Adrianne screamed and let go of the door. She fell forward against me so hard that I stumbled back. She was surprisingly heavy for a thin girl, the muscle I guess, and she had fainted away to deadweight in my arms.

Adrianne's father must've heard her scream, because he came running and clumped up on the porch just as I got us both down on the old milking bench. My foot was bleeding steadily and Adrianne was slumped with her head on my shoulder.

"What the hell?" he asked. He was in his mid-fifties, lean, and muscular. His eyes were an intense blue, and he looked tough and tan and damn good for his age.

Even as his gaze and mine moved away from each other and down to my blood on his porch, I noticed his shoes. Steel-toed work boots, like the ones Karen had described seeing in her visions.

I felt a ripple of excitement and something like nausea move across my stomach, and my hands were tingling. Adrianne moaned on my shoulder.

"She fainted," I told David Cannon. "And I've hurt my foot."

He shook Adrianne gently. "Honey, come on, honey."

He looked at me, apologetic. "She can't stand the sight of blood."

"Must be hard for her around here," I said. "Working cattle ranch and all. Must be cuts and scrapes all the time."

Adrianne came to, and drew back from me with a start. "Oh no," she said, looking at me.

"The lady just cut her foot, baby."

Adrianne jumped up and more or less cowered behind her

father. For a tall, strong, fast girl she sure was acting like a little kid.

"I'll get her a bandage," Adrianne whispered, and ducked into the house.

David looked mildly concerned about me and my bloody foot, and not especially worried about my presence there at the ranch. It was the cute sundress throwing him off.

"How'd you do that, anyway?" David asked.

"Running," I said. "After your daughter, in fact. I need to ask you both some questions."

"What kinda questions? You a census taker or something?"

"I'm a private investigator."

He raised his eyebrows and beneath them, those blue eyes took on an intensity that practically bore a hole in my skull.

"Investigating what?"

I improvised. "The disappearance of your wife."

He opened his mouth to say something, but Adrianne reappeared with a roll of medical tape and a spray can of sticky brown pine tar, guaranteed to stop bleeding fast, ostensibly before the person helping you apply it fainted again.

"You come on out to the barn to talk to me," he said. "I got chores to do. And Addy here, she doesn't know nothin' about her mother leaving. Nothin'."

He stalked off the porch and across the yard, kicking up little dust devils as he went.

Adrianne looked at me, wide-eyed. "You're here about my mother?"

"That's part of it," I said.

"You know where she is?" she asked, breathless.

"No, I don't."

Adrianne's face collapsed with disappointment. "It's something I dream about. Somebody finding her."

"You miss her a lot, huh?"

"Oh yeah, more'n anything. Why are you looking for her?"

"My client was worried about your mother. About you, too."

"Your client?"

"Karen Shaw. The psychic you and your friend Hayley—"

"I know who she is," Adrianne said, and her voice lowered to a whisper even though her father couldn't hear her from the barn. "Why would she be worried?"

"She asked you about your mother, didn't she, when you and Hayley went to see her?"

"Yes. And she was very worked up about it. She got me worked up myself."

"Did you know she grew up around here?"

"Yeah. I heard stories when I was a kid, about how good she was, how she was, like, the genuine article. I looked her up online, and I saw she was in Houston, so I figured why not take Hayley to go see her."

"Why not."

"I thought it would be a kick, you know. We could tell if she was a real psychic or a fake if she knew where we were from."

"Did she know?"

"She never said." Adrianne twisted her fingers. "Oh Lord, Daddy's gonna be angry at me for seeing that lady, when he finds out you're here 'cause of her."

"Why would he be angry?"

"He doesn't, um, approve of things like that. Psychics. Fortune tellers. He thinks they're trouble."

"Why'd you run from me at the bus station?"

"You scared me. I didn't know you were an investigator. You were just this woman chasing me, and I didn't like it much."

I had identified myself, but I guess she didn't hear me. I could buy that.

"You haven't been answering your phone."

"You can't hear it from outside. I've been working in the

garden. Dad let everything go the week I was with Hayley."

Okay, I'd buy that too.

She chewed on the edge of her lip. "If you find out something, anything, about my mother, will you tell me?"

"Of course," I said.

"And if you talk to your . . . your client, tell her I'm sorry, okay?"

"Sorry for what?"

"For being so rude. I thought she was running a scam or something. But I guess I misjudged her."

"You weren't the only one," I said.

I left Adrianne on her front porch and went out to the barn after her father. The barn was big, clean, and more freshly painted than the house. David was pouring grain from an enormous bag into feed sacks for the dozen or so horses stabled inside.

I tried to stay calm, and I kept my gun in my purse, but I wanted to be holding it on him. I wanted to have him cuffed in an interrogation room. I wanted to still be a cop and reading him his rights. Not that as yet I had the cause to arrest him.

All I had was a feeling that twisted through me from the first look I got of David's boots, and the first glimpse I had of the fierceness in his eyes.

That fierceness spoke of guilt. He was hiding something, and the way he hid it was through offense, not defense. It probably worked real well on a shy teenager like Adrianne. It didn't work so well on me.

"You follow my daughter four hundred miles, bleed all over our doorstep, and demand to know where my wife is? I don't have time for this craziness. I've got work to do," he said.

"So do I." I stroked the sleek nose of a pretty black filly, restive in her stall. The horse gave a nervous little whinny.

"My wife left me, that's what she did. Took two suitcases full of clothes, drove away in her car. Left our daughter sick in bed with pneumonia. It was three years ago, I don't know where she is now, and frankly, I don't care."

There was an air of righteousness about him, almost swallowed up in rage. My hands tingled again. He could be as righteous and as angry as he wanted, but he was lying. He cared very much.

"What kind of car was she driving?" I asked calmly.

He snorted like he was one of the horses. "A green '90 Dodge, like it's any of your business."

He emptied the feed bag and folded it up. He grabbed another bag of grain from a shelf, and struggled to open it. His hands were shaking as much as Karen's did coming off a bender. He reached in his pocket.

"Dammit. Keep forgetting I lost that knife."

"Silver, with a little turquoise on the handle?"

David looked up at me, doing a good imitation of surprised. "You see it lying around here?"

"Not lying around here, no."

"You messing with me?"

"No, sir," I said.

"You scared Addy half to death, chasing after her. I don't care for it much."

"Just doing my job," I said. "Her friend Hayley told me where to—"

He cut me off, sneered. "Hayley. Messed up little brat. Glad her folks left town. Somebody needs to give her a good whuppin'."

He ripped at the bag and finally tore it open, spilling some grain on the floor. The floor looked to be a relatively new, smooth concrete. It couldn't have been more than, say, five years old. If I lived way out in the middle of nowhere, and I had a body to dispose of, a new barn floor might be just the ticket.

He spun on me. "What's your client's name, anyway? Corelli? Is it Hayley Corelli's Daddy? Eavesdropping on the girls' talk? Like it's my daughter who's the bad influence? That it?"

I smiled slowly, watching his response. "Hayley's father isn't my client. My client's name is Karen Shaw."

Both his righteousness and his anger faltered.

He knew that name. He knew her.

"Just what are you after? Money? I don't have any. My land? Bank owns it."

I smiled sweetly. "Information. My client is trying to locate your wife."

"Somehow I doubt that, very much," David said. "Now get the hell off my property."

He stormed out of the barn, heading for his house, and I went for my car. This was his land, and I wasn't an officer of the law. It was time to back off a little.

I had my car door open when David crashed out of the house again, toting a rifle. He raised it, and pointed it at me.

It was a good-looking thirty-aught-six, with a clean, oiled stock.

I had my thirty-eight up and out and aimed at him, fast.

We froze, weapons drawn, barely breathing, with only the wind undulating the brown grass between us.

Naturally, he had a better chance of creaming me with the rifle at that distance than I had of taking him out with my Smith and Wesson, but then I had the car for cover, and aim so wicked good he might end up sorry he took me on.

Or I might end up his third victim. Time for a new barn floor.

Adrianne bolted out of the house, the door banging behind her. She grabbed at her father's arm, knocking the gun to the ground, where it fired, spitting dirt. David spun on his daughter, furious.

"Addy! What the hell . . . ?"

"Get on out of here!" she called to me.

I kept my gun on David while I climbed in my car, fumbled with my keys, and stuck them in the ignition.

David was just standing there, limp, exhausted. He made no move for his gun lying on the ground.

Adrianne was leaning against him, crying. Slowly he put his arm around her. I started the engine, gunning it to gain purchase on the gravel drive.

Looking in my rear view, I saw David push his daughter away and lunge for the gun like somebody awakened from a dream. As my car fishtailed away, he fired.

"Daddy! Don't do it!" Adrianne screamed.

A shot passed over my car, scratching across the roof. I expected him to jump in his pickup and take off after me, so I drove as fast as I could, sending showers of gravel against my hood. It really *was* the wrong time to have paid for all that body work.

When I reached the main road, such as it was, I found a turnout just before the box canyon, and I pulled into it. I climbed out of my car, my gun ready, and hunched down behind the trunk, waiting for David's pickup to show.

It was hot and quiet. I heard the sweat dripping off my arms and splashing down in the dust. After about twenty minutes, my quads cramped up and I felt the sun burning the back of my neck. If he was coming after me, he sure was slow about it.

After about ten more minutes, I gave it up and got back in the car, and did my snail's pace thing back down the side of the mountain and into town again.

CHAPTER NINE

Sheriff Charles Winton was carefully tacking "Wanted" notices on his office wall. It was one large room, crowded with filing cabinets and two desks, in the basement of the jail.

He was about David Cannon's age, I figured, but he looked older, his face mellow, rounder, lined. His hair, like David's, was silver, but it was thinner and flew up in little wisps around his ears. He had an easy smile and a weariness in his eyes.

It was clear to me right off that his role in the community was to act patient and understanding, settle disputes over trespassing cattle and water rights, dole out speeding tickets. He wasn't built to handle bad guys, at least not anymore.

Maybe that was the reason he was listening to what I had to say, but wasn't terribly impressed with what he was hearing.

"Why do you think David Cannon had something to do with your client committing suicide?" he asked me.

"She didn't kill herself. Someone killed her. I think it's the same person who killed Helen Cannon, five years ago."

He turned and looked at me, sharply. "Killed Helen Cannon? I have no reason to believe she's even dead."

I sighed. Assuming she was dead, I had absolutely no reason to accuse David Cannon of killing her, except for a pair of boots that looked like the boots Karen described to me, a description that had come from what some people might see as a psychotic break.

I didn't think it was a good idea to explain Karen's visions in great detail, or go into my theory that they were the manifesta-tion of something she had actually witnessed. The sheriff would think he was just hearing one lunatic defend another.

"I've got a hunch. I trust my hunches. You don't believe me, I can refer you to any number of satisfied clients. I can refer you to the Houston PD, where I had more case clearances than any other detective in the homicide division the last year I was so employed. Ask around and you'll see how many times I've been right."

Sheriff Winton raised one eyebrow.

"There's nothing I can do for you, missy. No matter how many times you been right. I'm not going to question David Cannon as to his whereabouts on Monday and Tuesday of this week, and I asked all the questions I'm ever gonna ask about his wife."

He turned back to his wall of felons. He didn't want to look at me anymore.

Of course it was possible that it wasn't entirely me he didn't want to look at. I took a wild shot. "You don't want to be around David Cannon, do you?"

"I'm getting ready to go on home. Been here since six a.m. helping the district attorney's office with the evidence on a drug lab operating over near Sanderson. Don't really have the time to spare on foolish questions."

I knew a prevarication when I heard one. "Why don't you like him? What do you think he's done?"

The sheriff swung around again, and folded his arms across his chest. "His wife, Helen, was a friend of mine, that's all. As far as investigating her leaving goes, I've been there and done that."

Something in the way he said it made me think she was more than just a friend.

"So you're telling me you never regarded Helen Cannon's

disappearance as suspicious? You're telling me you don't check with the DMV, every six months, look for her car?"

"Now, missy, you have no idea what I do or don't do."

"I know what cops do. I know what I would've done."

Sheriff Winton let out a long, low whistle. "Speaking of what people do. Cannon shot at you, but he didn't hit you, did he? Just fired a warning. I might do the same thing myself, scare off a trespasser."

"He said he lost his knife. It sounds exactly like the knife found by my client's body."

The sheriff scoffed.

"You should've seen his face when I said my client's name. He knows . . . knew her."

" 'Course he knew her. This is a small town, in case you haven't seen. Karen Shaw lived with her grandmother in the unincorporated area over to Onion Valley, 'til she was about fifteen or sixteen. Grandmother died, left her some money I guess, and off she went."

"She ever come back?"

"Not that I know about." He smoothed his wispy hair, and dropped down at his desk. "Look, what do you want me to do here?"

I wanted him to help me prove David was in Houston, in Karen's house when she died. I wanted him to help me link Karen's death to David's MIA wife, to something Karen had probably witnessed and forgotten she had, until Adrianne visited her on a whim. I wanted to establish that pesky thing called motive.

But what I said was, "I want you to ask David Cannon some questions. Or get him to answer mine in a setting where he doesn't have his shotgun quite so handy."

Winton sighed, but he picked up his phone, and dialed. After a long time, somebody answered. "This is the sheriff, Addy. Get your daddy on the line for me, okay?"

He pushed a button and the call went to the speaker phone; static and footsteps came across loud and clear.

"This about that woman?" David Cannon asked.

"What woman do you mean, David?" Sheriff Winton winked at me, and leaned back in his chair.

"We're playing games?" David sounded uncertain now, which was of course what the sheriff wanted.

"No game, no sir. I had a report made by a young lady that you shot at her in the course of a private investigation she was making."

"She's crazy," David said, and I heard the fury rising up in his voice.

"Admit her investigation is a little vague, but that's not the point here. You shot at her. She asks me to, I'm gonna have to bring you in. Might be easier if you gave her an apology and an interview."

David's voice vibrated with cold fury. "You do what you have to, Charlie. I'll take my lumps for actin' stupid, but I will not talk to that woman again."

"I'll be happy to moderate any discussion, make sure nothing gets out of hand."

The more angry David got, the more sanguine the sheriff sounded. I thought there *was* a game being played.

"Not gonna dignify the trash she's saying by giving it another listen," David growled.

The sheriff was silent for a minute.

"You there, Charlie?" David asked.

"Yeah. Say . . . you ever hear from Helen?" the sheriff hunched forward now, and his voice took on an edge.

"No," David said flatly. Suddenly there was no more emotion betrayed on his part.

"You don't think it means anything, she never even sent her

kid a Christmas card?" the sheriff prodded.

"It means she was so glad to leave, she didn't care who she hurt."

And with that, David hung up. I heard the click and the buzz on the phone line, but the sheriff got in the last word anyway.

"Lived too long with you, I guess," he muttered.

The sheriff hung up his phone and rubbed his hand across his face. "Well, you heard how he is. What are you gonna do next?"

"I might try talking to his daughter some more, if I can get her away from him."

"Good luck."

"Doesn't she ever come into town?"

The sheriff shook his head. "Other'n going to school, she doesn't leave the ranch much. Leastwise I never see her over at the pizza place or the movie theater in Alpine, where most of the high school kids go, or the café here in town, for that matter."

"Just out of curiosity," I asked, "that barn on Cannon's ranch, with the concrete floor. Any idea when it was put in?"

" 'Bout three years ago. Contractor did the courthouse parking lot the same time."

"Three years, huh? Before or after Helen Cannon disappeared?"

"I know what you're thinking, but the floor was in before she left," the sheriff said shortly. "There was a fire, old barn burnt to the ground. We were out there with ladders and buckets, trying to keep it from spreading to the house."

He shook his head, remembering. "When we got it contained, Helen said she wished it *had* spread. She was bitter. Said she'd given him too much, not just money either. She wanted out of the marriage."

"Why was that?"

134

The sheriff made a little sound in the back of his throat that could've been derision.

"Let me tell you how it was the night of that fire and a lotta other nights too. They started shoving each other around. Helen gave as good as she got, she was tough. I had to pull the two of 'em apart, with Adrianne watching, crying. Barn was still smoking." He lapsed into silence, remembering.

"Was that the end of it?"

"End of what?" he asked, his eyes opaque, guilty.

"The fight between David and his wife."

"Mmm, more or less. While I was holding Helen back, she spat at him, said he'd never change. 'Guess you think if it's not *her*, it doesn't matter,' she said."

"What'd she mean, not 'her'?"

"I don't know who she was talking about specifically, but David was at one time quite the womanizer. Not always the upstanding moral pillar of the churchgoing community he is these days."

"That's interesting," I said. "Any idea what women he was involved with?"

Sheriff Winton's lips twitched. "Try just about every female past a certain age in this town. But to his credit, he did offer to move out for a while. Helen refused. Told him she couldn't stand the place, he'd poisoned it for her. He could be the one to stay and deal with the triple mortgage. 'One of these days, you're gonna wake up and I'll be long gone. You'll never see me again. And I'll never look back,' that's what she told him."

Sheriff Winton wagged a finger in my direction. "That's probably just what she did, never looked back."

He sounded to me like he was trying to convince *himself* of it, more than me.

I thanked him for his time and efforts, and told him I would stick around another day, and try to talk to Adrianne again. I'd be at the hotel just across the street if he needed me, and I'd let him know if anything interesting turned up on my end.

"I'm sure you will," he said. He didn't seem either happy or unhappy about it.

I asked the young guy with a ponytail and a handlebar moustache at the Gage Hotel's front desk about doing my laundry, and was pointed an hour west, to Alpine, home of the only nearby laundromat as well as the movie theater and pizza parlor Adrianne did not frequent. It was also the home of the consolidated high school that she did attend. Although school didn't start up again until next week, I thought I'd nose around anyway.

The sun was sinking lurid and low in the sky. It was windy, and there were clouds stirring around in great cumulonimbus streaks as I headed up the highway.

As I told Sheriff Winton, I wanted to talk to Adrianne again. What I'd do after I talked to her depended on what she said. I hoped she'd say her father killed her mother and Karen Shaw knew it, so he killed her, too.

Without a statement like that, for the time being at least, I was out of luck. I couldn't get David Cannon arrested because my dead client had a vision of somebody in boots like his killing a woman, although it seemed prudent to me to lock the son of a bitch up while I found more standard evidence.

Even though I was pretty damn sure the knife found next to Karen's body was his, Houston forensics said the only finger-prints on it were Karen's. He must've wiped the knife clean, then pressed her fingers up against it.

But maybe his prints were somewhere else in Karen's house, on that bottle of rye, say. Of course the cops would say it wasn't the bottle that was the murder weapon. It would place him at Karen's, though.

Now if the knife was bought somewhere around this town, and it was unique enough, I had a feeling I could track its purchase to David. Still, I'd have to link him to Karen's death better than that. When you came right down to it, I needed something very much like a confession or an eyewitness.

I had my doubts about finding an eyewitness to Karen's murder, but if I believed the key to her death was Helen Cannon's, and I did, then that key might very well rest in Adrianne's recollections about her mother.

As I approached Alpine, I was surprised to find it was a big town, at least compared to Marathon, sprawling with fast food, motels, and sporting-good stores, where the unprepared could stock up on wilderness gear for a trip to Big Bend.

I parked in front of the high school. All the doors were locked, and the windows closed up tight. Behind the school there was both the football field and the track.

At the track, there was a perky looking, blonde woman in her twenties blowing a whistle and running a girl and a boy through their paces. I limped across the field to them. The blonde introduced herself as Coach Maynard, and she sent the kids off to the showers before agreeing to talk to me.

"I don't know what I can tell you about Adrianne Cannon. Other than she's a good kid, fast runner, gets fine grades. Somewhat of a loner, but that's probably 'cause her dad keeps such a close eye on her. Funny thing is, him doing that probably is the reason she gets involved sometimes with the wrong people."

"How so?"

"The other kids on my team do things together as a group. Plan picnics, go for a hike, go fishing. Kid stuff. Adrianne's shy to begin with, and then her daddy's real overprotective I guess, never lets her go on those kinds of outings so . . . she's left with the kids who don't care about participating."

"Kids like Hayley Corelli?"

She raised her eyebrows, nodded. "Best thing that could've happened to Adrianne was Hayley moving away. I'm hoping the visit Addy just made to see her was both the first and the last, yes, ma'am."

"Now that Hayley moved, does Adrianne hang out with anybody special?"

"Keeps to herself mostly. I'm making a real effort to get her involved in team activities, though. There's one she's promised to attend this evening, in fact. I cornered her father about it last week while she was away, and to my surprise he agreed she could go."

I smiled, pleased at my luck. "When and where?"

She hesitated. "It was so hard to convince her to come in the first place. I'd hate for you to make it an unpleasant experience for her."

"I'd hate to do that, too. But I'm investigating a murder that may or may not be connected to the disappearance of Adrianne's mother. And her father makes it difficult to reach her."

"Oh, goodness," Coach Maynard said, and some of her perkiness faded. "A murder."

She picked up her clipboard and walked back toward the school. "All right," she said. "We'll be at Nolan's Hot Springs, mile fourteen, between here and Marathon. The turn's on the right, heading south. We're making a couple of stops, picking up the kids without other transportation. We're going to have a barbecue and a swim. It'll be starting up at six."

I thanked her, and turned away.

"But ma'am," she called after me.

"Yes?"

"Try not to upset her. Addy's . . . emotional."

★   ★   ★   ★   ★

I had a little over an hour to myself. The pizza parlor was empty; the movie theater was closed. I found the laundromat, made change, and pushed my clothes in two washers.

Next door to the laundromat was a place called Roy's Steak Den. I went inside, in search of something like dinner.

Since it wasn't yet five o'clock, Roy's was deserted. Big brown glass-eyes stared down from the mounted heads of steers lining the dark wood walls. They looked mournful, overseeing the consumption of their relatives.

The waitress looked bored in her cute cowgirl uniform. "Welcome to Roy's," she mumbled, sticking a menu in front of me. "Home of the tenderest meat in West Texas."

The glass-eyed steers on the wall kinda made me nervous, and I'm not much of a carnivore to begin with. I ordered a baked potato, side of broccoli, side of corn, and a salad with blue cheese.

I asked for the wine list and she recited it. "House red or house white?"

I ordered a glass of red, and she brought that and a basket of garlic toast. I nibbled and drank and looked at my watch.

When twenty minutes slipped by, I ran next door to the laundromat and threw both washer loads into one, big, industrial-sized dryer. The windswept clouds were knotting together like Frank's eyebrows when he was mad, and the clouds were darker now.

Back at the restaurant, the waitress had left me my salad, iceberg lettuce cut up in little cubes, with Ranch instead of blue cheese, but I ate it anyway.

The steers looked down on me sadly, and I started thinking about David Cannon and his daughter, and wondering if she was in any danger from him.

It was easy to imagine all sorts of bad things going on at that ranch, way out in the sticks, with nobody around to help the kid. I pushed my salad away. I wasn't that hungry anymore.

Something loud rumbled, like a freight train, or a semi, barreling down on the roof.

I jumped and knocked my wine glass to the floor. The glass broke, and the dregs left in the glass looked like little drops of clotted blood. What was it with this case and shattered glass? I wondered if things would stop breaking when I finished working Karen's case.

The waitress stepped out of the kitchen, still bored, and slapped my food down on the table. "Have a little accident, honey?"

"Yeah," I said.

She called out, "José!" and a busboy materialized from somewhere with a dustpan.

The deep rumble shook the room again.

"What's that sound?" I asked.

"Thunder," José said.

"Big storm," the waitress yawned, and disappeared into the kitchen again.

The lights in the restaurant flickered. I heard the rain now, pounding down on the roof.

"Ten minutes ago the clouds were just moving in," I said.

The busboy shrugged.

"This is flash-flood country," the waitress was back, clunking a new glass of wine on the table. "On the house," she said.

I ate fast, tossed down the wine, and then ran out into the deluge to the laundromat. The storm was hard but fast; it was just drizzling when I shoved my clean clothes back in my big plastic bag, and wrestled the bag into my trunk again.

As I drove toward the Hot Springs, the sunset flashed thick red streaks across the sky. The water sprayed up off the road, catching the light, and shivering it all around me, reflective, like fragments from a mirror.

A pickup truck went skidding past, bolder and dumber and more used to the road than I was. Next came an old guy in an RV, fishtailing so much I slowed to let him get past me, too.

Then there was a gold SUV crawling up my ass. He was bearing down fast enough that I had to speed up to avoid another trip to the body shop. Accelerating, I missed the pull out for the Springs.

I made a U-turn when the divided highway let me, and swung back to the dirt road that led to the place. At the end of the road was a cement building painted in peeling, metallic blue.

Perched on the edge of raw, open desert, the building glowed with a ghostly light as the sun went down for good, and the moon came up through the last of the clouds. A faded sign on the building's roof read "Nolan's."

There were only two cars other than mine in the parking lot, a battered, ancient Army Jeep and a Volvo station wagon with a peace sign on the rear window.

One of them belonged to the skinny teenage boy at the admission counter. He asked me for seven dollars. I showed him my PI license, and explained my reason for visiting.

"Still seven dollars to get in," he said, "and the track team won't be here 'til seven-thirty, now. Rain killed the barbecue here, they're doing the Foster's Freeze in Alpine."

I cursed under my breath, I'd seen the Foster's about a block from the laundromat.

The boy sucked on his teeth. "You can stick around though, and wait for 'em." He held out his hand again. "That'll be seven bucks."

I paid him, and he stuck a lime-green plastic wristband on me.

I walked past him and down a narrow cement hallway. At the end of it, the roof opened to the sky, and the hall opened up to

141

a space large enough to accommodate a one-foot-deep wading pool about the size of a small house and a slightly larger three-to-eight-foot swimming pool with a fountain spraying up water in the middle of it.

Steam rose off the slippery cement between the pools from the rain.

Led Zeppelin blasted from a speaker. It was like somebody shouting, "hey, I'm here too, listen to me, not just the wind and the rain and the silence in this big empty land." I felt lonely there. I wondered if Karen did too, long ago.

A skinny, ancient woman splashed out of the pool next to me in an orange, high-cut tank swimsuit. It was not a pretty sight. She pointed a bony finger up at the open sky.

"Lightning struck here in nineteen forty-seven," she told me. "That's why there ain't no roof now. Don't scare me though."

"Good," I said.

"Still, it's time to go. I'm shriveling up more'n I'm already shriveled, I been in the water so long."

I returned her wave as she swung herself out of the pool toward the parking lot, agile as a monkey.

"Get on in that water and enjoy yourself," she called out to me. "You'll love it."

After I heard her drive away, I kicked off my flip-flops and stuck my feet in. The water was warm but not hot, and the fountain spray was cool. She was right. It was irresistible.

I hiked up my skirt and waded out into the pool toward the fountain. The cool spray fell in a fine mist. I looked up at the big open roof. I could see that the clouds were still drifting around, but a slice of moon kept tearing through the haze.

The surface of the water shimmered in the moonlight, an incandescent aqua. The water felt good on my foot, but the bandage Adrianne had wrapped around it was coming loose. I thought I should probably rewrap it, so I edged back toward the steps again.

The admissions kid stalked over to me and shouted over the music.

"Hey," he said. "I gotta go somewhere for a few minutes."

"Yeah, so?"

"Team gets here before I do, tell the coach, towels are in back, will ya?"

"Okay," I said.

I hoisted myself onto the side and tugged off the bandage. A shadow fell across the water, and I looked up and saw new clouds moving in, swallowing the moon. It crossed my mind that it was going to rain all over again.

And then I was down. Face-down in the water. Something had struck me on the back of my neck, and it hurt, a dull, glancing pain that spread on up to the top of my head.

My bandage slipped out of my hand and floated like a pale snake in the water. I felt dizzy and remote, and I realized I was losing consciousness. I scrambled for the side of the pool, but my reach exceeded my grasp and the water slipped up into my mouth, then my nose. Even as I fought against it, I was all the way out.

CHAPTER TEN

Frank was kissing me, again and again. He had me in his arms, he was holding me, pressing me close against him. I felt his hands all over me, warm and rough. It was the end of the world or something, and this was it, our last chance. My last chance anyway, to feel his lips on mine. God, it felt so right.

I wanted to get his clothes off, I wanted to rub my skin against his, both of us wet and warm, with the night opening up and raining again, raining down on us. Washing away everything but the two of us, rocking there together on the ground. I reached up, and pulled at his shirt.

I opened my eyes and saw that it was Johnny on top of me. And he wasn't making love to me, he was pumping his hands against my chest, blowing in my mouth.

"Breathe," he said, "Fucking breathe!"

I started coughing, and pushed him away. Johnny backed off. His clothes were soaked.

Sheriff Winton came charging around the pool, his feet slipping a little in the puddles. There was a paramedic coming up behind him, and then they were both leaning over me, checking my pulse, asking me if I was okay.

I found it very hard to answer.

"Lynn," Johnny said, "come on now, snap out of it."

"Never had three guys so interested in me all at once," I croaked.

The sheriff looked relieved; the paramedic cracked a smile

and stuck a stethoscope against my chest. Johnny squeezed my hand. "Jesus. I was afraid I was gonna lose you, too."

I gave him a hard look and he dropped my hand, embarrassed. He shoved wet hair off his face. He was wearing the same clothes he'd had on at Karen's funeral.

It was R.E.M. pouring through the speakers now. "Turn that noise off," the sheriff shouted.

Quiet blossomed like a rose, and my own breath sounded ragged and watery as it moved in and out of my chest. The rain tapered off again while everybody just stood around and listened to me breathe.

I had a lot of questions to ask, as soon as I got this breathing business squared away again. I wanted to know what Johnny was doing there, who or what had hit me, and what became of the damn track team. I tried to ask everything at once and ended up just coughing some more.

"Take it easy," Johnny, the sheriff, and the paramedic said. They were almost perfectly in-sync.

I sat up on my elbows and felt a little bit better.

The sheriff patted my shoulder. "How you feeling, missy? You fall in, like your boyfriend says?"

"He's not my boyfriend. What're you doing here, Johnny?"

He didn't quite look me in the eye. "I got worried about you. Couldn't reach you on your cell phone. So I drove out here."

"You came all this way?"

"I did."

"According to the kid up front, this man here pulled you out of the water. Gave you mouth to mouth before we arrived."

"I remember that," I said. I looked at Johnny and this time he looked away.

"Apparently, you slipped on the wet cement and hit your head a good one. You were out cold, face-down in the pool," the sheriff said.

The paramedic ran a bunch of little tests on me, waggling his fingers and making me count them, asking if I could read the wall clock, who the president was. I must've passed all of the tests, because he started to pack up his medical bag.

"Keep some ice on that bump you took," he said. "And stay out of the water awhile." The paramedic nodded to the sheriff, and took off.

"I didn't slip. I was sitting on the steps. Something hit me, and then I was down."

"Wonder what coulda hit you," the sheriff mused. It hurt when I turned my head but I followed his gaze. There was nothing around the circumference of the pool. There was nothing floating in the pool, nothing hanging from the corners of the open roof.

"You might've hit your head on the side, going in," Johnny suggested.

"I didn't hit my head. I was sitting down, fooling with a bandage I had on my foot," which I also didn't see in the water. "Now where did that get to?"

"Filter sucked it up, probably," Sheriff Winton said.

I raised my hand to my head and gently probed a pretty good-size swollen area just above the base of my neck. It made a nice companion piece to the two smaller bumps from my automobile accident and my fall off Karen's porch.

"Would the filter have sucked up some great big heavy thing that smacked me, too?"

Sheriff Winton frowned. He paced around the side of the pool, looking behind a life preserver and inside a trash can.

"How did you know I was here at the Springs?" I asked him.

"Track team bus skidded off the road a little, the rain made the highway slick. Nobody hurt or nothin', but I was called along with the towing vehicle." He waved his hand at Johnny, still kneeling beside me. "This fella here stopped to help, he mentioned your name to me, and the coach overheard, said you might be up here already."

"Good Samaritan day," I said to Johnny.

He shrugged. "I figured you'd contact local law enforcement, so when I saw the sheriff's car, I stopped to ask about you."

I looked back at Sheriff Winton. "Was Adrianne Cannon on the bus?"

He shook his head. "No, the storm would've kept her back at the ranch. But Hank Adams, my deputy, relayed a message that she called our office late this afternoon, trying to find you. Wanted to show you something, she said."

I picked myself up off the ground. Johnny offered his hand but I managed on my own, though I was a little surprised by how wobbly my legs felt under me. "Let's go out and see her, then."

"Hank told her where you were staying. She'll come by in the morning, I bet. Right now, you need to rest."

"No, I need to get on with this investigation. Before somebody else slams me."

Johnny and the sheriff exchanged a concerned glance.

I grabbed a couple of towels and went into the changing room to dry off a little. As I yanked my fingers through my tangled hair, I heard Sheriff Winton talking to Johnny.

"Smelled like she had herself some wine to me," Winton said.

"Yeah, I guess."

"Probably just lost her footing . . ."

"She was in a car accident a couple days ago. She tripped on a loose board after that, hit her head both times, too."

"Could've been the same spot?" the sheriff asked.

"I'm not sure."

"She have any wine then?"

"I don't think so," Johnny said.

I almost laughed out loud. The tables had turned. I'd blamed

Karen's so-called visions on booze. Now, other people were blaming my near-drowning on a couple glasses of house red.

I stepped out by the pool again, and the sheriff took my arm. "How you feeling?"

"Completely sober," I said pointedly. "And ready to go on out to the Cannon ranch."

He sighed. "Listen. Adrianne's gonna be a lot more forthcoming if you talk to her outside her father's home, I know you know that. Isn't that the reason you came here tonight in the first place, to talk to her one on one?"

"True. But if she's trying to contact me—"

His voice was soothing. "You shouldn't go out there tonight. You can help me look around here a little, but then I want you to go tuck yourself into bed, missy."

No large or heavy objects were found anywhere around the pool. In the back office there was a metal stapler that was kind of heavy, but it was also covered with dust, so it wasn't very likely that it was used to knock me out, unless somebody had cleverly replaced the dust on it.

To me, evidence pointed to my attacker taking his weapon with him. To the sheriff, evidence pointed to me hitting my head on the side of the pool and forgetting I'd done it.

I was annoyed, but since the rain had washed out all the tire tracks in the lot, and there were no discernible footprints as far as the sheriff felt like shining his flashlight, I gave up.

I hated to admit it, but I was more than ready to move on from the helping-the-sheriff-look-around part of the evening to the getting-myself-some-rest part. I still felt shaky enough that I left my car at the Springs, and Johnny drove me back to the hotel. If I'd realized what a junker he was driving, I would've asked him to take my car and leave his.

To replace his truck he'd bought a Ford Pinto, circa nineteen-eighty. It was under twenty miles back to town, but it took us almost forty minutes to wheeze there. He said he'd only paid two hundred bucks for it, and it had got him all the way from Houston, but I still thought he got ripped off.

There was a nasty little carbon monoxide smell seeping in from the engine, so we kept the windows open and my hair dried fast. I touched my head from time to time, tenderly.

When I was a kid in the Midwest going to school on my first bike, my mother told me "Always wear your helmet." I'd rolled my eyes.

"Don't you go rolling your eyes at me," she said, hands on her hips. "You get hit on your head too often, pretty soon you won't be able to think straight."

It seemed that she was right. I was having a very hard time processing what had happened to me that evening, and even more importantly, how it had transpired.

"You doing okay?" Johnny asked me.

"Okay enough," I said.

"Want to drive up to the hospital in Alpine? Get an x-ray or something . . . ?"

"Paramedic said I was fine, right?" I forced a smile. "You must imagine I go around falling down, knocking myself out ten times a day."

"You really think something hit you?"

"I'm thinking some*one*."

"But who? There was nobody around when I found you. The kid working at the place followed me in."

"Did you see anyone out on the road?"

"Just the kid who worked there, coming up behind me. It was raining again pretty hard when we pulled up. Saw your car, didn't see you, went inside, and there you were." He cast a sidelong glance at me, hesitated, then chanced saying what he really thought. "There's a real sharp edge on the pool steps. It's

149

not very well lit in there. Hard to see in the dark."

"Yeah, right, and you smelled the wine I had with dinner on my breath. I'm not Karen."

He kept his eyes steady on the road, chagrined. "I didn't say you were."

"I'm telling you, Johnny, I didn't slip and fall, and there was somebody else there."

"You weren't in the water that long, or I wouldn't have been able to help you."

We were both silent for a second, thinking about what would've happened if he'd been a few minutes later.

"If someone did hit you, whoever it was had to be in and out of there real fast. There's only the one road. I would've seen."

"Unless he went out on foot. Through the desert. Where he already had a car stashed, or a hiding place ready."

"No offense, Lynn, but why would somebody go to all that trouble for you?"

"You went to a lot of trouble. Followed me up here. Pulled me out. Gave me mouth to mouth."

"Was I supposed to just sit around waiting while the kid at the Springs called for the paramedic?"

"I'm grateful. I really am. I'm just saying, maybe you're not the only one who has me on his mind."

The town was shut up tight when we pulled in. Eleven bells rang from the courthouse clock tower, and it was a little spooky.

We walked into the hotel lobby. There'd been a fire in the fireplace and the embers were still glowing. Everything was quiet, except for the ticking of a clock and our footsteps.

"I don't want to get in your way," Johnny said. "But I could help out a little, if you let me stick around."

"I'll think about it, okay?"

"This is gonna sound crazy . . ." He looked at me in the half light from the fireplace and shook his head.

"What so far hasn't sounded crazy?"

He touched my shoulder. "I feel like Karen wants me to be with you."

I narrowed my eyes. He drew his hand away fast. "I don't mean like that! I mean to watch your back. Gas up your car, whatever."

"You can drive me back to it in the morning, and we'll take it from there."

I got out my room key. He followed me down the hall. I thought he was walking me to my door, but he pulled his own key from his pocket, and I saw he had the ground-floor room right next to mine.

"Goodnight," he said. "Get some rest."

"You too."

"If you need anything . . ."

"I won't."

We went inside our rooms and shut our respective doors.

We were sharing a bathroom between us and a little patio that stretched window to window about a foot off the ground. I opened the curtains and looked out at the black shadows of what must've been the mountains. With the moon still tucked behind the clouds you couldn't really tell. It was all just layers of darkness. I closed the curtains.

If I hadn't been too tired to care, I might've felt a little uncomfortable about Johnny having the room next to mine. As it was, I just waited until I heard him lock his side of the bathroom, then I went in and brushed my teeth, drank a glass of water, and locked my side of the door in turn. Then I fell down on top of the quilt with my clothes still on.

I would've been asleep in probably thirty seconds, except there was something tapping softly on the patio window.

I felt for my purse on the night table, pulled out my thirty-eight, and ripped open the drapes.

There was Adrianne, crouched down on the patio in Day-Glo green shorts and a grey, hooded tee shirt.

I dropped the gun and opened the window.

"What're you doing?" I asked her.

She held out her hand to me. I took it, and pulled her inside.

"Sorry to barge in like this, but the deputy said you were staying here, and the lady who owns this place knows Papa. He thinks I went to the track party. So I waited 'til I saw the light come on in your room. I didn't want word to get back, you know, that I came to see you."

I nodded, pulled the chintz-covered armchair next to the bed, and waved her into it.

She looked me over, my wrinkled dress, my windblown hair.

"Did something happen to you?" she breathed.

"Little accident."

"But you're okay? I'm not disturbing you?"

"I'm fine. I drove all the way from Houston to talk to you, and I got sidetracked by your father. Now we can talk."

"I'm sorry about my father this afternoon. You touched a real deep nerve, asking him about my mother."

I nodded, waited for more.

"And when you got the sheriff involved, well . . . he's beside himself."

"I'm sure he is."

"We never usually talk about my mother at all. It's painful for both of us, her leaving."

"I get it, yeah."

"I want you to know I don't obsess about my mama or anything. I try to keep my mother leaving out of my mind, really. I usually do a pretty good job. But since I saw your client, Ms. Shaw, Mama's on my mind big-time."

"Okay, so?"

"I was thinking about my mother just this afternoon, after

you left, while I was finishing with the garden. I was trying to hurry, get the last of the weeding done before it rained. And I got careless, dug down too deep with the hoe, took out a pumpkin vine I didn't mean to. When I bent down to take a closer look at the damage, I found this."

She reached in the pocket of her shorts and pulled out a gold wedding band.

"It was my mother's," she said.

"She lost it in the garden, before she left?"

"When she left, there was no garden there. That was where the old barn was. Dad didn't even clear all the timbers off the ground until months after she was gone."

"Did you show this to your father?"

Adrianne shook her head.

"You think something happened to your mother? Is that the real reason you went to visit Karen Shaw?"

She inclined her head, slightly. "I just wanted to watch the lady, see how she was with Hayley. And then if she was any good, then maybe I'd ask her some of my questions. But she went right after me." She gave a little shudder. "I got scared," she said. "I never got the answers I wanted."

"Maybe you had reason to be scared."

Adrianne turned her big eyes on me, beseeching. "I think finding this ring means something. And I think you know what it is."

I touched her arm, reassuring. "I don't yet. But when I find out, I'll let you know."

"But there's already something you're not telling me. I just know it. Please. Please tell me."

I sighed. "Karen Shaw's dead."

"Oh." She sounded disappointed. "I'm sorry and all, but I thought it was something about my mother."

"Ms. Shaw wanted me to investigate your mother's death.

And I think her request is what got her killed."

"Oh!" This time Adrianne didn't sound disappointed, she sounded shocked. "She didn't just, like, die? You think someone killed her?"

"I do, yes. The police think something different."

"Why didn't you say earlier that she was dead?"

"I was playing a little game with your father."

"You don't think he had something to do with—"

"With both the death of Karen and your mother? Yes, I do."

"My father wouldn't have hurt my mother. Not like what you're thinking."

"I hope you're right."

"Will you let me know whatever you find out? Will you tell me before you tell him, or *anybody* else?"

"I promise I'll tell you when I find out anything. But you have to promise me something too, that if you're afraid to stay with your father—"

She made a noise of protest, but I overrode it.

"If you're afraid of *anything*, you'll get in touch with me, okay?"

She trained her big, sorrowful eyes on me, and nodded.

"I'll look out for you," I promised.

"Thank you." She gave me a hug. "I'm glad I came to see you," she said. "I wasn't sure if it was the right thing."

She left the way she came, ducking through the window and onto the patio.

I made sure the window was locked, then I took my water glass from the bathroom and filled it. I sat it right on the ledge where it would fall and spill and smash if anybody tried to get through the window again. I pushed the armchair up against the front door, and wedged the dresser against the bathroom door. I hoped I wouldn't have to get up in the middle of the night to pee.

Then I reached in my purse, and pulled out the little sprig of lavender and sage I'd taken from Karen's house. I tucked it, and my gun, under my pillow. I was just covering all the bases.

CHAPTER ELEVEN

When I woke, white light spilled through the thin lace curtain, and danced off the mirror on the dresser I'd moved. It showered a fierce light that made my aching head throb, but that wasn't what had awakened me.

Someone was turning a key and unlocking the door to my room. I yanked my gun from beneath my pillow. I stood up fast, and pushed the armchair out of the way with my foot. I pointed the gun at the door. "Come on in," I called, real cheerful.

And there was Johnny, carrying a tray with cups of coffee and a couple of blueberry muffins. He saw the gun and jumped back, the coffee sloshing on him.

"You left the key in the door," he said. "I knocked and you didn't answer, so . . ."

"Sorry." I put the gun down, chagrined. I supposed that was what happened when you'd been hit on the head a couple times. I'd been so careful to lock the bathroom door between us, set up a whole series of booby traps, and then I left the key in the lock so that anybody could walk in. Well, once they got past the chair, anyway.

Johnny set the tray on the night table and handed me a cup of coffee. Our hands touched, briefly, and I remembered what it felt like with his hands on me at the Springs, and how I imagined it was Frank touching me like that.

Johnny pulled the chair over next to the bed and took a bite out of one of the muffins.

I put my hand on the base of my skull, and traced my fingers around under my hair.

"Still hurt?"

"Yeah, it still hurts."

I blew on my coffee, tried a sip. "How're you doing this morning?"

He dropped his muffin back on the tray. "I feel like I'm going nuts, you want to know the truth. I can't think about anything but Karen. I see her everywhere I look."

He stopped himself, and turned away from me.

I was glad he looked away, it wouldn't do to have Johnny seeing Karen when he saw me, and me thinking about Frank when Johnny touched me. God only knew where that would lead, but it was no place I wanted to go.

"I can't stop thinking that it all would have been different if I hadn't let her go home alone that night. I can't stop thinking . . ." his voice trailed off, tight and anguished.

"That you're the reason she's gone?"

Johnny leaned back in the chair, deeply weary. He nodded.

"And you want me to prove you wrong."

"If she did take her own life . . . I don't want to be why."

He looked bad enough that I took the time to fill him in about David and Adrianne, and Adrianne's midnight visit. As discreetly as possible, I also gave him my theories about David's involvement in his wife's disappearance and Karen's demise.

Predictably, Johnny wanted to take David on.

"I bet I'd get the truth out of him," he said.

Sensitive or not, when his face got all dark and he balled up his fists, I imagined he might give David something to worry about. At least until David shot him with his shiny rifle.

"I think we're going to try it a different way," I told him. "Starting with getting the sheriff to dig up the Cannon's vegetable garden."

I shooed him out of the room while I got cleaned up. All the laundry I'd just washed was in the back of my car, which was still in the parking lot at the Hot Springs. And the sundress was in awful shape. Not to mention Karen's theory about bad karma clothes. I'd nearly gotten myself killed wearing that dress, once at the ranch when David shot at me, and once at Nolan's.

I went back to the shorts and the Cabo tank top.

When I hustled into the sheriff's office a little after nine, his deputy, Hank, a younger, rounder version of Winton himself, looked me over, half admiring, half critical.

"Going fishin'?" he asked me, winking at the marlin on my chest.

"Apparently I am. I've been catching the attention of more than my share of idiots lately."

Winton growled at Hank. "Don't you have phone calls to make?"

Hank allowed that he did, and I took Winton by the arm and into the hallway, and told him about Adrianne and the ring she found.

I was afraid he'd tell me it was nothing, and I should let this go, it all had to do with the bump I got on my head falling down in the pool after two glasses of wine. But instead, he got a gleam in his eyes, and his whole body snapped to attention.

"I'll get a warrant and be out at that ranch by eleven a.m.," he said.

"Things move faster in a small town," I said. "Must be less paperwork."

"Must be that this is my warrant," Sheriff Winton said, and he slapped at the impressive looking forty-five tucked in the holster strapped to his belt.

I raised my eyebrows.

"Don't worry, missy. I'll get the paperwork, too." He shook his head. "Thing is, I kept thinking all last night about Helen.

And how you might be onto something."

"Adrianne seemed pretty scared when she came to see me. It might help if I was out at the ranch when you—"

"Use the girl's welfare as an excuse if you want," Winton cut me off. "Don't matter. You're welcome to come on out and see my cousin Jimmy's backhoe at work. And I'd like to see David Cannon try and stop ya."

Johnny's car chugged along the highway. It was another hot day. Johnny and I didn't talk much. Even without talking, I had the taste of his car exhaust in my throat.

He looked tense and twitchy, and I knew he was thinking about David Cannon. I felt tense and twitchy and I was thinking about Cannon, too.

As we approached the turn off to the Springs, I saw the old woman in the orange bathing suit from the night before, driving away from Nolan's in her jeep, and waiting to cross the highway. She saw us and she gunned the motor and zipped across the median.

Despite her age, she sure did drive fast. I noticed she had a big plastic bag in the front seat next to her, just about as big as the one in the trunk of my car.

When we pulled into Nolan's parking lot, I saw my trunk was popped open and there was nothing in it but my spare tire and half a flat of Arrowhead. Of course the old woman's plastic bag was the same size as mine. It *was* mine.

I got the trunk to stay closed by slamming it a few times, and pounding it with my fists. The pounding felt so good that I kicked at the tires, too.

Johnny just watched me, patiently, like he'd seen a lot worse. Of course, he probably had.

"I'll have Winton put out an APB on Grandma, I swear I will."

Johnny offered to go after her, but I figured she was long gone, holed up in some desert canyon some place, part of a latter-day Hole in the Wall gang of elderly clothes-thieves.

I asked the kid at the admission counter if he knew who she was.

He looked like he just got called before the principal for smoking in the boy's room.

"Said she was your mother," he explained. "I never saw her before last night."

The thought crossed my mind that this woman was my attacker, and that all along what she wanted was to steal my laundry, which she had somehow intuited was in my trunk.

I'd had my heart set on retiring the Cabo tank top, so I asked for one of the bright aqua tee shirts stamped "Nolan's Healing Waters" for sale behind the counter. The kid just gave me one for free, and handed me back the seven dollars I'd paid for admission the night before, too.

I used his phone to call in the theft to Winton's deputy; the sheriff himself was already headed for the ranch. Hank seemed mightily amused.

"You standing there stark naked?" he asked hopefully.

"Hate to disappoint you, but no."

"You get a license plate number on the oldster?"

I would've beat my head against the wall but my head already hurt too much. "No. But it was Texas. The Jeep was old, from sometime in the early seventies, and dusty."

"Dusty. Don't see too many vehicles like that around here."

Still, he promised to send out a report to traffic officers in neighboring counties and the state police in Alpine, and to be on the lookout himself. "She take your undies too?" he wanted to know.

I hung up on him.

I unlocked my car and slipped behind the wheel. Johnny was

sitting in the driver's seat of the Pinto trying to get the engine to turn over again. The only thing he was succeeding at getting it to do was belch large clouds of black smoke.

"Can you give me a ride?" he called out to me.

"Back to town. Not to the ranch."

Johnny climbed in my car. "I think I'm gonna leave that car where it is and take the bus back to Houston."

"If you're lucky, that woman will come back and take a car to go with those clothes."

"Why won't you take me out to the ranch?" he asked.

"Because I said so."

"Because you said so? What am I, five years old?"

I sighed. "I don't like people tagging around after me. Not in the best of circumstances, and these are not the best."

"I just want to see what the guy looks like. Adrianne's father."

"No, you don't want to see him. You want to judge him and prosecute him and execute him in one fell swoop, whether you're right or you're wrong." Of course, I felt much the same way myself.

"You told me you think he killed his wife."

"I think it's a *possibility*. But it's all just conjecture."

"I want to see him, that's all. I just want to look in his eyes."

"Yesterday he tried to shoot *me* for looking."

"I can wait in your car and make sure nobody steals any more of your clothes."

"I don't have any more clothes to steal."

"It might not be such a bad idea, just to have me hanging around. Think about it. If I'd been waiting with you by the pool last night, maybe nobody would've hit you."

"Now you believe me, that someone hit me?"

"Maybe it was David Cannon."

The thought had crossed my mind.

"It's not like we're in Houston, with all your police buddies just a phone call away."

"All my buddies?"

"Karen said you used to be a cop. But there's nobody you can rely on way up here."

Considering what had happened last night, I thought he might have a point.

"All right, you can come along to the ranch," I said. "But you make sure you do stay in the damn car. You just sit there, you don't do anything else." I gave him a stern look. "And, you even try to run anybody over, I'll tie you to my tailpipe and drag you back to Houston."

Out at the ranch, the backhoe had already torn up half the Cannon's front yard and all of the garden. Sheriff Winton wasted no time and was leaving no stone unturned.

Adrianne was kneeling in the tumbled dirt. Her father stood beside her, his arms folded, his face hard and cold. A great cloud of dust floated just off the ground like a mist.

Johnny slumped down in the car seat. He looked like he was just gonna take a little nap or something, but I could see his eyes were glued on David Cannon.

"Remember what I told you," I warned him.

"Yeah, I can handle it."

I wasn't so sure about that, but I took my chances and got out of the car anyway. I headed for Sheriff Winton. He was standing next to the backhoe, picking something off the bottom of his boot.

His cousin was a tall, bored-looking guy about twenty years younger than the sheriff, but still too old for the little goatee he was sporting. He gave me a wave.

"Find anything?" I asked the sheriff.

"Sure. Half a rake. A horseshoe." He shook his head.

"She coulda just thrown the damn ring away," David said.

"Helen did that kind of thing."

Adrianne brushed tears from her eyes.

"He's wrong, she never took that ring off," Winton told me, quietly. "But this looks like a dead end." He made no effort to hide his disappointment.

I tried to sound soothing. "We've just got to keep looking."

Adrianne spoke up in a quavering voice. "If you don't find anything more . . . doesn't it mean that Mama's all right?"

Nobody answered her.

"Mind if I look around back of the house?" I asked.

I expected David Cannon to object, if not the sheriff, but neither one of them said a word. Adrianne cleared her throat as if she was about to ask me something, but then the backhoe started up again in another spot, and all three of them turned and just stared, riveted, at the new hole in the ground.

I threw a glance back at my car; Johnny was still sweating in the passenger seat.

I hurried behind the house with my lock pick ready to go, but the kitchen door was already propped open with a brick and the screen unlatched.

I slipped inside. The kitchen looked a little grimy, crumbs on the table, a film of grease on the stove. It wasn't a place people lingered over a good meal.

Adjoining the kitchen there was a large dining room, with a fireplace and a cherry wood table designed for Thanksgiving dinners. The living room was at the front of the house, with a pretty oriental rug on the floor and a cozy plaid sofa and matching chairs that didn't go with the rug at all. There was an arrangement of silk flowers on the coffee table. Both of these rooms looked like they hadn't been touched in at least three years, say since Helen disappeared.

There was a crucifix hanging in the hall that led to two bedrooms and a bathroom off to the side of the house.

The bathroom came up first. Neat, but like the kitchen, a little grubby, like the people who lived here were too busy surviving to pay much attention to the surroundings they were surviving in.

I passed Adrianne's room, white and pink and little girl; she'd kept her childhood furniture, horseback riding trophies, third-grade achievement awards, everything. Maybe she thought if she hung onto all those objects, she could hang onto her mother, too. My guess was that until she saw Karen, she'd apparently refused to look into the possibility that her mother might be gone for good.

Across the hall from Adrianne's room was the master bedroom, now David's solo digs. He had a cork board on the wall with slogans like "One Day at a Time" and "I'm not an Angel but I have one on My Shoulder," pinned to it. There was also "An Alcoholic's Prayer," and little plaques indicating six months, one year, two years, three years' worth of sobriety.

There were also pictures of Adrianne from babyhood up, some framed. Okay, so he loved his daughter, and tacked up nice little sayings. That didn't make him a good man.

I rummaged quickly through his drawers, his closet. I didn't find the belt Karen described, or his missing knife, either.

I could hear the backhoe grind to a stop outside, and I hurried back down the hall and out through the kitchen again.

Outside, Sheriff Winton eyed me suspiciously. "Well?" he said.

I ignored his question. "Anything new?" I asked.

He shook his head. "This little digging expedition isn't raising anything but Cannon's blood pressure."

David and Adrianne were having a fierce whispered exchange. Adrianne seemed to be acquiescing to David, hunching her shoulders, and nodding miserably.

"Satisfied? Can we stop this nonsense?" David called out. He looked only at the sheriff, didn't even acknowledge my existence.

"Yeah. We can stop it." Winton gestured to his cousin, and the guy started backing off the grass.

"Do you forgive me?" Adrianne asked her father, her voice tremulous.

"Don't you worry. Everything's fine. You're still my little girl." He spun on his heel and slammed into the house.

The sheriff and I both waited a minute, watchful, in case David came out with his gun.

Adrianne slipped up next to me. "I guess finding Mama's ring meant nothing," she said.

"I won't give up just yet," I told her.

"My father swore he never hurt my mother. He swore to me there was nothing in the ground, nothing but carrots and corn. I shoulda listened."

"No real harm done, is there?" I asked her, wondering if there was.

"We'll have to replant," she mused. Then she looked at me, like a weight had been lifted off her shoulders. "I guess I just have to accept my mother's gone, by her choice, and move on with my life. Forget all this silly psychic nonsense. I mean that woman Karen was messed up, right?"

"Sure," I told her.

"She killed herself, that's what the sheriff told my Papa. I think after all these years I really believe it's over and done with, and we have to just move on with our lives. Doesn't that sound right?"

"More or less," I said.

"So I guess you'll be leaving town now?"

"Soon," I said, "real soon."

Last night she'd wanted to see me so bad she snuck in through my bedroom window; now she seemed anxious to get rid of me. She didn't hug me goodbye this time, either. She just went back inside the house, and closed the door firmly behind her.

The sheriff and I walked toward our cars.

"Wild goose chase," he said. "Not saying it's your fault. I was as eager as you to find something on that man . . ."

"You were, huh?"

"I won't pretend I like the fella. You got me on that one."

"Just because Helen Cannon's not buried here, doesn't mean she isn't buried somewhere."

"Along with her car?"

"Could've junked the car anywhere. It's a big desert."

"Won't argue with you there—" he stopped short, seeing Johnny in my front seat.

"I thought he wasn't your boyfriend, missy."

"He was my late client's boyfriend. And this missy stuff is getting kinda old."

"I'm getting kinda old too," the sheriff said, "too old for playing games. You find anything when you snuck into Cannon's house?"

I wasn't altogether surprised that he knew what I'd done. I shook my head.

"You looking for anything in particular?"

"Not really."

I wanted to tell him about the belt Karen described to me, but then we'd have to get into where the description came from, and I was afraid if I told him he wouldn't take anything I suggested to him seriously ever again.

"You looking for the old woman who stole your clothes?" He tossed me what passed for a smile. "Deputy Hank told me. You just keep getting into one scrape after another around here, don't you mis—" he caught himself, and amended, "Miss Bryant."

"Sure looks that way," I agreed.

We climbed in our respective vehicles and drove away.

CHAPTER TWELVE

"We're back to nothing, I guess," Johnny said. He sounded resigned.

"I'm back to nothing. You just wanted to come along for the ride," I reminded him.

"So can the passenger ask what's next?"

"Thought maybe we'd take a little drive, check out the scenery." And check out a place where somebody might've disposed of Mrs. Cannon and her car.

I circled the ranch, on a decent but narrow road that made a steep climb up and up some more into the White Mountains.

"What'd you think of David Cannon, anyway?" I asked Johnny.

"Good-looking. Tough. Mean eyes, except when he was looking at his daughter." Johnny paused, thoughtful. "Even if Cannon did off his wife, we still don't know that it had anything to do with Karen, do we?"

"Maybe *you* don't. Didn't you see his boots? Just like Karen was describing. I looked in his closet for that belt, but I couldn't find it. Doesn't mean it's not there, I only had a few minutes."

"You think Karen knew him?"

"Adrianne knew all about Karen, and she wasn't even born when Karen left town. I'm sure Karen was always the type of person who attracted attention, even when she was just a kid herself."

"I didn't ask if people knew Karen. I asked if you think she knew him."

"Yeah, I do," I said.

Johnny fell silent. I assumed the same thought was occurring to him as had already occurred to me, that it was entirely possible David Cannon knew Karen intimately.

"You thought they'd find a body today where Adrianne found that ring?" Johnny asked me.

"It would've been convenient. But awful easy." I swung the car around a curve so steep the drop on either side took my breath away. "I'm just feeling my way here. An investigation like this is hardly an exact science."

Johnny gave a short laugh. "That's what Karen used to say about her gift. It wasn't an exact science, quote unquote."

"There's very little that is," I said.

We were directly behind the Cannon ranch now. I saw the house, like something made out of Legos, crouched at the base of the hills far below.

"Here's my current inexact theory. The ring's all we found because it slipped off Helen Cannon's finger when her husband moved the body into the car . . . that's an educated guess, mind you. I worked in homicide almost five years."

The road veered back toward the ranch and went down, in a succession of hairpin curves. Even though I had it under thirty, Johnny looked pale.

"I wish you'd slow down," he said, clutching the dash.

"Oh, like I'm the one who drove right through a liquor store."

He tried to laugh but he was chewing his lip, nervous.

"Don't like heights?" I asked him.

"Karen was involved with a God-awful accident on a road not that much different than this. Six kids, trapped in the back of a van and the thing went up. She never drove again after that. Sold her car."

I slowed to a crawl. "She hit the van?"

"No, nothing like that. We were up near Big Thicket. Hiked up to a waterfall, real pretty spot. Stopped at this roadhouse on the way back, had a couple burgers, couple beers. She was driving. We got halfway down the mountain, and she slammed on the brakes so hard my head hit the windshield. She started screaming. She jumped out of the car, but shit, there was nothing there. She told me there were kids and their van was on fire. Said a tanker trunk hit them.

"When I got her calmed down, she said if it hadn't happened yet, it was gonna happen, soon, unless we did something to stop it. I tried to get her back in the car but she wouldn't leave the spot. She called the police, and a cop came, and she told him how she saw a terrible accident. 'Where?' he asked. And she gave him the whole story, begged 'em to put on a guy to do traffic control. Just for a day or two, anyway. The place was out in the middle of nowhere, why the hell would they do that? Instead they gave her a sobriety test.

"Humiliated the hell out of her. I drove home. She was real quiet. She said there was more she should've done. I said there wasn't anything. But she kept seeing the kids' faces . . ."

"Sounds familiar."

"It was worse this time, with the woman."

"So did the accident she 'saw' ever really happen?"

"Oh, yeah, it did. About a week later, she insisted we drive up there again. I thought it was self-destructive, and I wouldn't go. So she waited 'til I was working and went herself. When she got there, it had just occurred. An old car crammed with teenagers, a joy ride. The car sailed through that intersection from the south without stopping. A tanker truck coming from the east ran the stop, too. Those two collided. And six kids died in the van coming from the north, when the tanker spun out and hit it . . ."

I remembered the first page of the police accident report I'd seen on Karen. "Witness hysterical at the scene." I could only imagine what the missing pages two and three said about her. But the thing was, no matter what was said, she'd been right about the accident.

How she knew, was anybody's guess. You could write it off as her own morbidity focused on a dangerous intersection, and the law of probability that eventually, sometime, some day, someone was going to die there.

Of course, according to Johnny, she'd seen exactly who was going to die there, had described the exact circumstances. Maybe some stuff just couldn't be explained, whether it was what Karen saw, sometimes, and why and how she saw it; or for that matter, me and Frank still doing the same old dance after all these years. Damn, I wished he was with me now, working on this case. We had great moves when we were waltzing through other people's lives. And there were some times, there really were, when you just needed a partner.

I threw a glance at Johnny.

"I'm gonna need your help with something," I told him.

"That's what I'm here for."

More and more I got the feeling that was what made Johnny tick, helping out. Maybe the thing with him and Karen was that sometimes she didn't want his help, she didn't want anybody's, and he didn't understand that. Maybe his wanting to help all the time was what made her think she was just his latest do-good project, right there at the end.

My ears were popping as we made another twisting descent.

After the last curve, the road soared straight down, similar to the final incline on a roller coaster. It was there that I got a glimpse of the lake I'd spotted from a distance yesterday, now straight over the side. It was startlingly blue, a deeper shade than the sky, standing out like an enormous sapphire, a jewel dropped down in the rust-colored landscape.

If you weren't careful around that last curve, you'd sail straight off the hillside and splash right down into the middle of the lake. Such an accident could also happen if you put, say, a brick on an accelerator, and pointed a car in the right direction.

From the Cannon ranch, it had taken us a half hour on the switchback road to reach this trajectory. But there was the thin thread of a dirt trail cutting straight through from the back of the lake to a cattle gate that had to be ranch property. It would be a hell of a shortcut if you were walking home after you left a car and a body deep-sixed in the water.

I swung out toward the lake and drew Johnny the picture unfolding in my own mind.

He eyed me suspiciously. "How did you even know there was a lake over here?"

"I saw it from the highway, and then I looked at a map," I said.

He seemed relieved. I suppose he was used to Karen just intuiting things like that.

Dark-green pines ringed it on one side, but on the other, the side closest to the paved road, the trees were dead and withered. A weathered sign warned, "CO_2 Contamination. No fishing. No swimming. Ordinance Number 36, June 1994."

When we got out of the car, I saw thick, almost phosphorescent green algae, and a salt crust rimmed the edges of the lake. There was no way to tell if the lake was still badly toxic, but there was no noticeable smell at least.

I was not in the mood for a swim there, but then probably nobody else had been in the mood either for the last ten years. So if Helen Cannon and her car had left the Cannon ranch and made their way to the bottom of it, who would've noticed?

I dropped down on a rock and pulled off my sandals. The cut on my heel looked even better today, but it was still a little tender when I walked on it. The rocks along the lake dug into the new skin and stung.

I slipped off my shorts, glad that the Nolan's Healing Waters tee shirt was on the long and baggy side. I left it on; I didn't really want to go swimming with Johnny in just my bra and panties. I mentally resigned myself to the Cabo San Lucas tank top lying in the backseat.

Johnny was looking at me, scuffing his sneaker in the rocks.

"Hurry up, get undressed. You're coming in too," I told him.

"That water's not very pretty up close. And the sign says no swimming."

"The sign looks old. It won't kill us, but I don't want to stay under too long. Since you're here, two pairs of eyes are better than one."

I was getting annoyed at him standing there with all his clothes still on. "I told you I needed your help," I snapped.

That did it. Johnny tugged off his jacket and tee shirt. His sketch pad fell out of his jacket, open on the ground. He reached for it, but the wind came up and tore out a page, sending it drifting toward the water. I snagged it. It was a picture of Karen, luminous, dancing in the Empire Lounge.

"I thought you gave this to her," I said.

He looked surprised for a moment, but not for long. "You get around," he said. "That was another one, I got her eyes better. She took it home with her."

He tucked this sketch away in the back of the pad, and set his jacket and shirt carefully on top of it. I went ahead and splashed in the water while he was taking off his belt.

I got out past the algae rim and plunged on in. The water felt heavy, slippery. I kept my head out of it until I reached the middle of the lake, then I held my breath and made a dive.

I saw ripples above me as Johnny swam over top of me. He dove down, with a clean, sharp stroke, and we both circled around in different directions.

I surfaced considerably before he did, gasping for air.

"There's nothing down there," he said as he joined me dog-paddling on the slimy surface.

"You go left. I'll go right."

We swam in opposite directions, but dove down again at almost the same moment. It was murkier where I was this time. There were a lot of weeds, thick and silty. My eyes were starting to burn.

But there was something in the weeds. Something shadowy and big and I knew exactly what it was.

I surfaced again. My face was itchy in the blast of air. When Johnny came up at his end of the lake, I called out to him. "Come over here. I'm pretty sure I found the car."

He swam toward me and I went down again.

I pushed the weeds aside, trying to ignore how they felt, like rotting flesh rubbing up against me. There was Helen Cannon's green Dodge. Johnny splashed right next to me, and together we tried to open the front door, but we couldn't do it.

I pointed at a large rock lying on the lake bed. I couldn't lift it on my own. Together we dragged it over and used it as a battering ram, smashing it against the driver's window, over and over again.

There was no more air in my lungs, and pretty soon I had to get to the surface. I gave it one last thrust and the glass shattered. We dropped the rock. A hand floated through the broken window, just bones.

Along with the need to breathe I felt a sudden need to get sick.

Johnny rocketed for the surface, and I spun around to follow him, but I was stuck on something. I tugged at my shirt, but it was caught fast.

The bony hand drifted up and touched my cheek. There were

some gashes in the bone, they looked like the cuts a knife would make, if one could thrust all the way through the skin and sinew straight to the bone.

It was stupid but involuntary. I gagged, sucking in water. I choked and spluttered and pulled harder at my shirt. The material just wouldn't tear. I yanked it up over my head, pulled it off one arm, gave a huge tug, and what had to be Helen Cannon's skull with pieces of hair still sticking to it flew out of the broken window and banged against my chest.

Even after all this time, it was pretty obvious that the skull had been bashed in. Around her neck, there was a cross. It floated up next to my eyes and I saw it was engraved "Love, Addy."

This time the bile rose up in my throat. I felt my lungs burning. I couldn't breathe.

Waves of motion cascaded around me and pushed Helen's head and arm back inside the car. There was Johnny beside me again, and he helped me tear my shirt away and thrust me up, up, up to the surface.

The water seared my throat and lungs; I couldn't talk.

He put his arm around me and paddled us to shore. I just lay there on the gravel beach, gasping. I didn't care if he saw me in my underwear or not anymore.

"I thought you were right behind me," he said.

"Couldn't move . . ." I managed.

"Your shirt was caught. You ran out of air."

"No kidding, Mr. Watson."

I limped to the rock, and pulled on my shorts. I rubbed at my legs, wiping off handfuls of the slimy algae. I left the Nolan's shirt lying torn on the beach. Talk about clothing with bad karma.

I walked back to the car and threw on the tank top and settled in the passenger seat. I tossed Johnny the keys.

The taste of the lake and my own near sickness made my stomach heave and rock all the way back to town.

Johnny drove right up to the jail and courthouse, and I can't say that Sheriff Winton looked particularly glad to see us.

There was algae drying in Johnny's hair, so I suppose there was plenty in mine too. I raked through my hair with my fingers, and wiped my fingers on my shorts.

"Got anything to drink?" I asked. "I'm real thirsty."

"Hasn't anybody ever told you not to go messing around out in the desert without something to rehydrate yourself?"

"I guess I forgot."

"Soda machine's in the hall," he said shortly. Johnny left and came back with a couple of root beers just as I was telling the sheriff how we found a car in the bottom of the lake.

"What lake?" the sheriff asked, tapping a pencil.

"Ascher, it's called. Not that far from the Cannon ranch as the vulture flies," I said.

"What kind of car?"

"A mid-eighties, early nineties Dodge, looks like. Green-colored, but it could be what years in that water does to a paint job, I'm not sure. Female body inside, I'm guessing Helen Cannon. I'm also guessing you might want to take a look."

Sheriff Winton called the state police, who called in a diver and an underwater towing rig.

I drained my root beer, then Johnny and I went back to the hotel and took polite turns in the bathroom. I spent a long time brushing my teeth. I was wrapped in a towel when Johnny knocked. He offered me one of his tee shirts, clean, too big, splattered with paint. I thanked him and took it.

Then we went on back to the lake, where a large tow truck was grinding out a spool of steel cable. The diver had one end of it hooked onto the front bumper of the car, and slowly, slowly, the thing was gliding across the lake, like the biggest fish ever hooked.

"I'll be bringing Mr. Cannon in," Sheriff Winton walked up and told me. "Gonna hold him for questioning in the death of his wife, Helen. If I can, I'll charge him with her murder."

"Get a hold of his credit cards. See if any charges were made last week in the greater Houston area while you're at it."

His eyes narrowed. "You telling me how to do my job, missy?"

I sighed. "No. But I am telling you not to call me missy anymore."

CHAPTER THIRTEEN

While the sheriff prepared his second warrant of the day, this one for the arrest of David Cannon, I occupied myself in another part of the courthouse and sent Johnny out to the little café for some food.

A sweet, soft-voiced middle-aged lady named Betty was glad to let me look through the town records. It was quiet and warm and dusty huddled by her desk, tucked between filing cabinets, cozy almost. My second near-drowning had made me long for cozy. I folded my feet up under me and just waited for Betty to find what I asked her for.

"Oh sure honey. Sheriff's told me all about you, my files are your files, and I heard what happened to your clothes. Just want to tell you, there's a real nice selection at the Big Lots store in Alpine."

First, we went through the birth records. Karen Shaw was born to one Marlene Shaw in the West Texas Big Bend Memorial Hospital, which no longer existed. No father was listed on the birth certificate. The mother and child's residence was listed as 13 St. Nancy Terrace, where Marlene's mother, Mrs. Carol Ann Shaw, also resided.

Death certificates cross-referenced with the state of Nevada showed that Marlene had passed away in a hotel room in Reno less than a year after giving birth. Cause of death was "unknown." She was twenty-two.

Marlene's mother, Carol Ann, lived another fourteen years,

ostensibly raising Karen at 13 St. Nancy. Carol Ann died of congestive heart failure at her home at the age of fifty-eight. Apparently Karen had no living next of kin. Carol Ann was also on welfare, yet when Karen left town at approximately fifteen years of age, she'd had enough money to buy the house in Channelview, and pay cash for it.

I thanked Betty for her time and effort, and forced myself to vacate her comfortable corner. Then, for lack of anything better to do while Sheriff Winton arrested David Cannon, I decided I should go take a look at what had once been Karen's home.

But first, I wanted to call Frank.

Now that I'd nearly died a couple of times, it occurred to me to feel reasonably bad about not giving Frank a nice last memory of me. Almost running over his feet probably did not constitute a nice last memory.

I had no more cell service in Marathon than I'd had heading into town. Although Betty would've certainly let me use her phone, I wanted a little privacy. In the café, I'd have Johnny hanging around, so that left the bar with the gold-painted wooden Indian.

The bar was altogether a friendlier, cleaner place than the Empire, though it too had a contingent of grizzled afternoon drinkers clustered around the room. The bartender was a pleasant-looking woman in a pair of overalls, with her hair pulled back in a ponytail.

I asked for five dollars in quarters. I fed the change into the phone and prepared myself to get Frank's voice mail, but instead I got him on the first ring. He didn't sound very happy to hear from me.

"Been trying to reach you for two days. Forty-eight fucking hours."

"My cell phone isn't doing so well this far above sea level."

"Where the hell are you? And why?"

I gave him the short version.

"You need to let this suicide case go," he said.

I sighed. "I was getting to the reason I can't. It looks more and more like a murder, Frank. A local rancher named David Cannon has been arrested for killing his wife ten years ago. I found the body myself. His wife's murder may have been witnessed by my client; I'm looking at the link between the two, and I will bet you he was in or around Houston when my client was killed."

"Even if he was, what will that prove?"

I sighed. I'd thought of that myself. "He's missing a knife. A knife that sounds very similar to the one found at the scene of Karen Shaw's death."

Frank leapt right in, a lot more interested now. "They print him yet? We can match prints."

A computerized voice overrode him. "Sixty seconds remaining."

"The knife was clean. But I'd put money on his prints being elsewhere in her house. I'll make sure the sheriff up here calls Detective Hale, okay?"

"Look, Lynn," Frank began, but I cut him off.

"No, you wait. Let me tell you why I called. I'm sorry I almost took off your foot. I'm sorry you *make* me want to take off your foot sometimes."

He sighed. "You'd think we'd just forget about each other, except for the occasional Christmas card."

Neither one of us said anything for a moment, and then the disembodied computer voice of a telephone operator blurted "You have thirty seconds remaining."

"I'm gonna have to go," I said. "Out of change."

I brushed the stack of coins that was still left into my palm, in case Frank could somehow know I was lying.

"You can call me back collect," he said, undeterred. "We

should talk."

"No, I've got stuff to do."

"So you keep saying, whenever the going gets just a little bit rough."

The phone went dead, and I did not call Frank back collect.

Johnny met me outside the courthouse, and I explained my plan to visit Karen's grandmother's house. He was amenable. He offered me a large paper bag with a couple of cheese sandwiches and two big bottles of water inside.

I gulped some of the water.

"It might make you feel better to eat something," Johnny suggested.

I wasn't queasy anymore, so I ate a sandwich even though I didn't want it. Talking to Frank made me feel worse, not better somehow.

Outside it felt hotter, even though it was late enough in the day that the shadows were slipping off the mountains and sliding across the highway. I slipped behind the wheel of my car, and drove us north out of town to the unincorporated area that was St. Nancy Terrace.

The cottage where Karen's grandmother used to live was small, the type of housing people call a shotgun shack. It had a little screened-in porch facing the hills.

Smoke was coming out of a tin chimney stuck in the roof, so I knew somebody was home, although there was no car in the yard or parked along the road.

There were other houses, dotting the hills further down the lane. Just about a yard away, there was the cracked foundation of another house, and part of an old-fashioned potbellied stove.

For the hell of it, I knocked on the door to Carol Ann's old place, in case whoever was living there now was old enough to remember Karen or her grandmother.

The door opened with a smell of bacon and a cheery hello

from a woman who was definitely old enough, somewhere just shy of eighty. She looked familiar. And so did her clothes. She was, in fact, the elderly woman last observed leaving Nolan's Hot Springs. And she was, in fact, now wearing my favorite black Free People tee shirt.

"Oh-oh," she said, and tried to close the door on me.

I had learned the hard way at Cannon ranch not to stick my injured foot into door frames, so instead I just pushed my way in with my elbows, flashing my PI. license and grinning like a madwoman.

"You stole my clothes."

"Shit, you're a cop!" she wailed.

"I'm not police. I'm private. Which means I play by different rules. As in, give me my clothes back or I'll shoot you."

She started to pull the shirt right off over her head.

"That one you can keep," I said.

Johnny stepped up behind me. "What's going on?" he asked.

"This woman's trying to hurt me," the woman wailed. "Accusing me of things I've never done."

"We're together," he said quietly.

I got an odd feeling running through my body from my fingers to my toes. It was not dissimilar to getting an electric shock, only it was more pleasant. We were together? It was the kind of thing Frank used to say, but hadn't said in a real long time. I might as well admit it. I still missed Frank. I wondered if he meant it, when he said he missed me.

The woman hung her head. "Sorry," she whispered. "I still have most of your clothes. A few items I took over to the second-hand store."

She opened the door wide, to both of us. "Come on in."

It was basically two rooms. There was a living area, which included a kitchenette where the bacon was sizzling, and another room, the door open, in the back. In that room there was a twin bed and a whole stack of cardboard boxes spilling out toys, clothes, books, glassware.

"You steal all that?" I asked severely.

Johnny went and turned off the stove.

She shook her head. "There's garage sales. There's people just leave perfectly good stuff in trash cans."

I followed her into the bedroom.

"Where'd you learn to break into cars like that?"

"Oh, here'n there," she said vaguely.

She took two pairs of my jeans and five or six of my shirts out of one box, and a long, slinky royal-blue jersey dress out of another and thrust the clothes at me.

"Here you go honey," she said, like she was doing me a great favor.

"That dress isn't mine," I said.

"Well, like I said, I sold a few of your clothes already. That one's designer. Might make up for it. And you'd look good in it, too."

Johnny slipped in the bedroom behind me.

"Wouldn't she look good in it?" she asked him.

He smiled. "I'm sure."

"What the hell should I do with you?" I asked the woman.

"I'd let her alone," Johnny said.

I agreed with him, she had her age on her side.

"I already reported the theft to the county sheriff. I'd stay out of trouble if I were you," I warned her.

She sighed. "I don't even live here. A friend of mine's staying down by Matamoros, this is her house. I'm just house sitting, keeping an eye on the place. How'd you find me?"

"I wasn't looking for you," I said. "Miss . . ."

"Louise," she said, so quickly I knew she was lying. "Who were you looking for then?"

"Someone we know . . . used to live here a long time ago,"

Johnny added.

"Oh my, Carol Ann Shaw?"

Johnny and I exchanged a glance. Sometimes it's a lucky thing, getting your laundry stolen.

"That would be the lady," I said.

"I used to live up in Alpine, 'bout seventy years and several ex-husbands ago," Louise said.

"Did you know Carol Ann Shaw?"

"She drove the school bus for a while. And I rode it. She never waited, not even thirty seconds if you were late out the door. Conservative woman. Married young and once, once only, husband died, always poor, whole family, struggle and straggle, daughter left to go work the casinos way up in Reno, Nevada, but I hear the work she was doing was all in the horizontal position, you get my drift. Gotta marry 'em, you ask me, only way to get the good life. I had a good life once, I did, I married a banker, and then after that a doctor."

"Good for you," I said.

"You could get married yourself, you put on that blue dress. Get this young man here to pop the question. What do you want with Carol Ann Shaw anyway? She's long dead."

"I know she's dead."

"Daughter died, too. Heard she had a baby, Carol Ann raised the girl, she left town too, real young, I think her name was Carrie or something."

"Karen," Johnny said, and he took a step closer, urgency flashing across his face, as if anyone who knew anything about Karen brought her back to him a little.

"I'd moved away long ago of course. But my friend, Ruthie, she's the one got this house, you know she told me an earful about why the granddaughter left town in such a hurry."

She smiled at me, and nodded knowingly.

"Can you tell us what your friend Ruthie said about Carol

Ann and her granddaughter?"

Louise smiled again. "If I tell you, will you promise not to bring the sheriff out here, nosing around?"

"If you promise to stop breaking into people's cars."

She pursed her lips together. "I never actually broke into a car before, anyway. I didn't plan on doin' it this time. Just wanted to take another dip at the Springs before I had to give my uh . . . friend back his Jeep. And on my way, I found a perfectly good tire iron lying by the side of the road this morning. So of course I stopped and picked it up, and then there was your car, looked like it was abandoned there, and one thing led to another. Seemed like fate. Kid that works at the Springs was looking right at me when I went at your trunk, but I told him you'd locked your keys in and I was just helping you out."

"You said you were my mother."

"He isn't too bright, that boy. It's the hormones mess you up at that age."

"So you just *found* a tire iron." I put my fingers back against my head and pressed on the swollen spot. A tire iron could've done it.

"I didn't steal it, if that's what you're after. Last night I saw a fella in a shiny gold SUV had a flat out on the highway, right by the turn to the Springs there. Must've left the thing behind."

"Gold SUV," I said. I didn't know anybody who drove such a vehicle, but I clearly remembered one tailgating me in the rain just before I went out to Nolan's. Still, it was hard to believe road rage was the reason somebody tried to drown me.

"You get a look at the guy in the SUV?"

She shook her head, vigorously.

"Still have the tire iron?"

"Nope. Took it into the second-hand store along with a couple of your shirts. Got five bucks for it. Your shirts only brought three."

"You were going to tell us about the Shaws," Johnny prompted Louise.

"All right," Louise said. "We have a deal?" she asked me.

I nodded vaguely, but my mind was on that tire iron.

"My friend Ruthie used to live right next door. Her old house was a lot nicer than this little place, but it burned down, kerosene fire from a space heater. Rental company moved her in here, and paid her for some damages, so it worked out I guess. Like most things do. Anyway, she was living right next door, and she heard the Shaws having an argument."

She shook her head. "Ruthie always was a bit of a gossip, she kept her ears peeled and her eyes opened, she still does. Told me many a fine and lurid tale. This one wasn't all that interesting, but I remembered it because of my feelings about Carol Ann and how she more or less up and died."

Louise stopped talking and folded her arms across her chest.

"Go on," I said, a little impatient.

"No sheriff?" she asked me.

"No," I promised.

"All right then. According to Ruthie, it was a Tuesday afternoon, but the Shaws were in their Sunday best.

"Carol Ann was waving this manila envelope around in her hands like it was solid gold or something. She and Karen had walked up from the bus stop on the highway. It was a real hot day. Carol Ann, her heart wasn't in the very best shape, and she was too beat to get up the stairs into the house or something. She was sitting down on the bottom step with her granddaughter, taking a rest. Ruthie could hear every word passed between 'em. The girl was upset with her granny, told her it was bad what they did."

"Bad what they did?" Johnny said.

I gave him a warning look; you don't interrupt when somebody's spilling their story to you. You ask questions later.

"Yeah, I guess they'd done something naughty, 'cause the granddaughter was crying and carrying on so much that Ruthie almost came out to ask what in the world was going on.

"Then Carol Ann started choking, gasping for breath, like. The girl screamed, and Ruthie ran over to 'em real fast. Carol Ann was on the ground in her granddaughter's arms, holding her chest. Ruthie knew right away she'd had a heart attack.

"Now there were no phones out here or anything, so all Ruthie could do was tell her to lie quiet, and she'd go down to McTalley's place, he had a truck, he was just a half mile down the road.

"She said she loosened Carol Ann's clothes, tried to get her in the shade. Carol Ann paid her no mind at all, she was just looking right at her granddaughter. She said 'Keep this. You keep it.' She shoved that envelope right in Karen's face.

"Those were Carol Ann Shaw's last damn words. After the funeral, not three weeks later, the granddaughter, Karen, she was gone. It was a surprise, 'cause she couldn't have been more than fourteen or fifteen. Ruthie never did find out what was in that envelope. And oh yeah, this place sat empty 'til Ruthie took it over, and the girl never came back once."

"That you know of," I said.

"That I know of," Louise agreed. "Now about that envelope, any idea what was inside?"

She looked from me to Johnny, hopeful one or both of us would fill her in, but neither one of us said more than thank you until we were outside again.

"Money," I said. "That's what was in that envelope. Karen paid for her house in cash."

"I know she did. Twenty-five thousand. Had to lie about her age to buy it."

I threw my clothes in the backseat of my car, because I didn't want to hassle with getting the trunk to open and close again.

Johnny was slumped in the passenger seat, brooding about something. "She was pregnant," Johnny said. "She couldn't keep the baby. She wanted to, but she was only fifteen."

I frowned. "Why didn't you tell me?"

"I couldn't see how her having a baby thirty some years ago had anything to do with her death."

"Maybe you were wrong, huh?"

"Maybe."

"Why don't you fill me in now, okay?"

"All right. Karen left town right away, just like the lady told us. She didn't want to tell me where she was from, just that it was in the middle of nowhere. She never said why, but I definitely got the message something she didn't want to talk about happened to her.

"Anyway, she just got on a bus and left. She was thinking Florida but the bus went to Houston, and she took it as a sign and she stayed. Picked Channelview because it reminded her, kinda, of the ocean she could've been living near in Florida. First thing, she went to one of those women's clinics. She told them everything that was going on, hoping they would help her, 'cause she was having a rough patch."

"What do you mean? She was sick from the pregnancy?"

"She wasn't used to the powers she had then. She thought she was going crazy. She'd touch somebody's hand and see their whole life story. She'd walk down the street, she'd get bits and pieces flying out at her from inside people's heads."

"Oh boy," I said.

"She had to learn to direct it, she told me. It took her years to get it right and then still, like you know, there were times when she couldn't control what was happening. Back then, she was just a kid. Being pregnant, that made it harder. She told the doctor about hearing voices and seeing things that weren't there.

The doctor told a social worker, pretty soon they wanted to have her committed.

"They told her she wasn't fit to raise the baby, and she believed that part of it anyway. She was afraid she might hurt the kid somehow. She just didn't know what was going on. It was a little girl, and she . . . she gave her away."

"Karen ever try to find her daughter?" I asked him.

"She did. Long before I knew her, of course. She said the girl was happy, and had a mother who loved her very much. She wasn't going to mess with that. She said she'd know when the time was right to find the girl."

"But she never did."

Johnny was quiet. "No. And she never did tell me who the father was, either."

I turned the key in the ignition and started the car. The air conditioner blasted on, cold and delicious. I barreled down St. Nancy Terrace and back to the highway.

Johnny twitched in his seat and cleared his throat a couple of times. "You don't think Adrianne is Karen's daughter?" Johnny began.

"Do the math. She's way too young. Karen's daughter would be close to my age, early thirties now."

Still, I thought he was on to something. I knew Adrianne wasn't Karen's daughter, but I would not be in the least bit surprised to learn that David was the father of the very under-age Karen's child, and to save his marriage to Helen he'd offered grandma a payoff.

That fit. And maybe they'd stayed in touch, in spite of everything, and Karen had come back to visit, and she was around when David murdered his wife; but for whatever reason what she'd witnessed wasn't clear until Adrianne came to her and put it into focus.

I came up on a big rig, moving slow. I waited until the solid yellow line dividing the highway broke up, and gave me a passing lane, and then I swung around it.

But as I pulled out, I saw a flash of something bright behind me, and there was a low whoosh of rushing air. It was as if somebody had fired a very big bullet right at me. Coming up in the rear view, a gold SUV was on my tail, zipping around the truck into my lane, bearing down on us like a bull charging a red flag. Just a moment before, no one was behind me. The guy had to have been waiting, watching for me off some side road.

"What the hell?" Johnny asked.

The passing lane was about to end, so I swung sharply in front of the truck, leaving too little room for the SUV to tail me again. Instead the driver scooted in front of me, and slammed on his brakes. I had to hit my own, hard, to keep from smashing into him. The semi's brakes hissed behind me, and I headed for the shoulder at a right angle just before the truck would have smashed into us.

"Watch it," Johnny said.

"Great advice!"

I skidded to a stop, my front bumper grazing a guardrail. Below the rail there was about a hundred foot drop, studded with boulders.

While I was quivering at the edge of that drop, the SUV sped up, zoomed around a curve, and disappeared from sight, and the truck followed it.

I was shaking, but I grabbed my gun out of my bag and kept it in my hand. I swung back onto the highway, sending up a shower of gravel and dust from the shoulder behind me.

I dodged around a pickup and caught up to the semi again, but there was no passing lane this time.

"Take it easy," Johnny said, and he had that wary look on his face. Poor guy must think every woman he came near acted irrationally.

"That driver tried to kill us. How the hell can I take it easy!"

The highway went up and down a succession of small hills, and whenever I swung out I saw the reason for the double yellow. There was a lot of traffic, not a lot by Houston standards, but ten cars or so, strung out in a steady line, coming at me in the opposite direction. And there was no shoulder on either side of the road now, just the rocks the road was chiseled through.

If the SUV had forced me over on this stretch, I wouldn't be alive to chase him down.

At last the road widened, there was an actual passing lane again, and I sailed out past the semi.

The driver clearly remembered me. He blasted his air horn and waved his fist.

I barreled on down what was now a straightaway, but there was no gold SUV in sight. I was topping ninety-five and still no SUV.

"Lynn," Johnny spoke softly, soothingly. "He's gone now."

He was used to handling crazy women.

"The guy must've turned off somewhere. You're not going to find him."

My head was pounding with the chase, but there was nothing to be done. I forced myself to take my foot off the gas pedal, and think about the vanished SUV more rationally, so I could track him another way.

It was gold, . . . wow, that was some detective work. The glass was tinted dark and I couldn't see the driver.

It didn't have a license plate, only a cardboard advertisement, the type they stick on new cars fresh off the lot. It read "Thank you for shopping at Belfort Lexus," which meant whoever the driver was, he shopped in my neighborhood. I'd driven past the car lot with that name every day when I worked downtown. Of course, there could be any number of Belfort Lexus dealerships outside of central Houston.

If it was the same place though, that sure was a long way to go to buy a car if you lived up in the high desert, nine hours at least away from Houston.

CHAPTER FOURTEEN

I was itching to get on the phone and track that SUV down, but when we got back to the hotel, Adrianne was waiting in the lobby. She was sitting on the edge of a high-backed chair by the fireplace, breaking a piece of sponge cake into a million crumbs.

She set the cake on the table and ran to me, tears streaming down her cheeks. Apparently she felt bonded to me again. I patted her shoulder with one hand, clutching my depleted bag of clean laundry in the other.

"What's wrong?" I asked her.

"The sheriff arrested my daddy," she wept.

"He got the warrant quickly, then. We found your mother's car just this morning. In the bottom of Ascher Lake."

"Will you come with me, please?"

"Where?"

"To the jail. I have to see him. I just can't go in there by myself."

"I don't think that's such a great idea," I said. "I don't think I'm your father's favorite person at the moment."

"I know you're only trying to do what's right. Daddy knows it, too, when he's not all upset."

"He might be pretty upset about now," I said. Besides, I wanted to track down the gold Lexus. "Sheriff Winton'll take you to see your father, I'm sure."

Adrianne swiped at her eyes. "Sheriff was asking Daddy questions about Karen Shaw's death, too. That's just not right. He would never have had anything to do with her."

"I'll take the girl to see her father," Johnny volunteered.

I saw a new, eager, ugly light burning in Johnny's eyes. Sure, he'd held back at the ranch, but now he was putting the same stuff together I was. He probably had David scoped out as the father of Karen's child the same way I did, and was even more certain that David was a stone-cold killer.

I had a feeling that even if the sheriff and his deputy were standing there, service revolvers at the ready, that wouldn't stop Johnny from squeezing David's neck until his eyes popped if Johnny got his hands through the bars of the cell.

"That's okay. I'll go over to the sheriff's with Adrianne. Let me just change my clothes. You keep her company here for a little while," I told Johnny.

"Thank you," Adrianne whispered.

Johnny didn't seem pleased about it, but he poured himself a glass of wine from the decanter in the lobby and took out his sketch pad. Adrianne just sat there, dissecting the sponge cake.

My clothes smelled like the bacon Louise had been frying, but there was no way I was going back to that laundromat again. I slipped on a loose, black tank top and my oldest, lightest pair of jeans fast, before Johnny dashed over to the jail without my blessing.

Back in the lobby, I breathed a little sigh of relief. The avid light was gone from Johnny's eyes, and he was all wrapped up in drawing another picture of Karen. Adrianne was staring blankly into the unlit fireplace.

"Ready?" I asked her.

She nodded, numbly.

Johnny didn't look up from his drawing. "You'll talk to me when you get back," he said. It was a statement, not a question.

"I will," I agreed.

★　★　★　★　★

Deputy Hank told me he was the one who brought David in. At the time, the sheriff was occupied escorting Helen Cannon's remains to the county morgue.

Adrianne started to weep again, just hearing her mother's name. Hank seemed eager to get rid of her.

"Sheriff's just come back. He's down in the holding cell with David now. So go on down. You take two rights and then a left to get there."

"Anything interesting turn up at the morgue?" I asked.

"Well, autopsy's just started, but Charlie said cursory examination confirmed pretty much what you described seeing at the bottom of the lake—scars on the bones indicating deep cuts, a grievous head wound caused by a blunt object."

Adrianne was pulling on my arm, tears coursing down her cheeks. "I want to see my father," she said. "Please."

"Hang on one more second." I leaned close to Hank. "By the way, you can stop looking for the woman in the Jeep. I found her and she gave me most of my clothes back."

"You look nice in 'em," Hank said, and winked at me.

"There's something else though."

"Of course there is." He winked again, and I mentioned the gold SUV running me off the road.

"A lot of people don't like you, I guess," he said. "I do though," he hastened to add.

"Can you alert the highway patrol to that vehicle?" I asked him.

He promised he would, and I led Adrianne to the holding cell.

She clung to my arm and we blundered down one hallway and then another.

We heard the sheriff and David before we saw them. They were both shouting.

"I seen you two fight. She called me out a coupla nights, don't forget." That was Sheriff Winton, and his voice was cracked with anger.

"I swear to God, Charlie, she just up and left," David protested, and he didn't sound nearly so righteous and overbearing as usual.

"Left her friends without saying goodbye . . . left her daughter . . ." Winton raved.

We turned a corner. The sheriff stood with his back turned to us blocking a doorway, behind which were several small cells. David was pressed up against the bars in one of them.

"I told her I wouldn't let her take Addy," David said, his voice softer.

Adrianne froze. I had to give her a little push to move her up next to the sheriff.

David looked at us, his face contorted in a mixture of fury and grief. A lot of the grief was directed at Adrianne, and all of the fury pointed at me.

"Mama wanted to take me with her?" Adrianne asked, her voice just a tremulous whisper. "You never told me that."

The sheriff scowled. "This isn't an area available to the public."

"Hank sent us down," I told him.

Sheriff Winton did not look pleased.

David stood up. He pressed his hands against the bars, appealing to Adrianne. "Figured if I told her she couldn't have you, she'd stay. But she started packing anyway."

"And you tried to stop her," Sheriff Winton said, his voice thick and hard.

Adrianne buried her face in her hands.

"Take the girl back to my office, and you skedaddle too, missy," Winton said roughly to me.

"No, I want Adrianne to hear this," David said, sharply. "And maybe I shoulda had more to say to this other young woman here, and she'd be gone back where she came from, let the dead bury the dead as they say."

"See," Adrianne dropped her hands. "He understands you were only trying to do right."

She huddled against me and I put my arm around her, comforting, showing everybody I was a good guy. I wanted to make sure I got to stay and listen to whatever David had to say.

"You sure you want your daughter and this private investigator here while you tell your tale?" Sheriff Winton asked. "You sure you want to talk at all without your lawyer?"

"Yeah, I'm sure." David swallowed, hard. His voice was calm. The grief won out over the fury in his face, so that I almost saw what Karen must've seen in him. A yearning for understanding deep down in the man, a yearning she'd probably hoped she could meet.

"It was my weekend working volunteer at the fire station. We used to do those long rotations, remember?" David was almost pleading.

The sheriff didn't answer; his arms were crossed and his face was grim.

"When I got back, Helen wasn't at the ranch. And Addy was sitting out on the porch with pneumonia and a temperature of a hundred and five."

"You didn't even report her missing." Sheriff Winton rocked back on his heels.

"I spent two nights in the hospital with Addy. And it took me two *months* to realize Helen wasn't coming back that time. You know it wasn't the first time she left me."

The weird thing was, I almost believed him. Our eyes met, and he gave me a curt nod.

"See?" Adrianne said to me. "She just left. She had a car accident I guess, which is terrible and sad, but not something to lock my Daddy up over."

"The truth'll come out in court," Sheriff Winton said, and he turned to go.

Adrianne began to keen, a low wailing sound. "I lost my mama. Don't make me lose my daddy, too."

"Stop it, baby," David said, and to my surprise, she did, and fast.

"My lawyer's on his way," David continued, "go with Charlie now, wait for him in the office."

Sheriff Winton took Adrianne's arm and led her away from the cell. I tagged along in the corridor behind them, wondering what it was that made David sound so convincing. Almost innocent, except not quite.

The sheriff turned to me, his eyes red, like he'd been crying or got dust in them, maybe. "I got you those credit card receipts you wanted. David used his Shell card twice last week, at the same East Houston gas station. Used a Visa to pick up a roast beef sandwich and an extra-large coffee on Houston Parkway, not so far from Channelview, mid-afternoon on the Tuesday your client died."

I wondered if the son of a bitch had lunch right before or right after he killed Karen.

"Can I talk to him a minute alone?" I asked the sheriff, keeping my voice so even and calm I surprised myself. In Houston, of course, I would never even ask such a question. But here, I wasn't surprised at the response I got.

"Wear yourself out, if he'll let ya," Winton said.

"What are you going to talk to Daddy about?" Adrianne demanded.

She looked frightened, her eyes big and round, her lips trembling. I didn't blame her for being scared, but it would've been better if she'd been scared years ago. It might've saved Karen Shaw's life.

"Nothing to do with your mother," I said. "Go on up to the office."

I patted her shoulder, aiming for reassuring, but she shrunk back under my hand like I'd burned her. So much for my comforting, good-guy role. I spun on my heel, and marched back down the hall to David's cell.

He was sitting on a cot now, his shoulders hunched together. He looked years older, and smaller, diminished. He stared up at me, and I saw how much he wanted to stay angry, how much he wanted to hate me, and yet it slipped off his face and he just looked tired. All of a sudden, I felt pretty tired myself.

"Why'd you go to Houston?" I asked him, quietly.

"Thought you had it all figured out. Went down to murder your client."

"But why *then*? Why did you go when your daughter was there visiting her friend? Did you *know* Adrianne went to see Karen for a reading?" I figured that had to be it, but he shook his head.

"I had no idea Addy did something like that until she confessed to me this morning. If I'd known, I would've taken her straight home. All the fairy tales that woman told her."

"Sometimes fairy tales can come true, you believe in them long enough."

"Look, you want to know what's true, I'll tell you. Although I don't expect you to believe a word I say." His eyes met mine again, and held the gaze.

"I went to Houston to check on Addy. She'd called me a few days before, upset, without telling me why. And even though she changed her mind about coming home right away, I still wanted to make sure she was okay. I arranged for a hired man to keep the ranch running. But I didn't tell Addy I was coming east."

"Why not?"

"I figured I should keep my worries to myself. She needs to get out more, be with other kids. Even that Hayley's better than nobody."

"Her coach, the sheriff, Addy herself, everybody says you're the one holding her back, you scarcely let her out of your sight."

He passed his hand over his face. "She's the one clings to me, not the other way around."

"So she's a little dependent on her daddy, she called you upset about something, and you drove all the way to Houston to make sure she was okay. Have I got it right?"

"Yeah. I drove down and followed her around a day or two."

I made a face. "You followed your own daughter."

My reaction didn't faze him. "Addy and that Hayley, they were just hanging out at the mall and all. Weren't going to school, but they weren't doing anything awful either, and Addy seemed to be enjoying herself more or less. So I was gonna turn back around and come home. And I . . . I don't know. I knew Karen moved somewhere near Houston, of course. Thirty some years, and I never even called her. I suppose checking on Addy was the excuse I needed. All of a sudden, there I was in a phone booth, looking her up. Houston's a big city all right, but it didn't take me long to find her. But nobody answered the phone when I called."

"So you went to see her?"

With great effort, David stood up and met me at the front of the cell. He stood like that, eyes downcast, and I just waited. I waited a long time.

"You can tell me. I'm not a cop. Who knows, maybe I can even help you."

I've often found that when a person did something they were desperately ashamed of, something they'd lie, cheat, and kill to conceal, they were really just dying to tell somebody. All they needed was the slightest bit of reassurance they were doing the right thing by talking.

It was like an itch you knew you shouldn't scratch or you'd make it bleed, but something in your head said "go ahead, scratch," and it felt so good when you did, never mind the consequences.

David raised his head and the words came streaming out.

"Yeah, I went to her house. It was last Sunday night, around nine or ten. She wasn't home. I parked down the street and sat in the truck and I waited. My heart was beating so loud I thought everybody in the neighborhood heard it. I almost left three or four times, but it was like I was stuck there, and I couldn't go. Not without seeing her. She came home around, I dunno, twelve or so, crying like somebody just about broke her heart."

"So you thought you'd help finish the job?"

"Oh, Jesus, you see everything so black and white, don't you? I guess I used to see life that way myself, but that's not the way it is. It's just not the way it is." He slammed his fist against the bars and the cell door shook. He had that rage in him again.

"No? Tell me how it is, then." I had my hand inside my bag and my fingers curled lightly around my gun. Just in case the cell door didn't hold.

"Karen was pretty loaded. She was wearing this real pretty dress, and had her hair up, but it was kinda falling down over her face, and she was crying so much she didn't even see me watching.

"I went up to her on the porch. It was amazing to me, she looked just about the same as the first time I saw her, guessing weights at the county fair. She was just fourteen, and right every time. Couldn't take my eyes away. Shit, just fourteen."

David rubbed his forehead, trying to rub something out. A memory, or something he wished he hadn't done. "Promised Helen I'd never cheat again after Karen . . ."

"But you broke your promise, didn't you?"

"I didn't say I was perfect." He looked at me, he was willing me to understand. "But I've changed a lot since then. I was only twenty-four when I first met Karen. Not much more than a kid myself. In some ways she was a lot more together than I was."

"Right. At fourteen."

David fell silent. I tried for understanding, to get him talking again.

"So after all that time, you finally saw her again, and you said hello, at least?"

Slowly, David nodded. "She was searching around in her purse, looking for her keys, I guess. Pulled out some drawing, a sketch or something. She dropped it when I came up behind her, put my hands over her eyes."

"Was she scared?"

David shook his head. "Nah. She asked if I was Johnny, and I said no, took my hands away, and stepped right in front of her. She wiped at her eyes, and she didn't even seem that surprised to see me.

" 'My God, you're still beautiful,' I told her. She just shook her head, and gave a little laugh. I was a goner. It was impossible to stand that close and not want her. I told her so, too, and she just laughed again.

"It sure wasn't like thirty years had gone past. I wanted her so bad and so fast I couldn't think straight. She just stood there for a while, let me touch her, like she wasn't sure what was happening."

"She probably wasn't," I said, softly.

He twisted his hands together. "Funny thing, I tried to stick to the straight and narrow, had a hard time with it my whole life, but since Helen left me, I'm not the same man. Didn't look at another woman, until I saw Karen again."

"Why not? You were finally free to, then."

"Promised God. He let Addy live when she was so sick. I joined the church, promised to stop drinking . . ."

"You broke that promise, too?"

"Not until Karen. Old habits. They don't die hard. They don't die at all."

He leaned against the wall of his cell, and he smiled. "Thing is, I'm not entirely sure I regret it. Oh Lord, we went at it. Had a hell of a good time. I caught up to her pretty fast in the drinking department. Couldn't leave her alone then, not for a second. I didn't think she wanted me to, either. But I fell asleep once, toward morning, and when I woke up, she wasn't in the bed.

"Found her sitting outside on the front porch looking at that drawing that fell out of her purse, nice little picture of her. Grabbed her and brought her back to bed again. She was so wasted, had to cut that dress off her with my knife."

"With your knife," I said, my lip curling on the words.

But he didn't even seem to hear me. "Went through, I swear to God, two bottles of bourbon and half a bottle of rye by nine o'clock that morning. Found a card for a liquor store lying on her dresser, underneath a painter's hat."

"Red's," I said.

He was too into his story to even wonder how I knew. He just nodded. "Twenty-four hour delivery. I forgot all about Addy, all about everything. Just wanted to keep drinking and messing around. Figured once we'd both sober up, that'd be that, never see each other again in our lives. So I thought I'd keep the party going awhile longer.

"But while I was on the phone calling the liquor store, she went into the bathroom and took a shower, and when she came out, it was like she'd washed me right out of her heart. She was through with me. I tried to get her back in bed with me and that time, she wouldn't come.

"She was wrapped up in this little skimpy robe, her hair still wet, hardly able to stand up she was so wrecked, and yet she wouldn't get near me. Started picking up, the dress I cut up, things that fell off her bureau when we were going at it. She wouldn't stop with the tidying.

"I went, 'Come here baby, can't you read my mind,' and she looked at me like I just said something very funny.

" 'I can't read the fuckin' newspaper,' she said, and she threw my shirt at me. 'C'mon. Get outta here. I've been punished enough now.' That's what she said to me. Punished. Like we hadn't been having the best time two people could have.

"Damn, I couldn't believe it. I got up outta her bed and I grabbed her and I said 'I never made you do a thing you didn't want to. Not then, not now. You hear me?' She looked me right in the eye and she said she knew that."

He took a great gulp of air, and looked around him, like he was surprised by his surroundings. "It was all her grandma's idea, getting money out of me. At the time, they coulda put me in jail instead, statutory rape. Beat that one, but here I am all the same."

"So Mrs. Shaw knew you had a relationship with her grand-daughter?"

"Yeah. Caught us one afternoon, me and Karen in the barn, back of an old wagon. Gave Karen her first drink that day. 'It burns,' she said. 'Until you get used to it,' I told her. We shared a pint of bourbon and we lost track of time, I guess. Never could help myself around her."

He lapsed into silence.

"She was very attractive," I said. It was hard but I choked out, "I can understand."

"She had a beautiful smile, she did. I woulda done anything for her back then, except leave Helen. That's what she wanted of course, but I couldn't do that, it woulda meant I'd lose the ranch, it'd ruin me. Still she kept saying it over and over all that afternoon. 'Leave Helen, not me. Leave Helen.'

"Helen was somewhere, I dunno, doing charity work or some damn thing. I told Karen flat out I couldn't make any promises like that. Told her she was young, there'd be lotta guys she could marry . . . she started to cry then, and I was begging her to stop, when her granny walked in. Oh, she had a look on her face like she'd just chopped the head off a chicken and was ready to pluck it and throw it in the frying pan for dinner.

" 'She's under age . . . and I got you cold,' her granny said. Then she slapped me across the face and dragged Karen home.

"It all came back to me there in Houston, standing in Karen's room, getting my clothes back on. And I didn't mean to do it, but I slapped Karen, slapped her hard. She wasn't afraid or anything, she just looked at me, like I was as low as she'd thought I was all these years. I left her standing there in the mess of her room, and I bailed."

"Left your knife behind, didn't you?"

"So?"

He snapped out of his reverie then, and got the self-righteous look on his face that I really didn't like, especially from a man who'd just confessed to corrupting a minor and to smacking Karen around. He'd stopped short of confessing that he'd murdered her.

"When was it exactly that Karen Shaw asked you to find my wife?" Once again, David's eyes were burning, and he drew himself up and under the cover of that self-righteousness.

"You mean when did she have time before she was murdered, don't you?" I asked.

Everything went out of him, the anger, the sadness, the principle of the thing, the memory. He sagged and looked like somebody'd pulled the plug on him, and it was all over now.

"Did you kill her, David? I know you didn't mean to, but did you kill her?"

He shook his head, no, but he couldn't or wouldn't speak. The silence went on and on.

At last I walked out of the basement, and I found it hard to get my breath.

I'd planned to go to the sheriff's office and wait with Adrianne for David's lawyer, see if I got any more information out of the girl.

But I couldn't do it, I couldn't sit next to her and act like I wanted what she wanted, to exonerate her father. What I wanted was to excoriate him.

I played out David's visit with Karen in my head.

She obviously didn't connect Adrianne and David in the first place. From what she said to Johnny about not having any more of her visions, I didn't think she'd confronted David about his wife when he showed up at her door. Whatever she knew about Helen Cannon's murder, and however she knew it, she'd managed to subjugate her knowledge once again. And when she did, she lost what she thought of as her psychic abilities.

So it wasn't the fear of being uncovered as a murderer that sent David back to Karen's house again, and made him take her life.

My guess was that David returned to her place for his knife or to slap her around some more, whatever felt right to him at the time. And he saw her grappling with the delivery boy from the liquor store, misinterpreted that little encounter, and in a jealous rage, he waited 'til she drank herself into a stupor, then cut her wrists for her.

And the whole time, he probably felt justified in doing it.

As he must've felt justified beating his wife to death. Helen probably had a boyfriend of her own, with David cheating on her, it probably felt more right than wrong. But not to David.

David clearly thought he was the only one allowed to play outside the rules.

CHAPTER FIFTEEN

I lurched out of the courthouse, my feet pounding down the stairs and across the dry grass. Cicadas hopped out of the way.

There was nothing coming down the highway but a tumbleweed, so I ran across the street to the bar.

The place was crowded now, cowboy types and a group of guys passing through on Harleys; a family of backpackers sharing a couple of pitchers; three women dancing by the juke box; Betty, the woman from courthouse records cuddling with a big, bearded man.

"What'll it be?" the bartender asked me.

"Cola," I said, "extra ice. And change for a twenty this time."

"We sell phone cards here, be a lot easier and cheaper," she told me.

"That'd be great."

I might've had the story of David and his wife and Karen more or less all figured out, but I still didn't have a confession. And without one, where exactly was the proof needed to convict David Cannon? Sure, that was really up to Sheriff Winton now, but if *I* couldn't find the proof, would he?

I must've looked done in, because along with my soda and my phone card, the bartender returned with a cardboard box, pulled out a slice of pizza, and slapped it on a napkin for me.

"On the house," she said. "There's another couple slices left. It's good, brought it in with me from Alpine. If you want, I'll make that a double."

I grinned. "One'll do me for now, thanks." It was cold, and had black olives and mushrooms, not my favorite combo, but the kindness as much as the food revived me enough to get to the pay phone.

I dialed my new phone card's pin number and the three access codes necessary before I could punch in an actual phone number, and then I called Detective Hale's office.

I could've used the phone at the sheriff's of course, but I didn't want Adrianne listening in, or for that matter David's lawyer when he showed up.

Somebody else picked up Hale's phone and asked for my callback number, but I said I didn't have one and it was urgent. I leaned my head against the wall and looked out the plate glass window while I waited for Hale to come to the phone.

Outside the bar, the twilight hills towered over the desert, sucking up the last of the light. The shadowed desert itself ate up the edges of the town, pulling at the street lamps and all the lit-up windows, trying to swallow them down into its own vast darkness. That darkness could consume a *person*, too.

It had happened to Helen Cannon, out here on the parched edge of nowhere. It had happened to Karen, even if her particular nowhere was in an enormous city poised against the sea. The darkness was always out there.

Hale was out of breath when he picked up the phone, but he claimed to be glad I called. Our conversation had a whole different tone to it than my previous talks with the man.

The difference may have been Frank showing his interest in the case even if I hadn't called him back; or maybe the difference was how I was working it. There's a certain level of respect shown in law enforcement circles for simple persistence, no matter how ill-advised.

"The county sheriff faxed David Cannon's prints to us this afternoon, and the credit card receipts came through clear as a bell just a few minutes ago," Hale told me.

"And?"

"Well, now we can place Cannon in the Houston area, and in Ms. Shaw's house. There's a match between Cannon's prints and those found on that bottle of rye. Ms. Shaw's sheets bore easily identifiable trace elements of liquor, semen, and garden variety dirt, and they're being analyzed further now."

Hale had also examined Karen's dress. Fibers from the dress were found on David's knife. Unfortunately, that didn't prove he'd killed her. It just proved the knife had been used to cut up her dress, something he'd already admitted to me. Still, Hale was talking with Sheriff Winton about questioning Cannon himself.

"A lot depends," he said, "on whether these charges are gonna hold up regarding the guy's wife."

"In other words if he killed once, it's more likely he killed again?" I asked.

"No, if he killed once, and they've got him cold on that, maybe he'll cop a plea to this one, too. Maybe we can work out a deal. You know how it goes."

Yeah, I knew how it went. There were two women dead, and the best way to convict David for the most recent murder was to cut a deal.

"Lieutenant Wilson requests a word, by the way," Hale told me. "Can I patch you through right now?"

"Tell him I'll get back to him real soon," I said, and I hung up.

Talking to Frank was not what I needed right now. I already felt sad enough.

Outside the bar, the last of the twilight was spreading plum-colored fingers across the sky. A couple of guys came in the back room and started up a game of pool. Willie Nelson was on the juke box. The bartender passed me on the way to the Ladies and gave me a friendly wave. Not everybody was out to get me. But because some people were, my next phone call was to Belfort Lexus.

Eventually, I got to a sales manager who wasn't exactly eager to reveal his customer records, until I made it understood that we were looking at assault with a deadly weapon, and how much easier it would be if he'd help me out instead of making me call in the police, with whom I was intimately connected, and who would gladly go through the dealership's sales records, every last one of them. While they were at it, just to make the hassle worthwhile, they'd probably check everything from sales tax to interstate shipping fees.

Thirty minutes later I discovered that out of the eleven people who had purchased a gold Lexus SUV at that dealership in the past two months, which would be the maximum time the temporary tags were good for, there was only one whose name registered. And that was William Devins.

I called his lawyer's office and had his answering service page him.

"Hello? Hello?" Kincaid said. "Who is this?" He sounded panicky.

"This is Lynn Bryant," I said in my sweetest voice. "I just called to apologize for not having brought over those CDs yet. As you know, I'm out of town on business, and the actual passing of that evidence into your hands is going to have to wait just a bit longer."

"When'll you be back?" he asked flatly.

"Tomorrow, the next day, the day after that. I'll take care of *you* first thing." I tried to make the promise sound menacing, but he wasn't buying.

"Devins is losing it, Bryant. I'm a lawyer not a shrink, but you should come on back home and keep your promises."

"Or what? He'll run me over in his new gold Lexus? Hit me

on the head with a tire iron? Try and drown me? I'm losing it myself. Let him know that."

"What are you talking about?"

"I'm out of town, like I told you. And your client has been on my ass. I don't have any witnesses on the tire iron thing, but I have plenty of witnesses who saw him try and push me in front of a big rig and force me over an embankment."

Kincaid laughed, nervous.

"You think I'm a comedian? Is that why you're laughing?"

Kincaid shut up.

"I'm thinking your client called your secretary, your secretary informed him as to my general whereabouts, something like that? Or did she tell you and you told him? This is a small town, I'm not hard to find. Aiding and abetting—that's still a crime, I believe. And if I find out you've committed it, I'm not so sure I'd withdraw *those* charges."

I slammed down the phone, and leaned my head back against the wall for a rest.

The rest didn't last long. The phone rang about two minutes later, and it was Kincaid again, as I knew it would be.

"My office manager, Ginger, apparently she told him where you were going, yeah, but it was just conversational, nothing intentional," he told me.

"What are we going to do about this situation?" I asked.

"She's going to track Mr. Devins down now and I'm gonna read him the riot act. I'm sure he wasn't trying to actually hurt you, but he is a troubled man. Sometimes you get a client like that, I'm sure you've had your share, they need more help than you can give them."

I had to agree there. That was the truth with Karen, wasn't it? I was still struggling to help her now. I let Kincaid placate me a little longer, and then I hung up. All I could do was hope Devins would listen to his lawyer, or the highway patrol would hunt him down, or both.

I still wasn't sure how Devins had snuck up on me with that tire iron out at Nolan's. He was a persistent enough asshole to find me, follow me, hound me, try and run me off the road, but did he have the speed and the stealth in his fancy shoes to come up behind me and swing that iron?

I traded my empty soda glass for a beer, and occupied myself with peeling off the label. When I'd finished with the label, I drank the beer and went back to the pay phone. It was off the hook. One of the guys playing pool apologized to me. "It kept ringing."

I gave him a thumbs up and went through the ritual of the access codes and I called Frank.

And got his voice mail.

"I'm alone in this bar in Marathon and Detective Hale said you wanted to talk to me. And as it turns out, much against my better judgment, I wanted to talk to you, too. Why are you never there when I finally admit I need you? Why do you always piss me off so damn much?"

I sighed, got a grip. "But I didn't call to rant at you, as much fun as that is. I called because my murder case is coming together, as Hale will tell you, except there's no witnesses, no confession, it's all circumstantial and it makes me uncomfortable. I mean I'm sure the guy's guilty and all, reasonably sure, not positively sure. But I don't know if this case'll hold up.

"So, I thought I'd run some of it by you, confidentially. I thought hey, you'd have a disinterested perspective, a clearer line on what was going down. But I understand. It's a Friday night, there's no reason for you to be sticking by your phone.

"By the way, William Devins followed me up here and tried to run me off the road with his car this afternoon, and he may have come after me last night with a tire iron. But no worries, I haven't shot him, or his car, not yet anyway. Just also wanted you to know who's out to get me."

I let the phone dangle in my hand a minute, and maybe it was the beer going to my much-abused head, but I put the receiver up to my ear again and whispered into the mouthpiece. "Of course it meant something, Frank."

I hung up and sat there a minute watching the pool game, and the phone rang again. Both of the pool players looked up at me annoyed, so I picked up fast.

I was hoping it was Frank, but it was Kincaid again, telling me he'd tried to reach me repeatedly and thank God he had now, because I hadn't let him finish. "I swear to you, I will keep Mr. Devins in line, I will rope him in line, I will tie him up with the line, if he disturbs you again. I swear by . . . by my code of legal ethics!"

I disconnected the call and left the phone off the hook myself this time. I gave the pool players a little wave, and left the bar.

The hotel was quiet. Nobody was at the front desk, even though it was still pretty early. There weren't even any embers in the fireplace. The sherry decanter was empty and the sponge cake just crumbs. I snagged a Zane Grey and went down to my room.

Johnny must've heard me come in. He knocked on my door, softly, and called my name. I didn't particularly want to see him, but I had promised I'd talk to him. So I let him in, and stood there with my arms crossed by the bed.

"Well?" he said.

"I know who tried to run us off the road," I offered. "It has nothing to do with Karen."

Johnny was completely disinterested. "You talk to Cannon or just babysit his daughter?"

"I talked to him."

"He's locked up, right?"

"Yeah, for now. Until his lawyer springs him. Adrianne's real upset, and he won't cop to killing either his wife or Karen."

"That's not a surprise, is it?"

"Not a surprise. I'd almost believe he didn't kill his wife, but maybe that's because he's been denying it to himself for so many years he has the act down cold. But he admitted he was right there with Karen. He was right there with his knife."

Johnny slammed his hand against the wall and a little watercolor of the local hills covered with wild flowers in springtime fell off onto the bed.

I picked up the picture. "He was in Houston ostensibly to check on Adrianne. And he stopped to see Karen, out of the blue."

"And she said he killed his wife," Johnny's face was dark and tired.

I shook my head. "Karen told you she'd lost her gift. Whatever she lost, gift, memory, willpower, I don't think it came back again. If she'd said something to him, he would've been more suspicious of me when I first showed up at the ranch. He didn't even know his daughter went to see Karen, until today."

"Why'd he kill her, then?" Johnny asked.

I didn't want to lie to him, but I really didn't want to tell him that while he was moping around missing Karen, she was getting it on with a man she hadn't seen in thirty years. And then, she rejected him and he got mad. I was convinced this case had more to do with jealousy than Karen's mystical powers.

Even if Johnny was the prince of understanding when it came to Karen, I wasn't so sure he'd understand how she spent her final hours, doing what David wanted and hating herself for it, every bit as much as she must've hated herself years before when she went along with her grandmother's get-rich-quick scheme.

Johnny prompted me. "Answer me. If Karen didn't accuse the guy of killing his wife, why'd he hurt her?"

"Because he's a vindictive shit. And she didn't want him anymore." I busied myself with the little painting, carefully re-hanging it on the wall.

Johnny's fingers brushed my cheek, and he turned my face so that I had to look him in the eye. He smiled at me. "No wonder she liked you. You're the same way she was, so damn certain you know everything."

"What are you talking about?" I pushed his hand away, irritable.

"I used to think it was the psychic stuff that made Karen so sure she was always right, that she had the inside line on the rest of us. But I guess there doesn't have to be something cosmic going on. Life's just easier, in a way, if the only perceptions you really trust are your own."

"I'll tell you the perception I have right now. It's that pretty soon I'm gonna hit you if you don't get to the point."

"Karen didn't know everything and neither do you, that's all. I'm not gonna get all crazy and jealous if you tell me Karen was with David that last night."

"No?"

"She loved me. She just didn't love herself enough right then to understand I really loved her, too. And I wasn't strong enough to make her understand. I just wasn't strong enough."

He smiled again, but the smile was very sad. "If she turned to him, hell, it's on me," he said.

Before I shaped an answer, he was across the room, and out the door. He didn't slam it, but he closed it with a firm finality behind him.

He was right; I did believe mostly my own perceptions. They had taught me that people usually, if not always, behaved in particular, discernible patterns. There were psychological tomes by the score that backed me up.

Of course Frank used to say the truth was what I made it,

and I guess that's the case with just about everybody.

But what truth was I making out of Karen Shaw's death? I honestly wasn't sure. There was something I was missing, something I didn't quite get. That lack of understanding, that was on *me*.

I knew I'd never sleep, so I pulled off my jeans, threw on my old running shorts, and jammed my feet into socks and sneakers. My heel wasn't swollen anymore, and it fit easily in my shoe.

I didn't want to haul my purse around with me while I took a run, but since I had no idea where Devins was, I took my shoulder holster out of my bag and strapped it on. I double-checked the safety on the Smith and Wesson, jammed it in the holster, and slipped out of the room.

Outside, the night smelled sweet and the air was cool. The bar was still hopping, but the rest of the tiny town was shutting itself up tight again.

Coyotes howled somewhere in the hills, and even though I knew exactly what the sound was, it still made me shiver. I missed Houston. I missed my neighborhood. I missed the police sirens, the traffic, even the hissing sound that sometimes came from the power plant.

I pretended that out there across the dark desert sand, the city was waiting just around the bend for me, moving, moving, full of messy life and motion. It might've been the stillness, the lack of motion in the desert night that I found so disquieting.

I jogged around the quiet, pretty frame houses, keeping my pace steady. I wanted to get in a full thirty minutes. If I was Adrianne, I'd probably make it out to the ranch and back.

As I ran, I wondered if Karen's grandmother had hired a private eye like me to take pictures of Karen with David. I wondered if Carol Ann hadn't interfered, if she hadn't died, if

Karen had kept the baby, how would Karen's life have been different?

Everyone's life hinges on a series of decisions, some of them ours to make, some of them just plain out of our hands. Fate is an awkward thing, you try and shape it, and it ends up shaping you anyway.

I wanted to drive all the way back to Houston right then, and go over to Frank's and have a big fight with him. I wanted to shout at him about the chance he'd already missed with me, and if he ever wanted another one, he'd better get his act together fast.

And then we'd take off all our clothes and make up real sweet, and we'd go out for Mexican this time, some place like the Cadillac Bar on Shepherd, where they have cheese burritos with fresh cilantro and black beans inside, and great green corn tamales. We could toss back a few Cuervo's and talk about old times, and they wouldn't even seem sad anymore; they'd seem funny. It was time we stopped reexamining the past, forgave and forgot, and looked hard at the future, to see if we really saw ourselves together in it.

The wind came up, spraying dust against the back of my legs. It gave me a chill, and I felt a few drops of rain mixed in.

More weather coming. I picked up my pace, and circled the courthouse.

If the old woman who stole my clothes had gotten it right, David Cannon gave Carol Ann Shaw a cash payoff. There should be a record at one local bank or another to indicate such a withdrawal, on or near the day that Mrs. Shaw died.

But what would that prove? That Karen had a history with David, that David might've held that history against her, that David was with her the night before she died? All of it led nowhere. I wondered if David even knew he'd fathered Karen's child.

I reached the edge of town and turned back. I didn't want to go too far and end up shooting at coyotes. I ran past the courthouse one more time, and back to the highway again.

I slowed down in front of the bar almost without meaning to.

The guys were still at the pool table in the back. Behind them, I could see the pay phone still hanging off the hook.

Call him anytime, Frank said. It wasn't quite eleven. If Frank wasn't hitting on some girl, he'd be sitting at the office, going through his files.

I'd have to go back to the hotel, get that phone card. The idea of going back to the hotel and slipping past Johnny again was daunting. More daunting still was admitting to Johnny the conclusion I was rapidly reaching that even if Houston PD did get into it, David Cannon was more than likely going to end up walking away from his accusers, a little shaken, a little more self-righteous, and free as a bird, for lack of cold, hard proof.

If the bartender would trust me, float me for another phone card, I could use the phone now without dodging Johnny and pay her tomorrow. It was worth a try to ask.

As I took a step toward the door, Betty the records clerk walked outside the bar, a little unsteady. She had a cigarette in her hand and was snapping a lighter between her fingers, trying to raise a spark. The wind was more or less preventing it. The golden Indian watched impassively as she cursed. Betty shook her head at me, a little less sweet-voiced now.

"This damn no smoking law! I mean in a bar, for God's sake. Every time I light up, I gotta go out in the road. That's a deterrent all right. A deterrent against having a couple beers anywhere but home."

I made sympathetic sounds.

"Ooh, you're wearing your gun." She stepped out of the light and squinted a closer look at me. I could feel the sweat from my run drying in my hair and I was still breathing pretty hard.

"You've been running. Who're you after?"

"Just after some exercise."

Her eyes widened in disbelief. "Okay, if you don't wanna tell me . . ."

"Seriously. Funny time of night for it I guess, but I was just taking a jog around town. I had a man try to run me off the road today, the gun's in case he's still around and hoping to try something again tonight."

"You have been busy." She got the lighter to work, and drew a great big hit off the cigarette. "Don't suppose you want one, being a runner and all?"

I shook my head.

"You goin' in the bar?"

"I was thinking about using the phone, but I'm gonna give it a rest until tomorrow."

I wasn't sure I would take it well if Frank said something like just let go of the case if I couldn't make it work. I would take it much less well if he told me to just let go of him for similar reasons. And if I put any thought into it at all, I could see that both responses would be entirely logical.

"Goodnight," I told Betty, and I turned toward the hotel.

"Not surprised about David Cannon," she threw out after me.

I swung back. "You're not?"

"There was always somethin' kind of sneaky about him. Ladies loved him of course."

She sniffed. "Never looked his way myself. I prefer a man's gonna be true to you, like mine's been. David was formidable though in his prime. A formidable, good-looking, skirt-chasing, drunk." She inhaled again, deeply.

"So I've heard."

"He was always drivin' around in his pickup truck with a pint in his pocket, throwing a great big cloud of dust over everybody he passed by. He acted much the same when he wasn't behind the wheel, any time stuff didn't go his way. Tried to cloud the facts of a situation with his own anger."

"You should be a shrink," I said, impressed. "That's exactly right."

"Shoulda been a lot of things. Wanted to raise llamas." She tossed the last of her cigarette down on the porch, and ground it under her heel. Then she kicked the butt into the street. She was wearing boots with steel tips. They weren't entirely unlike David's work boots.

"Where'd you get those?" I asked her.

"O'Malley's Western Wear. My husband manages the place. Used to work in the Alpine location on Saturdays myself, but now there's only one location up in Pecos. Great boots, huh?"

"Yeah, they are. They sell work boots, too?"

"Yeah, work boots, and custom-designed vests, those tooled belts with the silver conchos on 'em. Real pretty. Adrianne Cannon bought one for her precious daddy, matter of fact, just before her mama disappeared. I remember it well. Cost one hundred and five dollars. Lotta money for a child to have around here. Told me she saved her allowance money for a year, and did other kids' homework for 'em, a quarter a page."

"That was enterprising of her." I managed to sound calm, even though my heart was pounding.

That belt. The belt that Karen described to me.

"Yeah, poor kid. She was still a couple bucks short. I kicked in the difference. Never saw her daddy wear it, though."

A little thrill shot through me and passed into a shudder. It was probably because of the rain that was really starting to come down now. A gust blew up on the porch, spraying both our faces.

"Better get back inside," Betty said. "Sure you won't join me?"

"No. I'm beat. It was good talking to you, though."

I ran the half block back to the hotel, letting the rain soak me. I'd come close but not close enough. I just had to prove incontrovertibly that David killed Karen. I had to, somehow. I wanted truth, I wanted justice, I wanted to see exactly how it all went down.

Of course, justice itself saw nothing at all; it was blind.

Whatever justice I was after for Karen Shaw and Helen Cannon was my own vision, as relentless in its own way as Karen's had been.

CHAPTER SIXTEEN

Back in the hotel, I took a long, hot shower. I pulled on a pair of sweatpants and a fresh tee shirt, and, filled with resolve, I knocked on Johnny's door.

If we ran through the facts of the case, if we ran through anything and everything Karen might've said to him about David, or someone who could have been David, anything about her life just outside this small town, maybe we'd come up with something I could use. He knew Karen better than anybody, didn't he? At least he acted like he did.

I knocked again and again, but Johnny didn't answer. I called out softly. "Johnny, hey, it's me."

Still nothing. I listened through the keyhole between the bathroom and his room; it was silent. If he was in there sleeping he slept very quietly and took very shallow breaths.

Maybe he was out. I'd gone for a run, he could've run after me. It seemed he was always following me around.

I lay down in bed with the light still on, and once again I tucked my gun and Karen's little herb bouquet under my pillow. I was waiting to hear Johnny come in, but my eyes were drooping and I fell asleep.

When I woke, it was five a.m., and when I went into the bathroom I drank a big glass of water, but it tasted faintly of iron, which reminded me faintly of blood.

I thought about the way Adrianne couldn't stand the sight of blood. Maybe her queasiness had something to do with her father murdering her mother.

It occurred to me that maybe Karen wasn't the only one who saw how it went down. There was something about the way Adrianne talked about her mother's disappearance, something that made me think she knew a little more than she let on. Maybe it was something she wished she didn't know. But wishing you didn't know something didn't make it go away.

I remembered telling my father I didn't want to know, when he came into my room to tell me the hospital had called, and my own mother was gone. But a few days later, there I was at the funeral.

There were things you wished you didn't know, but you did; there were things you didn't know and you wanted to know them. There was stuff you remembered and stuff you forgot and it didn't matter; in the end, ultimately, it was all still a part of you.

I went back to bed, and pulled the sheet up over my head as the sky grew light. Again, I wondered what Adrianne had forgotten she knew, and what she didn't know. It seemed to me she didn't know her mother loved her. She'd seemed surprised at the jail, when David said Helen wanted to take her daughter away with her.

I knew how fiercely my mother loved me, her love sustained me every day, even after she was gone and my father couldn't quite manage a goodnight hug. He always meant well, he did, but his heart was just—confined.

Sometimes my heart was pretty confined, too. I held back a lot, especially with Frank. If I still loved him, and I wasn't saying for sure that I did, but if I did, what was I going to do about it, pretend I didn't for the rest of my life, just because I was afraid he never loved me?

I remembered Karen telling me, confidently, like she had a clue, that he loved me. Maybe she did have a clue; who knew?

She'd been right about other things.

When the sun came up, I was up with it. I pulled on my jeans and a fresh tee shirt. I looked at myself in the mirror, and I remembered something else Karen told me, that I shouldn't hide my looks beneath a baggy black shirt. I glanced across the room at the slinky royal-blue dress Louise had given me.

It was clearly inappropriate for checking in at the jail or brainstorming evidence. But I could see the attraction of such a dress. I could see the look on Frank's face if he saw me wearing it. I could imagine his hands slipping it off my shoulders, in the front seat of his SUV.

An SUV not unlike the one William Devins just purchased, so he could drive around maniacally, trying to run me off the road if he couldn't drown me.

Of course he wasn't around when I almost drowned a second time at the bottom of Ascher Lake. The only person around then who wasn't a corpse, was Johnny.

Johnny had saved me. Saved me twice. I don't usually need saving. The idea made me uncomfortable.

I took my gun and Karen's lavender and sage out from under my pillow and dropped them back in my purse. The sage was crumbling all over everything, but I kept it anyway. I'd clean out my purse, organize my wallet, pay my bills, all that, when I got back home.

I was ready to go home, get connected with my life again, even if it was as messy as my purse.

But first, one more conversation with Johnny, digging for anything he might've left out. And one more conversation with Adrianne, one where I asked the questions and she didn't run away, not literally, as she did at the bus station; and not figuratively either, the way she sidetracked me by showing me her mother's wedding ring or weeping over her father's incarceration.

Despite my resolve to nail David, if nothing came from these conversations I'd have to tell Johnny it was over as far as I was concerned. We'd done what we could. The law would have to take over and do what it could, too. Karen would understand. To live a life worth living you can't turn away from things that frighten you, she said. Even if what frightened me most was admitting that I wasn't exactly infallible, and that I had feelings, which ran deep.

I left my room, and knocked on Johnny's door. There was still no answer. I scribbled a note on a piece of paper telling him I was going over to the courthouse, and stuck it in the keyhole. If he wasn't there when I got back, I'd ask for the master key.

The town was peaceful with early morning quiet; it was a warm, cloudy day, and the sky had a milky quality to it.

Over at the courthouse, Sheriff Winton was nowhere to be found, but Hank offered me a cup of coffee and some bad news. David Cannon had, just as I'd imagined he would, only a little bit sooner, made bail and taken Adrianne home with him.

Cannon's lawyer was working at getting the charges dropped altogether. Hank regretfully told me he had a decent chance at succeeding.

Hank scratched his chin. "Speaking of charges, you know that gold SUV? Temporary plates? Highway patrol caught the guy driving erratic outside of Ozona. Led 'em on a high-speed chase! I know you get six of them a week down in Houston, but out here, hey, it's exciting."

"So they have him locked up on reckless driving?"

"And evading arrest, too."

I felt a little relieved, but not a lot.

"Yeah, it's a shame it wasn't David Cannon driving. Might've kept him behind bars a few hours longer."

"I know this is a disappointment about Cannon. Anything I

can do . . ."

"Right now you could let me use the phone."

"You had a couple calls come in on the machine late last night," he told me, and hit playback.

They were from Frank. While I was glad he'd called me back, I resented the tone in his messages a little, considering he'd been MIA when I'd called him. He described his need to speak to me as "urgent," and that if I "knew what was good for me" I should call him immediately.

Hank handed me the phone, and tried to look busy shuffling papers.

I decided to call Detective Hale before I dialed Frank. He sounded sleepy but he picked up on the first ring.

"Yeah, I heard from Cannon's lawyer myself. He told me, quite rightly, that it's no crime to have been in the company of Ms. Shaw prior to her committing suicide. And we *are* still calling it that. Like I told you last night, it really depends how things look up where you are. Sounds to me like there's not enough coming out of that autopsy on Cannon's wife to keep things going." He yawned. "Things change, give me a call back right away."

"Frank say why he's been calling?" I asked Hale.

Hale sounded genuinely surprised. "Nah. I haven't spoken to him. If he'd heard something about Cannon he would've contacted me."

His tone indicated that he was reassuring himself that this was true, that Frank wouldn't do anything so insulting as go around the detective in charge of the case. Frank was usually quite politically correct at work, and I was pretty sure he hadn't.

"I'm sure it's about something else," I told Hale, and hung up.

Whatever it was, I wasn't sure if there was any point, any longer, in calling Frank or not. What I needed to say to him was best said in person. I realized I was mumbling to myself.

Hank misinterpreted. "Okay, I get the hint, I'll give you a little privacy. Gonna grab something to eat at the café. Want anything?"

I shook my head. After he left, I just sat there looking at the phone, like it could tell me what I should do next.

Apparently, it told me to dial it, because I had it in my hand and was halfway through Frank's number when Johnny strolled in, eyes dark circled, cheeks unshaven. He lifted two fingers by way of a greeting, and that gesture seemed to take a lot of effort. I set the receiver back in its cradle.

"You look worse than I feel," I said.

"I couldn't sleep. So I've been walking. Most of the night."

"In the rain?"

"Didn't really notice it was raining," he laughed. "You can walk for miles around here, it all looks the same, wet or dry. Everything looks the same."

"You're lucky the coyotes didn't eat you."

"Don't think even a coyote would want a bite of something this bitter."

"You already heard . . . ?"

"I came over here after we talked last night. I saw Cannon leaving, his arm around his kid, his lawyer talking a mile a minute about hearsay and probable cause and a stone-cold trail. They'll never get enough to convict him on a case years old, will they?"

"When they get the complete autopsy report back on Helen, maybe."

"The only person who saw it go down is dead and Karen didn't even see it, not in the conventional terms they use in a court of law."

Even though these were exactly the same conclusions I'd already reached, I felt duty bound to argue with him. "We've already placed him at Karen's the morning she died. Somehow, I'll get the cops in Houston working harder on this. I'll get them on our side."

"Cannon'll skate away. We might as well admit it."

Johnny had a blank look on his face;, he'd finally beaten his misery into exhaustion.

The phone rang and I answered it.

"Sheriff's office. Hey, Adrianne, how are you?"

I shot Johnny a thumbs-up, and I tried to sound bright and friendly. If there was a useful statement to coerce out of her I'd have a better chance of getting it if I didn't say something like hey, how's your murdering daddy this morning?

Johnny dropped into a chair, and buried his face in his hands.

"I'm not good," Adrianne said, her voice a hoarse, cracked whisper. "I called the hotel first. I needed to find you."

"Well, you have me now. How can I help you?"

"It's Daddy," she said, and she made an awful gagging sound.

"Did he hurt you?" I asked.

Johnny dropped his hands off his face and stood. He hovered over my shoulder, but I pushed him away. I didn't want the kid hurt, but if David was threatening her, waving that belt around maybe, surely something like that would turn her against him and into a state's witness.

"Adrianne," I said, "talk to me, honey."

Adrianne got herself together to speak. "Daddy's the one who's hurt. He's dead."

My hand dropped down on the edge of the desk, and I knocked a pencil cup over, spilling pencils all over the floor. Johnny knelt down and started scooping them up again, frowning. I suppose I looked as blown away as I felt.

"I'll track down the sheriff," I told Adrianne.

"I got him out of bed this morning. He's here now. But I was hoping you . . . you'd come out, too. Please. I'm not feeling well."

"I'm on my way," I said.

Johnny set the pencil cup back on the desk with a thunk.

"What's going on?"

"I'm going out to the ranch."

"He hurt his kid, now, too?"

I shook my head. "No, he—"

Johnny cut me off. "I want to see that son of a bitch try lying to my face. I'll make him tell the truth. Or I'll kill him. I'll kill him myself. If the law won't take care of him, I will."

"You're too late, Johnny. Adrianne says he's already dead."

A slight smile played across Johnny's lips. "God heard me praying," Johnny said.

"Maybe you ought to find a house of worship and give thanks," I suggested.

"You don't want me out at the ranch, do you?"

"If there's any chance of getting some answers from Adrianne, you're not going to be the one asking the questions."

He was pissed about it, but he didn't try to fight me. Maybe he was just too tired. "I hear what you're saying," he said. "I'll wait at the hotel."

We ran into Deputy Hank crossing the street carrying a big bag of something that smelled greasy and good. I filled him in.

"So that's where Charlie's gone off to this morning. Wonder if he's still gonna go snag that autopsy report on Helen over in Fort Stockton. Doesn't seem much point if the likely perp's gone to that great courthouse in the sky. I don't wanna bother him myself and seem pushy, but if you'd ask him if he's still planning to drive down, I'd appreciate it. He doesn't make that trip, I can still take my kid fishing this afternoon."

I promised Hank I'd ask, got in my car, and drove.

CHAPTER SEVENTEEN

On my third trip out to the ranch, the road hardly fazed me. As long as you didn't look over the sides of those cliffs and see how far away you were from the ground below, it wasn't scary at all.

That narrow road was analogous to life itself. Sometimes, if you didn't acknowledge how close you were to the bad stuff, you could almost fool yourself into thinking things were just fine. Or perhaps, also analogous to life itself, you could just get used to anything and not mind it anymore. I imagined that's what Adrianne had done.

As I drove up to the ranch, I could see her waiting for me on the porch steps, her knees drawn up to her chin, her hands wrapped around her knees. She was wearing a loose cotton man's shirt over a pair of jeans that were a little too big; the cuffs dragged on the ground.

David's pickup was in the yard, and there were tire tracks from other cars. The sheriff's squad car wasn't in the drive. I pulled up behind the pickup and climbed out. It was very still, except for the sounds of some insects buzzing around, and a crow calling.

"Well, I'm here," I told Adrianne, and stuck my hands in the pockets of my jeans. It was hot again, despite the cloudy sky.

"You missed the sheriff," she told me. "Coroner already came and got Daddy, too."

"That was fast," I said.

"I waited awhile to call you. I wasn't sure there was any point."

I wasn't sure there was any myself. Now that I was here, it seemed pretty awkward asking Adrianne to cough up any evidence she might have against her dead father. As I'd told Johnny, it was too late to hurt David. He was gone. What else could we do to him?

So instead I asked Adrianne what I could do for her.

She shrugged. "I just thought you'd want to come out. Look around I guess." She started to cry.

Adrianne sure cried a lot. I understood it in these circumstances of course; it's just that I wasn't big on crying. Usually if it hurt enough to make you cry, you sucked it in and kept it to yourself before your heart broke. At least that was how it was with me.

"I found Daddy in his bed this morning," she sobbed. "Oh my, Ms. Bryant, I couldn't believe it. I did his morning chores, so he could sleep in. Then his lawyer called to give him the good news."

"What good news?"

"Mr. Biddy, that's our lawyer, he and the judge go way back. Because of their friendship, all those charges against Daddy were dropped."

"They didn't care, in other words, if he was innocent."

Adrianne looked at me, surprised. "Which one of us is? Let him be the one to cast the first stone. Daddy always said that. It was one of the scripture readings he found most powerful when he became a churchgoer. Made me go, too, although I can't say I ever liked it that much."

"A little prayer might be comforting around now," I suggested, although I couldn't stop myself from thinking about Johnny, praying for David to die.

"I'm all prayed out. I have to believe he's gone to a better place," Adrianne said. "Just like Mama. I hope they'll be happy together there."

From everything I'd heard about the two of them, I couldn't quite picture them locked in eternal connubial bliss, but who knew.

"So he died in his sleep?" I asked her.

Adrianne shook her head vigorously. Her teeth started chattering.

"What happened to him, then?" I asked.

"All the blood," she said.

I'd been figuring a heart attack from the stress, something like that. It never occurred to me that David had not died of natural causes.

"There was blood?" I said.

"He killed himself," Adrianne wailed, and she hurled herself up and into my arms and buried her face in my hair. I felt her tears slipping down my neck along with a trickle of my own sweat.

"I came into his room and he was lying on his side with a sheet pulled up over his chest. I shook him, said, 'Daddy come on, good news, come to the phone, okay?' But he didn't wake up."

Adrianne began a low, keening wail. "I pulled back the sheet and I saw . . . I saw the cuts. I must've blacked out . . . you've seen how I get . . . I woke up on the floor, and I ran to the phone, and I called the sheriff.

"He was out here first thing, and then they took away Daddy's body and I felt so alone. So I called around 'til I found you. What'll I do, Ms. Bryant? Who'll take care of me now?"

The best I could offer was one of those sayings I'd seen pasted up on the cork board in David's bedroom. "One day at a time," I said. "Let's get through this one."

I led her into the kitchen. It smelled of stale grease and there was something unpleasant about it. I opened a window.

"Is there somebody you can stay with?"

"I'd say Hayley, but she's not around here."

"Did Sheriff Winton say he was coming back . . . bringing somebody to see to you?"

Adrianne shook her head. "He didn't say anything much."

He was probably as shocked as I was that David killed himself. In one way, it made sense. He took his own life in the same way he'd taken Karen's. Yet in the same way that Karen's so-called suicide didn't seem to fit her personality, David's death didn't fit his, either.

I saw the righteous gleam in his eye, even in a jail cell. It wasn't the look of a man who'd take himself out. It was the look of a man who believed he'd done no wrong, no matter how much wrong he really had done.

There was also his new-found religion. It was a mortal sin to take your life. Would he have really risked that, on top of his many other indiscretions?

I opened cupboards until I found a glass and filled it with water. A silver fish skittered around the edge of the sink. I slapped it down the drain, and gave the water to Adrianne.

"Maybe I should take you into town," I said, "I'm sure we can find someone to help you out. I can call your track coach."

"Okay," she said, and her voice was docile and young. "I'll pack up a few clothes."

She stood, chewing her lip. "He was the best daddy a girl could ever have, you know."

"I guess you think so," I said. I tried to soften my words a bit. "I am sorry for you, but beyond that, I don't know what else to say."

She pressed her hand to her forehead. I saw her trembling all over, and I reached out to her. "I'm okay," she said. "I'm not gonna faint again." She plucked at her shirt. "I put on Daddy's shirt. Makes me feel stronger."

Still, just to be safe, I eased her down at the kitchen table. There was a piece of white paper folded and held fast beneath the salt shaker. Suicide note, I thought. I lifted it, and opened it up. It was one of Johnny's sketches of Karen.

"Where'd this come from?" I asked Adrianne.

"The barn . . . when I went to feed the horses this morning. It was lying in one of the stalls. Look, I know this might sound funny, and I know you didn't like my Papa. But I was thinking somebody killed him, and made it look like he took his own life."

I gave a low whistle.

"I was thinking the killer might've dropped that picture," she added.

"Did you show it to the sheriff?"

"I forgot." She got all weepy again.

"Call him, right now," I said, "and tell him to get back out here." I thrust the phone at her across the table. "If you get Hank, get him out here. I want to go look around the barn."

I had the screen door open, but I stopped halfway through. "Adrianne?" I said. She looked up at me, tears spilling down her cheeks.

"What about your mother? Her body in the car. Your father had to be the one who . . ."

Adrianne wet her lips with her tongue. She took a deep breath. "It was a woman that killed her. I saw a woman beating her. A woman's hand, holding a knife."

"What?" I let the screen bump up against me.

"I saw. I saw . . ."

"Then why didn't you say anything? Yesterday, when the sheriff arrested your father! When I came to the ranch and you fainted. When everybody said your mother had run away! Before now," I finished, lamely.

She was sobbing. "I was a kid, I was scared, and sick with a terrible fever. The doctors said I was unconscious for days. I didn't remember anything much. Then this morning, seeing Daddy, it all . . ." She couldn't get any more words out.

"Who was the woman, Adrianne?"

"I don't know. It might've been . . ." she pointed her thumb in the direction of Johnny's sketch, still in my hand. "The woman in that picture. Karen Shaw. When I went to see her, like I told you, that was all she went on about. My mother. She said she saw her die. How would she know the way my mother died, unless she was the woman who killed her?"

"There's lots of ways, Adrianne."

"Name one."

"She might have seen the real killer."

"Is that what she told you?"

I didn't answer. I shoved the screen door open and left the stale little house with a heavy heart.

I walked across the dusty field to the barn. I had come to the ranch looking for answers, but maybe I was more particular about what they were than I thought.

I didn't want Karen to be the bad guy. I'd come all this way across this vast state to find out who killed *her*, only to find out that possibly she was a killer herself.

But I could see Helen's death happening the way Adrianne told it, almost in spite of myself. It was the first time I could understand, really understand, why Karen had the visions about the woman dying, and what it was about Adrianne coming to see her that had upset her so much.

The visions were not, after all, some strange phenomena of the spirit as Karen believed. They were not how I had them pegged either, as memories of a crime she'd witnessed, perhaps drunkenly. They were snapshots of her own actions.

I could've been right all along about the drunk part, and there could have been a fight between the two women that escalated out of control.

And maybe Karen had killed herself after all, remembering.

But David . . . why would he kill himself, too, in exactly the same way?

And why would he have brought the drawing of Karen home with him, evidence of his own indiscretion? Unless, as Adrianne had just suggested, he wasn't the one who left the picture in the barn.

I opened the barn door. It was heavy and it slammed shut behind me with a whoosh of wind that sent the smell of horse manure and hay and dust swirling up around me.

There was another smell too, something metallic, like wet rust. That's not what I thought it was, though. I found the cord to the overhead light and I pulled it, but the light didn't come on.

I leveled a curse at the universe under my breath. The universe's only response was to put a bale of hay right under my foot and trip me. I picked myself up, and then the hay. The thing was heavy. I propped the barn door open with it, to let in the light.

I really needed to do some more weight training when I got back to Houston. I hadn't even run for days, except my pitiful circle through town last night. Perhaps that was the explanation for why I felt so out of breath all of a sudden, so weak in the knees, as I wedged the hay against the door, and saw something red and sticky on the side of it.

At first I thought it was my foot, bleeding again. I hadn't even looked at it after I came in from my little run. But I slipped my foot out of my sandal, and I saw the cut was still closed, healing nicely.

Something flipped in my stomach, and I reached for my gun.

One of the horses whinnied, restive. I turned toward the sound. The mare that whinnied appeared to be pawing at something on the ground, pushing at it with her hoof.

I opened the gate to her stall, and I saw Sheriff Winton. He was half-covered in hay and he was pretty badly beaten. He could've been stomped by the horse, but since the horse wasn't doing anything like stomping him now, I doubted it.

Winton blinked up at me. "Addy," he said, weakly.

"It's Lynn Bryant, Sheriff. I'm gonna get you some help."

I leaned down and brushed off some of the hay.

"Who did this to you?" I asked him.

He closed his eyes and just moaned.

I pulled him out of the stall, in case the horse got more restless.

A gust of wind sailed through the door I'd propped open, and rattled the eaves of the barn. The door flew all the way open and all the way closed, knocking the hay bale aside. I was ready to shoot, but I couldn't see anything to shoot at in the thick, furry darkness.

I ran to the door, and pushed against it, hard, but it wouldn't budge. It seemed like somebody had bolted it shut from the outside. Of course, it was entirely possible somebody had.

On the other side of the door, out in the daylight, there was the sound of car wheels on gravel. I was hoping it was Deputy Hank. I'd be happy to have him crack lame jokes at my expense right now.

Then somebody screamed. It sounded like Adrianne.

I ran back to the sheriff. Quick but careful, so I wouldn't hurt him any more than he'd already been hurt, I slipped his gun from his holster. It was a nice solid forty-five. I decided right then and there that I wanted a forty-five of my very own, a companion piece to the little thirty-eight. There were times when only a big-caliber bullet would do. This was one of them.

Sheriff Winton opened his eyes and blinked at me, a question.

"I need to borrow this . . ." I told him.

He let out a large, rasping gulp of air. "Loved . . . Helen," he said. "Wanted her to leave . . . with . . . me." He passed out.

I knew he thought that was his deathbed confession, but I checked his pulse, and found it was weak but steady.

God, what a mess everybody's life was, not that mine was any exception. Karen wanted David. David wanted Helen, or at least her family's money. Helen wanted out. And the sheriff, he was hoping to give her a way.

There were a couple of people left out of this complex equation. There was Adrianne, and there was Johnny.

Another scream rose up outside, high-pitched, hysterical. I heard a car start again, and wheels spitting gravel, and the engine revving up and roaring away.

I ran back to the barn door and fired Sheriff Winton's big bore gun over and over, until the wood splintered and there was a nice big hole in the door.

I pressed back against the side of the barn, keeping myself out of sight. It was quiet outside, but I waited a minute, my heart pounding and my head rushing. It was really awfully quiet out there.

Carefully, I pried the splintered boards back until I reached the latch on the barn door. I slid it up, and the bolt swung free with a loud, rasping wail.

My car and David's pickup were still in the yard. The wind was blowing hot, and rain was spitting down again. God, this was a desolate place in a brown, empty land.

I looked around at the beige grass, the chocolate-colored hills, the ochre dust, the grey sky. I supposed it could be singularly beautiful, if you liked your world in monochrome.

I was quite frankly tempted to jump in my car and go. Return only with the state police, an ambulance for Winton, lots of eyes, hands, and guns.

Still, it must've been Adrianne I'd heard screaming. I couldn't leave her alone with the badly beaten sheriff, and maybe whoever it was that had done that to him. And where was the sheriff's car anyway? Who had driven up just now and who had driven away again?

"Adrianne! Adrianne!" I called, but there wasn't any answer.

On the amazing off-chance that I'd get a signal, I plucked my cell phone out of my bag. Oh yeah, right, sure. I couldn't get a signal standing in the middle of the highway in town, but I was expecting to get one on a ranch an hour off the main road, with Cathedral Mountain cracking through West Texas on one side and Santiago Peak climbing toward Mexico on the other.

I went for the house, still shouting for Adrianne, and waiting between shouts for something, anything, to stir. But there was only the sound of crickets. It felt like I was alone here, the only sentient being in the middle of the desert.

The wind swirled up, the rain petered out, and I tasted dust and regret. There were a lot of things I should've done differently. A lot of things I should've *seen* differently.

I crossed the yard to the back of the Cannon house, and stepped inside, crouching and ducking and plastering myself up against the walls.

Nothing but silence. I snagged the phone off the kitchen table. I wondered if Adrianne had reached Winton's deputy, and how long it would take him to drive out from town.

I wondered where the hell Adrianne was. Maybe the deputy had come and gone, and Adrianne jumped in his car, just said drive, get me out of here, there's something bad here, there's something bad . . .

When I put the receiver to my ear there was no dial tone.

The long cord hung loose from the wall. That was enough for me.

I bolted out of the house and I made it to my car, panting. There was something here that made me afraid, more afraid than I'd been on any stakeout, on any dark night in the projects. Some of it was people unexpectedly turning up dead or hurt and that whoever was killing and hurting them was out there, and maybe they were after me. But there was something else, too. It was that emptiness, that darkness that hung out over the desert at twilight. That darkness had a permanent home at the Cannon ranch.

I jammed my key in the ignition and threw a glance in the rear view and there was Johnny, groaning up from the backseat.

I spun on him with the gun so ready to fire. He was holding the side of his face, where an enormous purple bruise was rising.

"Don't move. I'll shoot you right here," I said.

"What the fuck are you doing . . . She hit me. Hard."

"Adrianne," I said flatly.

"She cracked me with something . . ."

"She did, huh. What are you doing in my car?"

"I crawled in here, locked the doors. But she didn't come after me again. She ran after the guy who gave me a lift out here . . . I don't know if she caught up with him or not, I blacked out for a couple minutes, I guess. Why do you have the gun on me? What the fuck, Lynn, what the fuck is going—"

"Why're you here?"

"I got worried about you."

"You keep telling me that. Just after someone tries to kill me. What happened, Johnny? Were you afraid Karen chose him over you?"

"What are you talking about? Take that gun off me."

But I didn't waver.

"C'mon, you're making me nervous," he said.

"That's the whole idea, Johnny. You gave a good show of being the understanding, ever so sensitive artist, am I right? You accepted Karen Shaw, and everything about her."

"Of course I did. I loved her. I still love her."

"I found the sheriff."

"Found him?"

Right now he was giving a good show of being incredibly confused.

"And Adrianne found the picture."

"What picture?"

"Get out of the car, Johnny. I won't shoot you, if you get out of the car. Out!"

He did what I told him, but he had a hard time with it. It seemed the blow he'd taken to his head was making him dizzy. He was staggering in the dirt.

I jumped out after him, the gun still on him. "Get in the house. Move it. March!"

I kicked the door open and pushed him into a kitchen chair. "Sit."

His mouth opened and closed, as if he couldn't think what to say. "Please. Tell me what's going on."

"You'd be the one to tell me," I said. I yanked the cut phone cord out of the wall.

"Don't even breathe," I said, and I wrapped the cord around his hands, and bound them to the back of the chair. Johnny struggled, but I pulled the cord taut, down from his hands. I trussed his feet, too.

"I didn't do it, whatever it is you think I did. Cannon? Is it Cannon? You think I had something to do with his death?"

"Not only his," I said.

"Oh, Jesus, Lynn. You think I hurt Karen? You're nuts, you're nuts!"

I held the gun steady. I looked him right in the eyes and he looked at me right back, and damn he was giving the best show I'd ever seen of playing innocent and distraught.

"Jesus," he said again. "You're so sure, huh? So sure! No wonder she picked you out of the phone book. You look like her, you act like her, you fucking smile like her, you just don't smile very much. I don't know why I didn't see it before. No wonder she picked you out of the phone book. No wonder she thought you'd understand."

If he thought he was gonna rattle me, he was dead wrong.

"But like I already told you, she wasn't always right either."

Without even realizing it, I had the hammer pulled back.

"Don't do it, Lynn. I loved her! She loved me!"

I released the hammer, slowly, carefully. And I plucked his drawing from the pocket of my jeans. I waved it in his face.

"Recognize this?"

"Sure, of course, I gave it to Karen. In the Empire Lounge."

"Then how did Adrianne find it this morning? In the barn."

"I don't know. Cannon took it, I guess. From her house, when he . . ."

"The thought crossed my mind. But that's not the thought crossing it now. It's a shame *I'm* not a psychic. Maybe I could've gotten a better read on you."

Johnny just gaped at me.

I drew a deep breath. "It was you the neighbor saw, knocking on her door. I was thinking it was David coming back for his knife. But it was you, wasn't it? And you heard her inside with the delivery boy."

Johnny opened his mouth to say something, but the back door flew open, and Adrianne charged in with her father's rifle in her hands, and her eyes wide with fear.

"Murderer!" she shrieked at Johnny. She had the rifle up and the hammer back, and oh my God, the girl knew how to shoot it.

I jumped forward and slapped the barrel with my hand, just in time to keep Johnny's head from exploding. A bullet slammed into the wall and ripped a big gash in the flowered wallpaper.

Adrianne just stared at the hole in the wall.

"Give me the rifle," I said. "And go get us some help."

Adrianne was glaring at Johnny. "He came to hurt me! I woulda shot him before, but I didn't have time to load the bullets. So I hit him with the stock, and then I just ran 'til I caught up with the man who drove him out here. I got in the truck, but I realized I couldn't just leave you, Lynn. So I sent the man for help, and I ran all the way back again."

"You're gonna give the gun to me now," I said.

"Not 'til the sheriff comes."

"The sheriff's up in the barn. He's hurt pretty bad," I told her.

"And I'm supposed to have hurt him, right?" Johnny asked.

Neither of us answered him.

Tears rolled down Adrianne's cheeks, but she was still holding that rifle. I stepped closer to her.

"Lock me up then, 'til the sheriff can tell you I didn't do anything! He'll tell you, it wasn't me!" Johnny shouted.

Adrianne raised the rifle. "You were her boyfriend, weren't you? That crazy bitch."

I was pissed off that she had the gun up again instead of handing it over. Now I had to sweet-talk a thirty-aught-six out of the hands of an seventeen-year-old high on grief and adrenalin. I moved closer.

"The law's going to handle this, not you. If you help me, we can put Johnny in the back of your father's truck, and drive him into town. He won't go anywhere all tied up. There's rope in the barn. We can prop Sheriff Winton in the passenger seat. You can fit in the jump seat; I'll drive."

I had my hand on her rifle now, but Adrianne wouldn't give it up. It was unbelievable how strong she was. It was the strength you get when you've got nothing left to lose. It was the strength of a three-hundred-pound convicted felon on PCP, the grip of a man facing three strikes with only you between him and the open door.

I backhanded her across the face, and pushed her against the wall. But just like in a nightmare, she still had that gun and she was charging at me. She slammed up against me so hard and so fast that she knocked my gun out of my hand.

I hit her again, a solid thunk on her jaw, and she fell back against the kitchen counter. That knocked the wind out of her.

I pried the rifle out of her hands, ripped open the breech, and shook the bullets out all over the floor.

"I'll tie you up, too," I told her. "Get a grip."

And Adrianne got one, but not the kind I'd intended. She got her hands around a paring knife lying on the counter. And she clenched it in her fist, and she was ramming the thing straight at me.

I dodged it, but by way too close a margin for my liking.

Johnny rocked in his chair, and kicked at Adrianne. She turned on him, and she slashed at his throat.

I jumped on her, put my arms around her neck, and pulled her over backwards. We fell down on the floor together with her flat on top of me, her back pressed against my chest. She still had the knife.

Johnny writhed against the phone cord, but I'd done a fine job tying him down.

Adrianne twisted in my grip. She smashed her body against me, over and over, until I lost my hold. Then she flipped, cat-quick, so she was facing me. In that instant I saw the ugly truth that had been eluding me.

She was wearing David Cannon's steel-tipped work boots. And under the long man's shirt, her jeans were held up by the belt with the silver conchos on it. Wearing her father's clothes made her feel stronger, she'd said.

And suddenly, I knew Adrianne saw things right. It *was* a woman's hand that stabbed her mother. At least it was a teenage girl's; Adrianne's own. She'd been telling the truth when she said she'd forgotten everything about that night, at least until very recently. But now she knew. And worse for me as her eyes met mine, she knew I got it too.

She pinned me to the floor with her body, her forearms, her fists. Her strength was surreal; I was hurting. She still had the knife. I forced myself to go passive, let her think she didn't have much to worry about. Maybe she'd relax a little, maybe I could snap the crazy switch in her head from on to off.

"It's okay, Adrianne. Let's just both get up now and sit down at the table."

"That sounds like something Mama woulda said. 'Be reasonable, Addy. You're sick, I'll come back for you.' How was I to know she meant it, that she wanted me with her? She was always chasing me out of the way. How was I to know it was Daddy said she couldn't take me. It was all his fault, really."

"Just get off me now, Adrianne," I said. "It'll be all right."

She laughed at me. "I had Daddy's belt, I had Daddy's shoes, I had Daddy's temper! And I had a kitchen knife in my hand, and I used it. Then I put her in her car, with all those bags she'd already packed."

I reared up and banged my head against Adrianne's, making her nose bleed. I was hoping the sight of her own blood would send her into a swoon again but no such luck. She didn't even seem to notice.

She rocketed forward, and threw me back against the floor like a rag doll. An seventeen-year-old track star, three inches shorter than me, was kicking my ass. I felt something crack in my right arm. The pain itched and burned.

I grabbed for her foot with my left hand, twisted her ankle. Latched on to each other, we writhed around on the floor.

Johnny was working at the cords with his teeth. It was a good idea, but the wire was thick and I didn't think he'd break it, not in time to be any help to me.

I saw the thirty-eight lying on the floor next to the sink. I dropped her leg and inched my hand toward it.

"Give up?" she asked.

"I don't want to hurt you," I said. What I wanted was to keep her attention away from my hand and that gun. "I want to listen. Tell me the rest of your story, Addy. Who drove your mother's car to the lake?"

"I did," her eyes looked inward, like she was seeing it all unfold inside her head all over again. "Daddy'd already shown me how to drive, it was no big deal, getting up the mountain. When I got to the bend overlooking the lake, I put one of Mama's bags on the accelerator, and the car in gear, and just let it go. Down, down, down it went."

My fingers arched out a little more, a little more.

"You must've been scared," I said.

"Yes. I ran all the way home. Daddy was already there."

I almost felt the gun now, the smooth, cool metal. I didn't dare look; I didn't dare let her see.

"Did you tell him what happened?"

Adrianne's own voice was just a whisper, as if something heavy was pressing her down, too. She leaned close, her face inches from mine. "When you get found out, it's like a poison that takes a few minutes to seep in. You feel sick to your stomach, numb. Then it hurts so bad, and you're so scared. Then you stop being afraid. Or you forget that you are. You die, a little."

Adrianne was panting, her breath ragged, the smell of it repellent, like a cornered animal. "Papa knew, but I never told him. He protected me."

Tears ran down Adrianne's face, mixed with the blood from her smashed-up nose; it dripped down her chin and onto my cheeks.

"I was so sick, I wished I would die. I wanted to be with Mama. But my daddy took me to the hospital. He prayed I'd pull through. His prayers were more powerful than mine."

Please, God, I thought, praying myself. My fingers curled around the handle of my gun at last.

But Adrianne sensed the motion, and bore down harder on me. It felt like she was gonna push me straight through the grubby linoleum and into the ground, like my bones were gonna splinter. I didn't dare lift the thirty-eight, not yet.

"And Karen Shaw . . . she was around that night? Visiting your father?" I whispered.

"No!" Adrianne screamed. "She woulda been afraid to set foot in this town again. My mother would've ridden that slut out on a rail. She ruined Daddy for all time, Mama said so. She ruined him for all of us!"

I gasped, trying to sound understanding instead of like she was crushing me to death. "Then why . . . go see her, Addy?"

"I just wanted to know what she looked like. That's all. But she started in with this talk about Mama. I didn't remember anything until she started talking. She *couldn't* have known, but somehow she knew! She shoulda kept quiet, because then I had to go back and make sure she did. I tried to keep you quiet too. That tire iron I found didn't work, so I tried another way, make you look foolish, chasing down that wedding ring. But nothing works on you, does it? Nothing."

"You don't have to do anything else, Adrianne. I'll go away now. I promise."

She blinked, and let up on me a little. She wanted to believe me. "Really?" she asked.

"I swear." I slid the gun beneath my palm, and slipped the trigger back in the same motion that I used to draw it up off the floor.

Her eyes flashed, she saw, she kicked, and the gun went flying. The shot it fired shattered the glass on the kitchen door.

All that care, all that patience, all that time listening to her shit, and she saw me pick up my gun anyway.

"Liar! You think I don't see? I see everything."

She didn't have eyes in the back of her head, though. She didn't see Johnny still straining at his bonds.

She moved a few inches forward; I couldn't tell if it was the heat of the story moving her, or if she was trying to stop my heart from beating.

"I'll accept the blame for Mama," Adrianne said. "But you made me take Daddy. Who knew what you told him? He might've left me this time. Lord, I thought, please, not him, too."

Her moving forward gave me a little leverage with my legs. I bent my knees and jammed them as hard as I could against her. It was a move that usually worked to loosen somebody up, but it didn't work on her.

I felt my ribs cracking under her weight.

"Now the psychic, she pretty much asked me to take her. Delivery boy left the door open. I waited 'til nobody was around, and then I just walked right on in. She was staring into her stupid crystal ball. She didn't even see me, and I was right there in front of her. She was so wasted.

"Then I saw Papa's knife. I couldn't believe it. It was horrible that he'd been there, but perfect that he'd left it for me. It was a gift. I told her so. She looked up then, and she said, 'I can see again.' I was the last thing she saw."

Adrianne lifted the paring knife, still clenched in her fist, and she took up my hand, the one with the wrist she'd broken, and slowly, dreamily, she drew the blade into my skin.

I tried to twist away, but rotating the broken bone hurt so much that I screamed.

Johnny tugged one hand free, and grabbed at Adrianne. All he snagged was her hair, but he pulled for all he was worth, and some of her weight lifted off me. Her knife slipped away.

My ribs burned, but I lunged for her, snapping at her with my teeth.

She ripped her hair out of Johnny's hand, shrieking.

"Shoulda let Papa just shoot you!" she spat at me. "I was afraid he'd get in trouble!"

Johnny yanked his other arm free. He lunged for my gun, the chair scraping against the floor.

Adrianne turned at the sound, but she was too late to stop the nice pass he made, kicking the gun right to me. I drew the hammer back and I shot her, a clean hit just below her left shoulder. She fell next to me with a thud.

I crawled up on my knees, I snatched up her knife. My chest hurt, and so did my wrist, my cut hand.

I crawled over to Johnny with the knife in my good hand. He reared back, a look of pure horror on his face.

"Oh, for God's sake, hold still so I can cut the cord," I said. "What do you think, everybody's a wacko now?"

I slashed through the cord. He kicked it off his feet.

I tried to stand up, but it made the ribs hurt worse.

"I was afraid you still thought I was the one," Johnny began.

"I made a mistake. I'm sorry. I'm really, really sorry. But everybody's entitled to make a mistake," I mumbled.

And then I crumpled down on the floor, cheek to cheek with Adrianne.

★ ★ ★ ★ ★

When I came to again I was in the passenger seat of my own car, and Johnny had dish towels wrapped tight around the cuts on my palm and my wrist. His hands were shaking; he was having a hard time fitting the key in the ignition.

"Want me to drive?" I croaked.

He gave what almost amounted to a smile. "Just want to get out of here, get everybody some help."

"Did you tie Adrianne up?"

He got the key in, revved the engine. "I don't think there was any need."

He made a sharp U-turn, and we were headed down the road, when I begged to differ with his assessment of Adrianne. There she was, stepping out on her front porch, seemingly oblivious to the gunshot wound below her shoulder, and stalking toward my car.

She had her rifle up and apparently she'd reloaded it, because when she pulled the trigger the kick made her stagger backward, and the bullet cracked my rear window.

I ducked, and shouted at Johnny. "Get down and floor it!"

He hunched low, and rocketed the car forward, but the wheels hit a rough patch of road and the car swung out of control. He rammed the front end against a fence post.

Adrianne fired again, and this time the bullet tore into the car's rear door.

"Drive!" I shouted.

He threw the car in reverse and broke free from the post.

He shifted into drive while the car was still moving and we fishtailed down the road. Adrianne ran behind us, keeping a damn-good pace.

I was rooting through my purse with my left hand, looking for my Smith and Wesson. "Where's my gun?" I asked.

"Oh. Might've left it in the kitchen," Johnny said.

"You didn't tie her up, and you left her rifle and my gun—"

"I was a little busy rescuing you!"

"And a fine job of it you've done, too!"

The car careened around a curve, dipping into a ditch. Adrianne was advancing on us.

"Drive straight," I screamed, "or she's gonna kill us!"

Johnny skipped the next bend in the road, hurled right through the Cannon's barbed-wire fence, and straight across the field. He was dragging wire and a couple of fence posts along with us.

"I meant stay straight on the road! You think I have four-wheel drive?"

Racing like a greyhound on acid, Adrianne flew across the grass behind us shooting round after round. The good news was she had to run out of ammunition soon.

The bad news was how slow we were going. "Speed it up," I smacked Johnny's shoulder, and he hit a gully hard.

The front of the car flew up, and the back smacked down, and I hit my head on the ceiling. We both let loose a string of invectives. The car lurched out of the gully, tires skidding, engine straining. And there was Adrianne, panting, bleeding, lifting the gun, lifting the gun.

I prayed she'd miss. This had to be her last shot. It had to be. I hunched down in my seat. I closed my eyes. Boom.

It didn't come anywhere near us. I saw the rifle pointed down. I saw the great hole in the earth opened up before her. I saw Adrianne sink on her knees and collapse, face-down into it, crying.

"What have I done? What am I doing?" she sobbed.

It looked like her crazy switch had finally moved back into the off position.

Johnny hit the dirt road to the lake. We bounced along, and with every bounce I felt my ribs shake and hurt.

We passed an old pickup on the side of the road. There was a plump young man in it, lying forward on the dash. Johnny's ride, I presumed. Something that resembled a rifle blast had ripped a hole in his seat.

In a gully, tall grass almost hiding it, there was the sheriff's car. I muttered at Johnny to stop, and he did, and we used the radio.

CHAPTER EIGHTEEN

An ambulance met us in town and took me to the hospital in Alpine. They wanted to start me on the pain meds right away, but I insisted I didn't need anything at all when they set my wrist. They assured me I did need something, because the break was bad enough that it would require pinning.

But not to worry, the orthopedist was the best the town had to offer, used to treating all sorts of rock-climbing-related injuries, arms, legs, fractured this, fractured that. My wrist would be nothing to him. Still I saw him blanch when he got a look at it, and that was enough for me to okay the medication after all.

"It's my gun hand," I told him. "You better hope I can still shoot straight when you're done." It wasn't the drugs talking, but they passed it off as that, and probably it was just as well.

When I opened my eyes again, it was dark outside the hospital window, and a slice of the moon was shimmering over the hills. It was clear for once, not a cloud in sight.

The nurse told me I had four broken ribs, plus the wrist, now successfully pinned. I had six stitches in that same wrist and eight across my palm.

If Karen was still alive and she was reading palms instead of the cards she'd lost faith in, I wondered what she'd make of mine. Probably that we make our own fate, no matter what anybody tells us.

Deputy Hank and Betty from records both came in to tell me

Sheriff Winton was in stable condition, and thanks to me, everybody was sure he'd pull through.

Adrianne had made it, too. She was under police guard even when she was in surgery. Hank said she had no recollection, or at least she pretended to have no recollection, of how she'd gotten herself shot, her father's death, or any of the rest of it. Arrangements were being made to transport her to a mental health facility in Fort Stockton for evaluation.

The nurse left, Hank and Betty left, and Johnny came in. He had a bandage plastered around the big bruise on his face, and his sketch pad tucked under his arm.

"I've been waiting for you to come around," he said.

He poured me a glass of water without me having to ask, and I took it in my good hand and drained it, grateful.

"Careful, or you'll be sick," he said.

I set the glass back down. "I sure wish I hadn't tied you up," I said.

"Me, too."

I drew a deep breath. I hate apologies.

"I'm not good with people trying to help me out. That's how I went so wrong with you." It wasn't great, but it was something.

"Yeah, you expect to do everything on your own. You're a lot like Karen," he said.

"Look, I'm not sure I want you saying that. I mean I know she was a good person, I do know that, and I realize you think there's a chance that she was my . . ." I stopped, I shook my head. "My mother died in Houston. Years and years ago."

"I'm sure you'll investigate. Reach your own conclusions. And whatever they are, they'll be right."

It was probably all the drugs they had me on, but I started to cry, and I just couldn't stop. Johnny leaned down and he held me, patted my back like I was a little kid.

"Shh," he said, "it's all right."

He kissed my forehead, and I leaned back on my pillows, swiping at my eyes.

"Need a handkerchief?" Frank's voice sounded low and disembodied, and seemed to belong to a different universe from the one I was inhabiting at the moment.

But there he was, crashing into my hospital room, broad of shoulders and chest, his dark hair wild and curly, his brown eyes snapping. Johnny stood back, and Frank dropped a big, crisp, white hankie on my chest.

"What are you doing here?" I asked, surprised.

"Interrupting, I guess," Frank said.

Johnny shook his head. "No, I was just leaving. I'll be back in the morning," he told me. He tore a page from his notebook and handed it to me. It was me, looking at a picture of Karen. The resemblance was, truly, striking.

Frank dropped down at the foot of my bed. He snatched the sketch out of my hand, grunted at it, and set it on the chair.

"That the guy who wrecked Red's Liquor?" he asked.

"Yes. Karen Shaw's boyfriend."

"Looks like he wants to be yours."

I shook my head. "I think he wants to be my stepfather."

"Why is it, that whenever I see you, there's always some complication?"

"Life's complicated, Frank. It's not just a matter of breathing in and breathing out."

"Not when you're around," he admitted. He patted my shoulder, gently. "I'm glad you're still breathing, baby."

"I want to talk to you," I said.

"I want to talk to you, too."

Whatever he had to say couldn't bother me now. I'd faced Adrianne, I'd faced death, I was facing some very weird personal possibilities, plus I had a bloodstream full of narcotics. It might not even hurt to tell Frank how I felt about him. Maybe I wouldn't even have to use too many words. Maybe I could just pull him down on the bed next to me, and show him. I could use one of his kind of lines, something like, "c'mon, never done it in intensive care before?" The idea made me almost giddy, and I laughed.

"What's funny?"

I shook my head. Maybe I ought to slow down a little here, let him make the first move. I drew a deep breath.

"You go first, tough guy."

"Okay. I will. Just promise me something. I want you to hear me out and then ask questions, okay? No interruptions."

I nodded. Since he seemed so serious, I made a big effort and squashed down that stupid giggly feeling still rising up in my throat. I was really, truly, planning on listening, but I was still out of it enough that for a minute, I just wanted to close my eyes, and then I'd give him my full attention.

But when I opened them again it was six hours later and he was gone, and if I'd heard anything at all that he had to say, I'd forgotten it.

Except for the blood-stained clothes the hospital staff had left neatly folded in my room, I was once again temporarily without wearable attire. It seemed that in finding a plastic bag of not-so-new clothes in my room, and assuming I'd left the hotel without checking out, the manager at the Gage donated the bag to the town church's annual clothing drive. Only that slinky blue dress, left on a hanger, survived for Johnny to claim.

So before I checked out of the hospital, Johnny went down to the gift shop and found me a long-sleeved purple tee shirt and some sweatpants to match. It was better than wearing a hospital gown all the way back to Houston.

The bill for the clothes plus hospital stay came to just over two thousand dollars. Karen's payment just about covered me.

While they were processing me out, I checked my phone messages.

Frank had called, several times; still, at this point I thought we might as well wait for our talk until I was back in town. What I had to say to him was better said face to face anyway.

Johnny drove us home, because it would've been hard steering one handed with sore ribs for so many miles. He swung by Nolan's and told the kid to keep his Pinto junker.

After so many hours on the road, the most striking thing about sliding down into Houston again was how green everything was, after all that desert brown. The second most striking thing was how nothing was still. Gone was the solitude of sand and stone, and in its place were cars and people and the great tumultuous perpetual motion of an enormous city sprawled out there in front of us. You might feel just as lonely in Houston as out in the West Texas desert, but you would never feel as alone.

We stopped at a florist's, and Johnny bought an enormous bouquet of daisies. We both knew who they were for, but we didn't talk about it. He pulled onto the six-ten freeway in the low golden slant of a smoggy late afternoon to make a stop at Tranquility Garden.

I saw that all the unseasonable rain had already started the grass growing over Karen's grave, as rich and emerald as in any River Oaks garden.

Johnny left the daisies and I left the little sprig of sage and lavender I'd taken from her house. I held it up to my face and breathed it in for a moment. The scent of my childhood. My mother told me once that someone had given that sachet to her to give to me. Had she ever told me who that someone was?

"You okay to drive yourself home from here?" Johnny asked. "I'd like to, you know, visit here awhile."

"I'm okay," I said.

"Call anytime."

"You too."

"You won't call, will you?" he asked.

"I might."

"I hope you do."

We left it at that.

"He was distraught yesterday." The nurse at Sunrise House stopped me outside my father's room. "He might not express it in words, but he counts on your visits."

I nodded and opened the door to my father's room with my good hand. He wasn't watching television like he usually was when I visited; he was just sitting in his chair, facing the window. The last sunlight was streaming in, making his hair look shiny, haloed.

"Hi, Dad," I said.

He didn't turn, so I moved next to the window, and looked out with him. "Whatcha see out there? Anything interesting?"

He didn't say a word, so I filled in for him. "Coupla cars. Light going green, yellow, red. Crows. Mmm. Dive-bombing that trash can . . ."

He lifted his face to mine, still silent. His face was remarkably unlined, his eyes serene. It was that serenity that spooked me the most. Where was the irritable intensity, the military reserve, the cold scrutiny? Where was the question that even now hung between us, "Why're you so late, young lady? What have you gotten yourself into this time?"

As much as that question used to piss me off, I missed it.

Pretending he had asked, I answered him.

"I was working on a case that got pretty ugly," I said. "I'm fine, but I was in the hospital the last few days, getting this wrist set. Have some ribs taped too. Gave me too many meds; you know how they are, doctors. I woulda called here if I hadn't been all drugged up.

"It's a long story but the short version is, this woman hired me to look into a murder, but someone took her out in the meantime. Yeah, I got the bad guy, except it wasn't a guy, it was just a kid. And I didn't get her before another person lost his life. It makes me feel humble. And lucky."

I stopped there. I ran down like one of those little wind-up toys that teeter over to the edge of the table and fall over. He just looked at me and I just looked at him.

"Anyway, heard you were upset yesterday, which surprised me. I mean I'm not even sure sometimes, Dad, if you know I'm here, much less what day of the week I usually show up but . . . I know it's not your fault or anything. I know you're doing your best. That you always did. You and Mom both."

He looked away from me, and back out the window.

"There's some questions I wish I could ask you. I mean I know I can ask, but I wish you could answer them. I'll look into it all myself, but still, I'd like to hear it from you."

His head rotated toward me again. A little spark of something flicked across his eyes, curiosity, or interest, or just awareness. Whatever it was, it gave me enough incentive that I stumbled on with things.

"See, I might be, um, related to my deceased client. What do you think of that? Her name was Karen Shaw. That mean anything to you?"

"Crows," he said, looking out the window again.

"Yeah, lots of birds this time of day. Sorting through the garbage, looking for treasure. Kinda like my job," I squeezed his hand. "Anyway, I'll be back next week, and hope you know I would've been here yesterday if everything hadn't gotten so out of control."

He closed his eyes and slumped back in his chair. I thought he was falling asleep, much as I'd fallen asleep on Frank. I wanted to see Frank. I wanted to listen to him this time.

My hand slipped from my father's, and I stood and picked

up my bag. I figured he'd already nodded out, but for some reason my lips kept moving and words kept coming out.

"What I'd really like to know is if I'm adopted. One of the last things Mom said to me was that she wished she had more time, because there were things she'd never had a chance to tell me. I wonder if that could be one of them. I mean I don't look a lot like you or Mom.

"This woman, Karen, she looked like me, Dad. I guess lots of people resemble other people but . . . there's gotta be records. Even if the records were sealed. I mean my birth certificate lists you and Mom but . . ."

My father's eyes were still closed, but he spoke in a crisp, lucid tone. "No records. Were on vacation. Your mother lost her baby. Doctor said no others. This gal, she was in the bed next to your mama. Giving her baby up for adoption. Come to us in the parking lot, wearing her hospital gown. Put you in your mother's arms. 'You just take her,' she said. 'You must. I want you to have her. Not somebody whose heart I don't know.' Was peculiar."

He stopped there and drew a great, deep breath.

"Yeah, yeah, I guess it must must've been strange." I was so excited I was stammering. Between the news he was giving me, and his remarkable coherence, I was getting pretty worked up.

" 'S why we never said. The girl ran, we snuck out of there like thieves in the night. Afraid she'd take you back. Medic, owed me a favor, wrote up the birth certificate. Tell you when you were sixteen, your mother said. But she was gone, then."

He had never spoken so many words to me at one time, even before he went into Sunrise House.

I lifted my father's hand in mine, and stroked it. "Dad. Why didn't *you* tell me?"

His eyes opened, and they were clouded, and the clarity was gone from his voice. "Relentless, those crows."

★ ★ ★ ★ ★

I knew I should go ahead and take the car in to Three Crowns Auto Body again, and get the bullet holes out of the door, the rear window replaced, and the trunk lock fixed, but it just seemed like too much effort. I'd do it tomorrow. My mind was already on overload.

I had to go home for a little while, lie down, and try and deal with the fact that my mother and father were not, biologically speaking, my mother and father; that I carried in me the genetic indiscretions of Karen Shaw and David Cannon.

When I pulled in to my apartment garage, Rita was there, sliding Amber's soccer gear out of the van. She took one look at my car and one look at me. She opened her mouth and then closed it again. "I don't think that auto body place did such a good job," she said.

I managed a laugh.

"And what happened to your arm? Last I heard you were hanging out in the desert with that artist with the cheekbones. Come on Lynn, talk to me. Don't just look at me. You should've called. How did you even drive home like that? My God, you're wearing purple."

I gave her a *Cliff Notes* version of my case, and watched her bravely try not to flinch over the matricide and destruction. I tried not to flinch myself.

A kid not that far from Amber's age was locked up in a ward for the criminally insane. Sure, she was a stone-cold killer, although how aware she was of what she'd done and the havoc she'd wrought, I wasn't sure.

That same poor, crazy, violent lunatic was the kid people referred to as a good student. A great runner. Her daddy's little girl. And very likely my biological half-sister.

I gave Rita a one-armed hug, and told her there was more to tell, lots more, but it would have to be later.

"I'm glad you're okay," she said. "You are okay, right?"

I told her I was. And then I turned and lurched out of the garage, stiff-legged and sad.

I made it to my front door, unlocked it, and had already stepped inside when somebody grabbed me around the waist with one arm, which hurt like hell because of my ribs, and put something over my face with the other.

I couldn't open my mouth to scream, I couldn't even breathe, because if I did, then whatever it was that was on the thing he put over my face was gonna knock me out cold.

So I just let him close my door quietly, and holding my breath so long I thought my lungs and my poor messed-up ribs were gonna burst, I went limp, and let him drag me into my bedroom and toss me down on the bed. The cloth he'd put over my face slipped away. Finally I could breathe.

I opened one eye just a crack and I saw the shoes. Nope, not steel-tipped work boots. Nice loafers. William Devins had apparently made bail.

The guy thought he had me, but he was wrong. It was just like it was a little over a week before on the roof of his office building's parking garage.

Well, there were a few differences. This time I didn't have my gun in reach, and I already had broken ribs and a broken wrist, and no way to get my good hand around to punch him in the nose.

So I reared up and used my teeth instead, and bit him. He screamed and drew back, and I rolled toward him across the bed, kicking out with my feet, reminding myself to exchange my flip-flops soon for, say, motorcycle boots, or better yet, motorcycle boots with spurs.

Flip-flops or not, the surprise factor got him in the groin, and he staggered back against the wall, and let out a loud cry.

As I lurched up from the bed, I saw that my dresser drawers

were open and the pitiful amount of clothing that the drawers still contained was cut into shreds. That made me angry enough to punch him a few times with my good hand, nice and hard in the solar plexus.

The only comfort was that maybe all my clothes had bad karma attached to them, and he was saving me from myself.

There were footsteps; my door was being kicked in, I heard the chain break. Devins was still bent double when Frank put a chokehold on him.

On Frank's heels came Rita's husband, Paul, ready to help Frank grapple with Devins, except Frank didn't really need any help. He had the guy down and the cuffs on him, and he was saying something into a walkie-talkie like this had all been a stakeout. And maybe it was, and it was just that nobody had bothered to tell me about it.

Rita advanced from the living room brandishing a lamp, Amber swinging her backpack like a cudgel behind her.

"Unnecessary," Paul said.

Rita set the lamp down, Amber stopped swinging, and about a dozen officers poured into my bedroom. The other cops got Devins up even as Frank was reading him his rights. Paul and Frank shook hands, Rita gave me a kiss. Amber looked from me to Frank and Frank to me.

"He's cute," she said, while everybody trooped out again.

Frank was in my kitchen, rooting through my refrigerator. I was lying down on the sofa, trying to get my heart to stop beating quite so fast. I honestly wasn't sure if it was Devins' attack or Frank making himself at home that was doing it to me.

"You don't have anything to eat," Frank noted.

"I've been out of town, remember?"

"You didn't have anything in here before you went out of town," he said.

"I had a bag of salad."

"You still have that. It's fermented."

He clicked on his cell phone to call for pizza, and then he shut it off again. He actually shut off the cell. That was absolutely unheard of, for Frank.

I sat up and he joined me on the sofa, and held my good hand in his. "So you wanna catch up?"

"Yeah. Start with how you knew Devins was gonna come after me tonight."

"From his lawyer, believe it or not. Devins thought Kincaid was lying about not having the CDs he was supposed to get from you, and actually tied the guy up, and ransacked his office, got your address. Kincaid called me soon as he got his hands free, in fear of his life and charges of aiding and abetting. So he offered the juicy information that Devins was likely to come after you next, chasing the CDs. So I put surveillance on your office and here. I wanted you to come to headquarters, not home, but you didn't return my phone calls. Again. So I figured you were still out of it."

"Understandable," I said. "I didn't call you back because I thought you wanted to talk about personal stuff. You know. You and me stuff." I felt that old disappointed feeling creep in, because in spite of everything that had happened I wanted to talk about *us*.

"I do," Frank said, patting my knee. "But that wasn't why I asked you to call me before you headed home. You know, I actually considered asking the police out in Alpine to arrest you, hold you without bond until you called me back." He shook his head. "I'm just glad, once again, that you're okay. Anyway, I left a couple uniforms watching your place, and I looked everywhere for those disks. I didn't want Devins to get them back. I went home just to clean up, and I remembered the note you'd written me about leaving something at my place. That's what you'd done with the CDs! I tore my place apart. Couldn't find 'em. I go into the kitchen to fix myself a drink, and there were the damn CDs, behind the scotch in a baggie. It's lucky I was frustrated enough to turn to drink. Or I never would've found them."

"Okay, okay, I should've told you; in fact, I tried to tell you, several times. But if we didn't have our signals crossed, I would've already picked the disks up, and given them to Devins' lawyer. And then there'd be no evidence of his fraud at all."

"Anyway, after I found them, I came back over here. I was just getting a stakeout set up. I didn't even think you were home when I heard you scream."

"It wasn't *me* who screamed," I objected.

"I assumed you were still in Alpine, with that kid, Johnny."

"He's not a kid, but he's not competition either, if that's what you're thinking. Wait'll you hear my story."

"Tell me just one part of it, straight up. How did your client know about Helen Cannon's murder, anyway?"

"I'm not sure exactly. Right before I found Helen's body, it crossed my mind that some things just can't be explained, not easily, anyway. Like what Karen saw, or why and how she saw it even without any real proof."

"Speaking of no proof, I was a little bit taken aback by those messages you left me Saturday night inferring I was engaged in sexual acts with someone other than yourself."

"Well, were you?" I asked.

Frank sighed. "You know, every once in a while my eye wanders. But I have kept my hands and all other appendages to myself since the day I met you."

My mouth dropped, I mean this was almost a bigger surprise than William Devins trying to chloroform me.

"Seriously?"

"Seriously. I want you back, Lynn. I want *us* back."

"I want us back, too," I said softly. "But, Frank. What about that file clerk? Susie Hawkins, I think her name was. I bet you didn't just *look* at her."

"Susie Hawkins. Wow. I tried to forget about her," he sighed, while my spine stiffened.

"She mixed up the 'P's' with the 'R's,' and the 'T's' with the 'F's.' She always had this stupid grin on her face. 'C'mon, turn that frown upside down' she'd say to me unless I smiled back. And then you handed in your resignation, and I couldn't stop you, and there she was, making things a bigger mess. Even had to start locking my office door, so she wouldn't jumble up everything I left on my desk. What a fool."

Apparently she wasn't as big a fool as me.

"I thought you and she . . ." I began.

He looked at me like he couldn't believe whatever it was I was about to say.

I shook my head. "I guess it doesn't matter what I thought. Now."

The pizza arrived while I was telling him all the details of my case. And about Karen and David just about certainly being my mother and father. Frank paid, shooed the delivery girl away, and plopped a couple of sodas and an extra-large, extra-cheese down on the coffee table in front of me. He handed me a stack of napkins and tore us each off a slice.

"I'm not sure of the right thing to say. You gain this whole other family you never knew you had, and then you lose 'em. It must hurt."

I hadn't thought about it quite that way, but yeah, he was right.

"I liked Karen. I really did. I thought she was crazy when I first met her but . . . she had a beautiful smile."

"Like you," Frank said.

"Flattery's not gonna get you anywhere, not tonight, I'm too beat. Besides," I said, gesturing at my pizza, "I wanted pineapple on it. That's my favorite. How can you forget that?"

"Couldn't tell you how many sugars you put in your coffee, either. There's some things I never was any good at remembering. But you have to give me credit that there's a lot of things I'll never forget." He leaned over and kissed me.

That kiss lasted a long, sweet time, and when we came up for air, we were both grinning.

"I wish more stakeouts ended like this," he said.

"I wish you would've nailed Devins before he cut up the last of my underwear," I sighed. "I don't know what I'm gonna do. I have hardly any clothes left."

He nibbled my neck, and gently, very gently, mindful of my ribs, he put his arms around my waist.

"Oh, maybe that won't be so bad," he said.

ABOUT THE AUTHOR

Genie Davis is a multi-published novelist and multi-produced screen and television writer. Her novels include award-winning romantic suspense titles *The Model Man* and *Five O'Clock Shadow* (Kensington), the literary fiction of *Dreamtown* (FictionWorks), and an erotic romance novella *Rodeo Man,* released as Nikki Alton in *The Cowboy* anthology (Aphrodisia).

In film, her work spans a variety of genres, from supernatural thriller to romantic drama, family, teen, and comedy. A member of the Writer's Guild of America, she's written on staff for ABC-TV's *Port Charles;* written, produced, and directed reality programming and documentaries for TLC, Lifetime, PBS, and HGTV, as well as numerous television commercials and corporate videos.

She's also written dozens of articles on travel, the arts, writing, sex, food, parenting, and more.